Mr Tambourine Man

Graham Whalan

roundtuit
publishing

ISBN 978-1-904499-23-7

Enquiries should be directed to the author at:
graham@whalan.fsnet.co.uk

First published in the UK in 2008 by
Roundtuit Publishing, 32 Cookes Wood,
Broom Park, DURHAM DH7 7RL
www.roundtuitpublishing.co.uk

Printed and bound in the UK by *Prontaprint* Durham
0191 384 3220
www.durham.prontaprint.com

Prologue

The young girl who greeted me reminded me of her – the long brown hair, the gentleness of her manner, and that same wistful look. But this wasn't Jeanne. I knew from the name tag pinned to her chest that this was 'Michelle'. She spoke.

"Monsieur?"

"Bonjour. Je m'appelle Nigel Broadbent. Je …"

"Ah, Monsieur Broadbent! You are very welcome! Madame is expecting you. Please, follow me."

And there it was again – that instant unmasking of myself as an Englishman as soon as I opened my mouth. I smiled to myself. Michelle led me through the Restaurant, down a long thin corridor and then down a small flight of stairs. I thought the Restaurant seemed a little shabby and in need of re-decoration but, despite its old-fashioned appearance, the atmosphere was warm and homely. A varied collection of customers were already tucking into lunch.

I had come to Nice to satisfy an itch I'd had for some time, to have a nostalgic trek around some of the old places, and to see if they still looked the same. I had found Pip's old *studio*, and the Hotel where Sue and Steve had stayed – neither of which had changed much at all, but Bobbi and Marcel's old flat was now a hair salon, and Mistral's print-works had been demolished to make way for a modern apartment building. I had also been sad not to be able to find *La Grange*. I thought I'd found the street, but no-one had ever heard of it. Needless to say an L.P. featuring that famous picture of Mike and me playing there, hunched over our guitars, was never released. Perhaps if it had been, *La Grange's* place in history would have been more secure.

Well, probably not actually.

As I followed Michelle's lead, I felt as if I was walking back in time. After all, we had not met for about 30 years. Soon we arrived at a heavy black door, and the thought of seeing her again suddenly made my heart beat faster. Michelle knocked and a thin voice from inside bade us enter.

And there she was. She had changed surprisingly little. She was older of course, but the same pretty face was evident despite the wrinkles.

i

Her hair had turned silver too, but instead of falling freely it was now scrunched into a disciplined bob, held in place by a large silver clip. A silk scarf puffed out from the collar of her suede jacket and I noticed a couple of bangles which clanked on the table as she quickly put down her coffee cup. She was sitting behind a large wooden desk awash with papers. The room, like the Restaurant, had a cosy, comfortable feel about it with well-worn furnishings somewhat dated in style.

"Nigel!" she said excitedly as she jumped to her feet and embraced me. "I couldn't believe it when you telephoned."

"Hello Bobbi," I said. "I'm amazed you remembered me."

"Of course I remember you. They were very important days we had together all those years ago. Can you believe it is now nearly 30 years?"

"No, I can't ... and especially when I look at you Bobbi. You haven't changed."

"You think I looked like this 30 years ago!" she laughed.

"Well you're older of course, but you are still the same Bobbi I remember."

"And you too, Nigel – you are how I remember you too."

Michelle smiled, excused herself and left us to it. My heart was still pounding. I don't know why I felt so anxious – perhaps I'd worried that she wouldn't actually recognise me, or that her memories of our time together would have faded faster than mine. And of course, I was aware that Jeanne was on my mind and, sooner or later, she was going to ask about Mike.

PART ONE

DOWN THE HIGHWAY

1

I woke up feeling wet and cold. Standing at the end of my bed, staring fixedly at me in that languid sort of way cows do, was a cow. I rubbed my eyes and sat up warily as I heard a shout from somewhere in the distance.

"Over here!"

The cow lost interest in me, bent down to tear up some more grass and shambled off. Mike came running over.

"It's O.K. I've moved the stuff over by the wall. I thought the bugger was gonna stamp on the lot for a minute".

I peered through the mist towards the wall Mike was pointing to, and dimly made out our 'stuff' – two guitars and two rucksacks. Given the choice between protecting my head or the guitars from the cow's hooves, it was a reassuring thought that Mike had instinctively chosen the guitars. They were to be our livelihood over the next few months after all.

"Come on. Let's get out of here!"

The dim shapes of more cows eerily appeared out of the mist at the sound of Mike's voice, and headed towards us. I shuffled out of my sleeping-bag, hurriedly picking up my shoes, and ran over to the wall, naturally stepping into a cow-pat en route.

"Shit!" I said, and I was right.

I always liked to think of myself as something of a rebel. In truth, I don't think I was so much an "angry young man" as "a young man in a fairly bad mood." Protest and unrest were all around me but I was never exactly sure of the appropriate target for my discontent. In any case I found the choice of causes too difficult – I didn't know whether to join the Civil Rights movement, demonstrate against the war in Vietnam, or go on long CND marches and do my bit to rid the world of nuclear weapons. I even considered putting my weight behind the fight for women's rights and sexual emancipation although, I have to admit, my qualifications were somewhat on the thin side in that particular quarter.

In the end I never went on marches or demonstrations or anything – I mean, with a name like Nigel Broadbent I don't think I was ever really destined to set the world on fire. And anyway, I was living in Morecambe, Lancashire where folk didn't go in for protest rallies much. But I did buy all the badges, and I had a picture of Che Guevara stuck to my bedroom wall, with *drawing pins* defiantly piercing Aunt Doris' precious anaglypta. You could say my protests were of a more passive kind, like growing my hair long, singing *We Shall Overcome* at the Merry Neet Club, and handing my homework in late. On one famous occasion the Head at school even asked me why I wasn't wearing my school cap, sealing my reputation as someone who liked to live life on the edge.

As for the folk-singing, I made up exactly one half of *The Outsiders*, a resident duo based at the Merry Neet Folk Club in Morecambe, Lancashire where, via the gift of our music, we spread the word about life's hardships and the injustices suffered by the down-trodden. The other *Outsider* was my mate Mike who, as well as being considerably more angry than me, was also a much better guitarist. He had a daring, fearless sort of streak which was fun to watch from a distance, but disturbing when he wanted you to become involved – like the night of the Highfield Estate gnome caper.

We'd been struck by the growing number of these odd little ornamental creatures appearing in people's gardens, and Mike took great exception to them for some reason.

"I mean, what's the bloody point?" he'd rant. "If people want to see little old men with beards sitting on a toadstools, why don't they just get stoned or something?"

Basically the plan was that, under cover of darkness, we would transfer as many of them as we could find to one particular garden, and make it look as if they'd all gathered there by themselves during the night. It sounded hilarious in theory, but it soon became clear that we hadn't thought through the logistics very well. After a good hour of our best hole-and-corner cunning, we'd only managed to re-locate 7 gnomes and one plastic flamingo. We were just putting the finishing touches to our gnome circle on some guy's lawn, when he appeared from nowhere and set his border collie on us. It was three streets before it gave up the chase, and twenty minutes before my heart regained its normal rhythm.

Shortly after this Mike kept talking about how great it would be to break into someone's house. "It'll be a laugh," he'd say. "And it's not like we're going to steal anything. We'll just nose around for a bit, and see how the fat cats live." It was always the big posh houses he'd focus on, as if he had some grudge against people with money, and he got irritated with me when I refused to join in. It was bad enough being his accomplice on shop-lifting adventures – just a few packs of ciggies from Patterson's shop

4

maybe, but enough to turn me into a cringing wreck. I definitely drew the line at house-breaking.

It was Mike who first introduced me to Bob Dylan, in whom we both found a kindred spirit. In turn Bob taught us about Woody Guthrie who, thanks to Lonnie Donegan, I was already dimly aware of. Woody lived through the Great American Depression and wrote songs about real people, their lives and the hardships they had to endure – in other words, things that mattered. Bob had absorbed Woody's romantic hobo lifestyle and made it his own, and in passing this dream on to us, we thought we had found a real modern-day 'outsider'. He was a new raw force to be reckoned with, a restless spirit, someone who brought a rebellious sense of freedom and justice to an oppressed and disaffected youth - or so the *Melody Maker* said. I found myself totally caught up by the spell that he cast. Mike and I found the stories of Bob's early years as a sort of folk-singing rambling boy irresistible, fitting in perfectly with the image we had invented for ourselves as latter-day wandering minstrels, drifting around Morecambe Bay, unattached and free.

And so it was, back in 1966, that I found myself in a field outside Strood, England, cold, wet and miserable with a sock full of cow-pat. It had all seemed like a good idea at the time. We had decided to tread the rambling boy path in earnest, follow in the footsteps of our heroes, and become cool folk-singing road-buddies, rambling down the highway. In our case the highway in question was to be the iconic National Seven – that's the road that runs all the way from Paris to the south of France. We were going to hitch lifts from passing strangers, sing for our supper, ride on box-cars (if we could find any), possibly liberate even more gnomes from their capitalist oppressors, and then shake the dust off our boots (or in my case, cow-dung from one's sock) as we moved on from town to town.

I have to say that, up to this point, my experience of rambling round and hitching rides had been fairly limited. Mike had organised my initial induction via a trip to Liverpool - to an actual Bob Dylan concert. This was a strange sort of time as Bob had just 'gone electric' which, for some, had turned him into a traitor to the cause. As for me, I had been so enraptured just to see the man in the flesh, I wouldn't have cared if he'd gone Scottish and taken up the bag-pipes. (Although, to be fair, that's not an image I would wish to dwell on.)

Anyway, we had set off early and quickly got our first lift with a lorry driver who was on his way to Lancaster. It was a noisy, bumpy sort of ride so there wasn't much opportunity to discuss matters of topical interest. We'd then stood and shivered on the roadside for about an hour before a guy pulled up in a grey Ford Cortina. He was a travelling salesman I think, but conversation was again limited as he had the radio on full blast. When a song by Bob Dylan happened to come on Mike tried to tell him that this was the guy we were going to see. Oddly, he just nodded and said, "Yeah. He's rubbish isn't he?"

Prior to this I'd tried some local hitching, just for practice. I went for the full Dylan look by taking my guitar with me, turning my collar up against the wind and perching my denim cap loosely on my tousled curly hair. Looking back, I think it was more likely that I just looked like a bit of a pratt. After about half an hour of fruitless thumbing a car stopped. I felt a brief frisson of excitement followed quickly by a surge of despair as Jim Rooney-the-Loony stuck his head out. He was evidently out for a drive in his Dad's car because sniggering next to him was Susan *'I've-got-a-lovely-bunch-of-coconuts'* Pickles. I cringed. Rooney was well known at school for taking the piss out of everything and I was now directly in his firing line. In fact it was Rooney who had originally saddled me with my horrible nickname - 'Jelly Fish', as in Ni-*jell*. I hated him for that alone.

"Hey, look who's blowin' in the wind! It's me ol' mate J-E-L-L-E-E!!," he yelled. "Jellyfish Broadbent, as I live and breathe. Oh and he's got his 'instrument' with him. What's the name of your group? I keep forgetting – something to do with arses isn't it? No hang on, sorry, back-sides. Yes that's it, he's one half of the famous Back-sides, aren't you Jelly?"

"Out - Side - Ers, actually," I said, spelling it out for him in as sneering a tone as I could muster.

"Oh yeah, that's it. How's the revolution going anyway?"

"Oh sod off, Rooney."

"Eee, did you hear that? And we were going to offer you a lift too."

I considered for a moment that telling the first person who had stopped to sod off, even if it was Rooney-the-Loony, probably wasn't what hitch-hikers usually did. Still, he'd started it. Then Miss Pickles chipped in, "Hey, give us a strum on yer banjo."

"It's not a banjo, actually," I announced loftily. "It's a guitar. Technically, it's what's known as a Jumbo."

6

"O.K. big boy, give us a strum on yer *Jumbo'* then."

They both thought this was hysterically funny for some reason, and collapsed with laughter. Then when he'd got his breath back, Rooney persisted, "So come on then Jelly boy, where're you going, really?"

"None of your business."

"Well we can't give you a lift if you don't tell us."

"I'm just going down the road," I said testily.

"Oh what a shame. We're going *up it,*" and he turned and gave a stupid wink to Susan.

"Yeah," she laughed. "Completely the other way!"

"Still, since he's fighting for world peace and all that, we should try and help him out, shouldn't we Sue?"

"Yeah."

"Oh just p-e-a-c-e off Rooney and leave me alone."

"Ooh, charming. Well alright then, please yourself. No, but seriously though Broadbent … just before I go … I was wondering, how many roads *must* a man walk down? You know, before they call him a man like?"

And he roared off with a brash 'up yours' sort of honk on his horn. I stuck two fingers up after him, just as a bloke with a dog walked past. "You won't get many lifts like that son," he offered. "Try with the thumb".

So by now actually *feeling* like a pratt, I pretended I didn't want a lift anyway and set off walking. When Rooney was safely out of sight I thought I'd try a different tack, and waved my thumb whilst *simultaneously* walking along. I figured that if I looked like I was contributing something to my progress it might encourage more people to stop. I had walked about a mile when a car pulled up beside me. It was my Auntie Pat.

"Where are you going love?"

"Oh, just trying to get to Lancaster."

"Eee, why are you walking? Is it them useless buses again? Always being cancelled aren't they? Well you're in luck, I'm just off to Lancaster myself! Come on then, hop in".

"No, it's all right thanks. I'm trying to thumb a lift."

"Thumb a lift? Don't be silly love. I'm *offering* you a lift. That's why I've stopped. Come on, hop in."

"No I'd rather not if it's all the same. Getting a lift from a relative doesn't actually count. I'm trying to see how far I can get on my own."

She looked upset. "Well you won't get very far if you ask me, not if you keep turning down perfectly good offers." And she drove off in a huff.

I stood and watched her car disappear, feeling somewhat forlorn. Of course she had a point. First Rooney, and now her. I'd waited hours for a lift, two people had stopped and I'd effectively told them both to go away and leave me alone. I figured that, in the ordinary way of things, hitch-hikers probably made more progress by being less choosy.

When Mike and I had set off on our European adventure however, I knew I was with a professional. He knew things like the proper orientation for the thumb when you stick it out, the importance of making eye-contact with the driver as he drives towards you, how it was always helpful to carry cigarettes to offer to your host, and how it was always bad to tell someone to sod off once they'd stopped for you. Even so, with all his knowledge and experience, the first leg of our journey, down to the South Coast, had certainly taken longer than we'd thought. We hit major problems when the M6 ran out at Birmingham and we somehow had to cross the outskirts of the city to get to the M1. Then we'd ended up in London without really meaning to. Does anyone ever actually *mean* to go to London?

As we were changing trains on the Underground we passed a guy with a guitar singing *Blowin' in the Wind* at the bottom of one of the escalators. We stopped to listen and he gave us an angry stare as if challenging us to even think about setting up in any kind of opposition. When he'd finished his song Mike asked him how he was doing.

"Piss off", he said.

It was clear that he hadn't quite grasped the sentiments of the song he'd been singing. I don't know what I expected but I did think the camaraderie he showed towards us as fellow-buskers lacked a certain warmth. But perhaps 'fellow-buskers' was pushing it a bit actually. It has to be said that, up to now, we hadn't had much practice. We certainly never ventured out on to the streets of Morecambe. If we had, I can imagine that, rather than attaining any credibility or even retaining our anonymity, we would have brought the same kind of shame and disgrace on our heads as if we had been caught performing a sexual act in public. *"You don't expect to see that these days Doris – not outside Marks's. Playing with his banjo he was. Your Nigel! Right there in the middle of the street!"*

So our public performances to date had been limited to the Merry Neet Club where at least we were only under the scrutiny of people who had already paid up front. But here in London, Mike was clearly fascinated at the sight of someone actually *busking*, and he was determined we should give it a go before we left England.

We chose a pitch on Oxford Street, tossed my denim cap on to the pavement in front of us, along with a few coins to give people the idea, and then hit them with *San Francisco Bay Blues*. Surprisingly, things went very well at first as a trickle of coins began to jangle into the hat. But as time passed it was clear that we were getting mixed reviews from the passers-by – everything from contempt, to mild amusement, and total disinterest. I also noticed we were being watched by a bloke who was minding a tobacco kiosk just up from where we were standing. After about 10 minutes he came out from behind his counter and walked towards us. I couldn't gauge his expression at first and was hugely relieved when he said, "Do you do requests?" I felt a lurch of pleasure and, smiling pleasantly, told him that indeed we did.

"Right, well sod off then", he said.

Looking back, I really ought to have seen it coming. Feeling somewhat chastened, but also encouraged by our busking initiation, we caught a train out to the suburbs. Then somehow or other, mainly by accepting the first lift that was offered I suspect, we had ended up in the cow field just outside Strood. But at least we were heading in the right direction.

I finally decided I couldn't do much about the cow muck, apart from removing the excess with a twig, so I stuffed my feet uncomfortably into my shoes and we loaded up and hit the road for our final push into Dover for the ferry crossing.

You'll find that folk-singers do quite a lot of travelling down roads. Roads symbolise the journey of life, and rambling down them with no particular destination in mind means that you're restless and unattached, it means that you've chosen to embrace a lifestyle of insecurity and uncertainty with a boldness of spirit that rises above the cold and oppressive system that threatens to trample on your individuality. Except at that particular moment I could have killed for a cup of tea and a warm bath.

But as much as the journey from Morecambe to Strood had been difficult, Strood to Dover proved relatively easy – two lifts was all it took. The first one was a bit strange – after about 20 minutes the chap stopped and said something about having forgotten his briefcase and that he needed to turn back. He dropped us off but then continued on his way, not apparently turning back at all.

"It's your bloody socks!" wailed Mike.

And sure enough, they were giving off a certain aroma. Just as I was wondering what to do, Mike had thumbed down a lorry-driver which turned out to be a stroke of luck on several counts: (a) he was going all the way down to the port, (b) we hadn't been going long when he stopped at a roadside café where he bought us life-affirming bacon rolls and cups of coffee, and (c) there was a pungent stink of diesel in his cab which effectively drowned out all essence of cow-pat.

Once on the boat I was able to clean up my sock (somewhat successfully), and we then stationed ourselves with our luggage in the bar. We sat next to a group of lads who turned out to be French school kids – a school football team in fact who were returning from a brief tour of fixtures against schools in Kent. They eyed up our guitar-shaped luggage and fell into conversation with us about where we were going, and what we were planning to do.

"Aah! Beet-e-neek!" one of them piped up, and before long we had got out the guitars and were playing them some tunes. Mike always reckoned this was a smart move in pubs and bars as it generally led to people buying you drinks or giving you cigarettes. Since these lads were penniless school kids, this seemed a bit optimistic, although it did produce an even better result as it happened. They said they were all bound for Paris and had seats booked on a train departing from Calais. If we wanted we could pretend to be a part of their group, and get a free ride to Paris! Things were definitely looking up as, in my estimation, this was the European equivalent of riding a box-car, or jumping a freight train – or in other words, riding on a train without a ticket.

The only drawback was a certain Monsieur Pierre Dubois, the maitre d', or whatever he was called, who was in charge of the lads and their trip. I thought it would be hard to get him to accept us as members of his team, although the French lads were equally confident this wouldn't be a problem. When Monsieur arrived on the scene we could see why. He was a bearded hippy-type, with pierced ears and long hair tied in a pony-tail, and he appeared just as we were playing 'Monsieur le Tambourine Man'.

"Aah! Les Beet-e-neek!" he exclaimed and, beaming at us in an excited kind of way, he sat down to join in the party. He seemed to me to become gradually more sort of spaced-out as he swayed along to our songs with his eyes closed. Anyway, it proved an easy task to get him to agree to our free lift to Paris and we had a thoroughly enjoyable train ride. Mike thought the fact that he was called 'Dubois' was significant, meaning of-the-woods in French, or 'Woody'. I thought his first name was more significant – 'Pierre' as in the French word for stone, i.e. 'stoned'. He was smoking as I recall, and I don't think it was Gauloises.

Once in France our first aim was to get to Paris. Here, or at least nearby, in a village called Gif-sur-Yvette, we were to rendezvous (as the French say) with Pete, someone we'd met in the Merry Neet Club who was spending his summer holiday at the home of his sister and her French husband. Pete had promised us a bed for the night before we headed on down the long road to the South – the so-called National Seven. Given the length of the walk from the Gare du Nord to Gif, and the general shortage of freight trains on that route, we decided to make our way there by Metro and bus.

The journey was fairly uneventful. There was just the toilet stop that we attempted in a street café, where the *garçon* chased after us and, going purely from his intonation and gesticulation, we deduced that he wanted to know why we'd used his *toilette* without having ordered any drinks. So to preserve the entente cordiale we ordered 'deux tasses de café' in our best secondary school French.

By the time we arrived in Gif it was dark and fairly late – too late in fact to go knocking on Pete's sister's door, especially as at this point we had no idea which door it was. We had an address, but no street map, and therefore no clue where the house was. On the edge of the village, near to where the bus had dropped us, was an old woodshed, so we decided to doss down in there for the night. There was a pile of old railway sleepers in particular which, as well as being raised off the damp ground, gave us a level resting-place.

As I settled down in my sleeping bag, a gentle tune started up and fluttered by on the breeze. Not being the type who could go for long periods without picking out a tune, Mike had got out his guitar. The tune was instantly recognisable – an instrumental piece called *Angie* written by another virtuoso guitarist called Davey Graham. Mike was working on it constantly, perfecting his mastery of it. The furthest I'd ever got was the base-line, which you play with your thumb, but I could never get my other fingers to coordinate the melody.

Mike and I had been in the same class at school and he was one of the first people I met when I moved in to live with my Aunt Doris and Uncle Fred, which happened when I was about nine. His parents owned the Post Office in a street behind my Aunt and Uncle's house in Morecambe, so we took the same route to school. The routine became that he'd call for me as he went past and we'd walk down together. He always seemed to know a lot of girls which of course became part of the charm of walking down with him as we got older. He was also one of the few people who didn't stoop to calling me by my stupid nickname. I don't know why he did that, perhaps it was something to do with the fact that he and Rooney hated each other.

He didn't talk about it much but the general impression was that he had a pretty rough time at home. He had a younger sister Rosie, who was in some way brain-damaged. I think there'd been something wrong with the birth, a shortage of oxygen to the brain or something during the delivery. It had a devastating effect on Mike's Mum anyway, who subsequently had long periods away from home "for a break", although we all knew she was actually in the local mental hospital. This was another of our shared connections. You could tell when she was going off it because she'd drift off into a kind of trance and become pre-occupied and sad. His Dad's escape was to busy himself in the Post Office and Mike, from the age of 10 or so, was more or less left to get on with it.

He emerged from all this as a sort of funny mixture of soft and hard, very caring and protective towards Rosie, but sometimes very cold and cruel to his friends. Altogether he was fiercely independent, and that's what I liked about him really. One thing was sure, you never *ever* made fun of his mother or sister – unless you were either an unfeeling thug, a thick bastard, or just plain tired of living. I remember one occasion vividly, outside a chip shop, when a very ugly fight broke out between Mike and thick Baz Newby who referred to Rosie as 'the spasmo'.

There were lots of times when he could easily turn into a callous bully himself though, and he took particular pride in sneering at others' tastes in fashion and music. He once wrote "shit" on another of our mate's prized Elvis L.P's which I thought was particularly unkind. But equally he could be this other type of considerate and kind bloke, and he was always patient with me when teaching me new songs or guitar runs. Once when I was off sick he called round with the new Bob Dylan L.P.

which had just been released and had bought only the previous day. He told my Aunt Doris he thought it would cheer me up and that I could borrow it as long as I didn't breathe on it or touch it, and actually left some woollen gloves and a surgeon's mask along with it. Aunt Doris thought this was hilarious. His manner was also generally shy and unassuming in a way that clearly impressed her so that her overall conclusion was that he was "a nice boy".

That was why she hadn't kicked up too much fuss about my trip to France – once she had come round to the idea that is. She was resistant at first, and managed to upset me quite badly when I first talked to her and Uncle Fred about it. "I don't know," she said, "you're just like your father, wandering off to who-knows-where at a moment's notice." I felt rage surge up in me at the very suggestion that my plans resembled my father's selfish abandonment of his family in any remote way, but luckily Uncle Fred came to my defence. "Nay lass," he said. "Don't be saying things like that to the lad. He's young and after a bit of adventure, that's all." Then again, I think the whole Ramblin' Boy ethic was a bit lost on Aunt Doris anyway. That much became clear when, after I'd tried to explain to her again what we were planning to do, she asked me why we didn't try to get a few chums together and go to France by double-decker bus or something – "like Cliff Richard did in that film."

But on the whole she thought I'd be alright with Mike. Luckily she didn't get to hear that, just before we left Sandra, his girlfriend of the day was mysteriously whisked off to her Aunt's in Brighton for an extended holiday. One might have called it maternity leave, except that the two families had come to the painful conclusion that there was no way Sandra could actually see the baby through to term.

Our trip has begun soon after all this, which I guess was very timely from this point of view although Mike's attitude to the whole thing was pretty despicable, referring to his unborn child as "the sprog". He even treated poor Sandra as if it was all her fault. I didn't know her very well actually. She came over as rather excitable and somewhat annoying, but she was hardly deserving of the contempt Mike appeared to show towards her. And now here he was with the gentle touch – here he was bent over his guitar in the darkness entirely focussed on picking out this beautiful tune, delicately blending and bending notes so that the song became alive.

He'd had been playing since he was about 12. Music became an important therapy I suppose. It concentrated his mind and gave him a necessary distraction from the worry and tensions within the family and, from his parents' point of view, I guess they were happy that it kept him occupied and out of trouble. They bought him quite an expensive guitar, maybe to ease their guilt at not giving him much else in the way of time and attention. It was a Gibson, which Mike considered to be the 'Royal Family' of guitar manufacturers. Anyway, he'd undoubtedly become a very proficient guitarist who could play with flair and competence. Meanwhile I came puffing up behind as a very definite also-ran. I'd only been playing for about 18 months and my technique was certainly more primitive. I could flat-pick and strum out a reasonable tune, but I had to learn every new tune very carefully, chord by chord. The kind of finger-style guitar Mike played was mostly out of my range. My guitar was also of a decidedly cheaper make. Mike sneered at its 'action' – that's the space between the strings and the fret-board – and referred to it as the 'Bob Scratchit' of guitars. I, on the other hand loved her dearly.

I listened to him play and became aware of the stillness around us, as if everything else around had also stopped to listen. That's the difference between me and Mike I thought – I carefully learn the notes, whereas he knows how to play the song.

14

2

Next morning there were some worrying signs of activity nearby, so we got up, packed our stuff together, and headed off into the village. There was a fine drizzle in the air – the kind that gets you wet through in record time without you even being aware of it. We accosted one or two of the locals to seek directions. They all looked at us very quizzically, with a curious mixture of puzzlement and disgust. It was as if our innocent enquiry about the street - "Connaissez-vous cette rue s'il vous plait?"- was being freely translated in their heads as "Can I sleep with your daughter please?" But eventually, after one or two false leads, we found our way to the house and I knocked on the door.

Perhaps because it was 7.30 in the morning, or perhaps because we weren't altogether expected, I felt our welcome was a little on the cold side.

"Non, non" said this thin little voice through a crack in the door. "Allez-vous en … vite, vite".

"We are friends of Pete", I protested quickly. "Amis de Pierre – from Angleterre".

"Merde!" said the voice, adding as she shut the door, "un moment s'il vous plait – I mean, hang on a sec…."

We then heard the muffled sound of Pete's name being called, then some more muffled sounds from upstairs, and after several more minutes Pete finally appeared at the door, dripping wet and wrapped in a towel.

"What the hell are you two doing here?" he moaned.

"Yeah, nice to see you too mate," said Mike. "You said you'd put us up you tosser – you know, when we were on our way to St Tropez?"

Pete banged his head against the side of the door, nearly losing his towel in the process. "Bloody hell", he said. "I didn't think you were serious! St Tropez? Good God! How the hell did you find your way here anyway?"

But we didn't have to answer as just then an older man loomed up behind him, looking fairly menacing. "What's going on here then?" he boomed. "And who the hell are you two scruffy-looking articles?"

"It's O.K. Dad. It's just Mike and Nige. I know them from … er … from the Club. They're … er … passing through."

I felt anxious, both about Pete's attitude towards us, and the contemptuous tone he used when he described us as being 'from the Club', but luckily his Dad didn't pick up on that part.

"Passing through?" he said. "You bet your life they're passing through. On your way lads. And what do you think you're doing inviting people to your sister's house anyway?"

"I didn't invite them, honest Dad. I didn't know they were coming! They've just sort of turned up."

I'd never met Pete's Dad before. In fact I didn't know Pete all that well. He was a regular down at the Merry Neet and it was when we were packing up one night and happened to mention we were off to St Tropez that he'd said, "Hey, call in on me on your way down!" And I clearly remember him giving us this address. I imagined that he was either being a twat, or he had really forgotten. I suspected both were true in fact. But by now the pleasure of being reunited with our old chum was beginning to wear a little thin, and it seemed clear that the most rational thing to do was to make a strategic exit and leave them to it. Mike intervened.

"Look, Mr Saunders," he said, "we really don't want to cause you any trouble. We're on our way to the South, and we thought Pete had invited us to call in as we passed by. It's just a big misunderstanding that's all, and we have no wish to cause you or your family any offence. We'll just get on our way. I'm sorry again that we've troubled you."

Yes, Mike was good at this. The mixture of a polite middle-class apology with the doleful little-boy-lost tone of voice worked a magic charm on Pete's Dad and he melted before our eyes.

"It's O.K. lads," he said. "Look, I can see you're both wet and cold, and I don't want to seem unkind. This has just come as a bit of a shock, that's all. I'm sure we can rustle you up a bit of breakfast or something before we send you on your way."

I sensed a certain emphasis on the idea of "sending us on our way" but he then invited us in. As we gradually warmed through, so did the general atmosphere between us all. I wouldn't say a family atmosphere developed exactly, but, with the exception of Pete who seemed determined to treat us like scabby lepers, the warmth of our welcome did raise a few degrees over a lovely breakfast of coffee, croissants, and cold meats.

It turned out that Pete's Dad had just arrived unexpectedly himself, so perhaps that helped him to empathise with our predicament of being yet more unexpected arrivals. Pete's sister was also warm and friendly, particularly when Mike and she discovered they had mutual friends in Morecambe. As it happened, her husband had left early for Paris on a business trip, so we'd missed him, and actually it felt that we were more easily accepted because we could all be Englishmen (and woman) together.

Pete's Dad seemed a nice enough guy in fact – sort of bluff and severe, but warm and friendly underneath. He reminded me of my Uncle Fred, who was usually fairly fixed and uncompromising in his views yet had been oddly supportive of me taking this little trek. I suspect that he and Aunt Doris were pleased to see the back of me actually, having been dumped on them after my Dad left and my mother went well, strange. Still, that's another story. Probably the fact that I had a University place to come back to helped. Uncle Fred was actually quite proud of the fact that I was going to read Chemistry, taking it as a sign that it reflected some kind of vocational choice. In fact I only chose it because I was entranced by the lovely Miss Rosemary Benson, my Chemistry teacher, and hadn't a clue what else to do.

As well as that, Uncle Fred had also spent some of his teenage years in National Service when, as he never tired of telling me, he'd had to 'rough it'. It was something of a conceptual leap, but I think he saw this trip as a means for me to get some character-building experience in the real world of work and self-sufficiency before I came back to get a 'good college education' and 'a good job'.

Of course I left him to his misapprehensions – I had no intention of seeking proper 'work' in France (which he had fixedly determined was picking grapes), nor did I see University as a route to a good education, well not in the academic sense anyway. I was putting the emphasis more on the benefits of boozy nights, the social and music scene, and the general kipping around. And 'a good job'? I hadn't a clue what he had in mind on that one. I did once tell him that I thought 'good' and 'job' were contradictory concepts. I might have got away with it had I not over-reached myself and tried to use the word 'oxymoron' to seal the argument. At that point he gave me a clip round the ear and told me in very plain terms not to be a smart-arse. I thought that might be an epithet, but didn't want to risk further injury, so said nothing.

"So where are you headed anyway lads?" Pete's Dad asked as we hungrily munched our croissants.

"To the south coast, to St Tropez," Mike said.

"St Tropez? Wow, that's a hell of a long way you know. Hitch-hiking? All that way?"

His pessimism wasn't helpful, but Mike just shrugged it off.

"It'll be O.K. There's a road that runs all the way from Paris to the south coast – the National Seven? All we have to do is fix ourselves on that and keep heading south."

"Well I wish you luck," he said, and had a little unkind chuckle to himself. Doubts about the wisdom of our trip started to sprout in my mind.

"How far do you reckon it is Mr Saunders?" I asked.

"Ooo …well…it's got to be at least 450 miles, maybe more." I think he saw my disquiet. "Why do you have to go all that way in any case?" he asked.

Of course there were very important reasons, but probably not ones he would easily understand. It was all to do with Bert and John, especially John. They were two guitar virtuosos who put out amazing L.P's playing tunes and folk songs in the context of fantastically intricate guitar work. As far as I could make out, they lived in some flat in Soho, played music all day whilst smoking Players Gold Leaf, and sang about rambling down highways, running away from home, and generally not giving much of a toss. Needless to say, as soon as I got to know about it, their music was so far up my street it was in the kitchen and making itself a cup of tea in no time at all.

Anyway, on one of his L.P's John had a song called *National Seven,* basically a song about a disillusioned guy hitching down this road all the way to St Tropez whilst trying to forget some tortured experience of unrequited love. We had thought it was going to be just so cool to follow in his footsteps, and not only would we be just like John, but also like Bob and Woody. I wasn't sure Mr Saunders would appreciate the thinking behind all this though, so I just muttered something about wanting to see what the French Riviera was like compared to Morecambe. He laughed so hard I wasn't at all sympathetic about him almost choking on his coffee.

After breakfast Pete's Dad offered to give us a lift out to the 'main road' where we could carry on hitching lifts down to the South. He was clearly taking no chances that we'd actually be leaving – although that's somewhat unkind, as he pressed a 20 franc note into my hand as he dropped us off. "Good luck lads" he said, "and remember me when you're famous!" Pete on the other hand was less than generous. He scowled at us, and gave us the finger out of the window as the car sped away.

18

Of course, being roving ramblers on the hobo trail, we didn't go in for soft things like maps. So when Pete's Dad dropped us off we quickly came to the sudden realisation that we didn't know where on earth we were. It looked like a 'main road' in that it was wide enough for two cars, but there were no road markings and, even more worryingly, no sign of any cars. Luckily Mike had a compass function on his Swiss Army knife, so at least we could work out which general direction was south. We set off walking and after about 10 minutes, miraculously really, a guy in a tractor-like machine rolled by, and stopped just up ahead of us.

"Alors!" he shouted back. "Où allez-vous mes amis?"

Marvellous, I thought – he even speaks French I can understand.

"Vers le sud", Mike shouted back confidently.

"Le sud! Hé hé hé! C'est loin, non?" and then set off laughing again. His French then seemed to go up several gears, way past A-level and probably up to degree level, as he spoke and gesticulated quite quickly and energetically. The gist of it seemed to be that we could climb into his trailer and, we assumed, he'll give us a lift somewhere – *vers le sud*, hopefully.

As we were getting in I tried to shout "Connaissez-vous le National Sept?" but I don't think he heard me. He just gave a sort of funny wave, turned away, and shoved his machine into gear. We then bumped along uncomfortably for what seemed like an hour or so. All we could do was trust him, as there was no way any further communication was possible given the distance between us in the trailer and him in the tractor, and the noise of the engine. We anxiously watched as we crossed over various promising-looking highways, any of which I could swear would have taken us *vers le sud*. Eventually he drove into a village where he stopped and indicated for us to get off.

"Le National Vingt – c'est là-bas", he said, pointing in some general direction to the right. "Bonne chance mes amis!" and he drove off.

National Vingt – didn't '*Vingt*' mean 20? What the hell was that, and where did it go? We had imagined getting on to the National Seven would be easy from Gif – everyone would know this famous road to the south, and all we'd have to do was follow it till it ran out. Why would you need a map? Now I was beginning to think one would come in handy. In the end we resolved to go down the N20 to the next major town, buy a map, and plot a route over to the N7. Simple.

Four hours later we were still standing on the National *Vingt*, exactly one kilometre away from the village where we started and several hundred away from St Tropez. By now it was about 6 o'clock in the evening, it was starting to rain, and we were both feeling fed up and hungry. Pete's sister had kindly given us some baguettes and cheese as we'd left Gif, which we'd scoffed during our tractor ride, but now we generally agreed that a hot meal wouldn't go amiss. So we plodded back into the village, found a little bar/café and had a 'slapsie' (as we called these kind of treats) of soup, roast beef and frites. I feared such treats were to come less and less often as our journey wore on.

The café owner was a big burly chap with a huge bushy moustache, as if he was carrying a pet hamster under his nose. He bore a chilling resemblance to Stalin, which unnerved me rather, plus the fact that you couldn't actually see where the sound was coming from when he talked. He created a certain air of menace and I imagined the welcome we got had a similar quality to the one Trotsky might have got if he ever unexpectedly called on the Stalins for tea. As he served us our food he asked us where we were going, so we gave our usual '*vers le sud*' reply. It seemed to cheer him up as, even though I couldn't tell if he was smiling or not, he went off muttering, "Bon, bon, très bon" to himself. He went over to join a guy sitting at the bar. This guy also had a moustache, but it was Zapata style, and I thought he looked vaguely Mexican. I tried to think what joint interests Stalin and Mexico could have.

"Bit strange in here, isn't it?" I said to Mike.

"What?" He seemed pre-occupied.

"Over there ...." I nodded towards Stalin and his mate.

No response.

"You O.K?"

"Yeah".

"You seem a bit ... I don't know .. somewhere else".

"Oh, just feeling a bit pissed off really".

And then he took me completely by surprise when he said, "Well actually I was thinking about my Mum". I can honestly say I have never ever heard Mike say such a thing before. I was so taken aback, I didn't know what to do. So I just sat there, numbed, wondering what was coming next. Nothing. So I decided to risk a little prompt. Something safe, and inoffensive.

"Are you missing her?"

"Piss off! *Missing her?* Course I'm not *missing her*!"

Oops .... something even more safe and less offensive then.

"Sorry". Yeah, that was safe enough.

"She just wasn't right when I left ... you know? She just seemed more out of it than usual. Didn't know what to make of it ..." and he looked thoughtful. More silence.

I tried something a bit riskier.

"Do you think it's all that stuff with Sandra and the baby?"

He visibly winced, and shot me a dark angry look. I wished I'd just kept quiet. He breathed in deeply and looked down again. As I was clearly on dodgy ground, I decided to try another tack.

"Did you say anything to your Dad?"

"No", he sighed, now breathing out. "No use talking to that bastard – not unless you want to buy a postal order or something".

We lapsed into silence again. I wanted to hear more, but I still hadn't a clue what to say. I just felt confused. I'd never really known Mike to worry about anything. It was one of the big differences between him and me that I liked. He could always seem to find some optimism that things will work out, whereas with me, it was generally the painful feelings of hope that did me in. In the end I just said, possibly rather stupidly, "Mmm, it's sad". It animated him.

"Sad? Did you say sad? What's sad you pillock. I was just thinking, that's all. I don't need you to go all Marjorie bloody Proops on me".

Now I felt stung and not a little bit fed up with him.

"Do you have to swear at me so much?" I said, "I'm only trying to talk to you."

He looked at me sharply and I stiffened, preparing for another tongue lash, but instead he softened and then ... he actually apologised to me.

"Yeah, sorry mate," he said. "You're right. I shouldn't be shouting at you. Sorry. Let's just leave it shall we?"

He looked away, and started fiddling with his thumbs. We sat for a bit longer, and I found I was now starting to feel depressed, as well as somewhat anxious at this glimpse into his vulnerability, so eventually I said, "Not doing so well with the lifts are we?"

"Oh, we'll be alright", he said. "Be there in no time".

Then I caught sight of Stalin eyeing us up.

"People don't seem to like us".

"Yeah well we're freewheelin' hippy betta-neeks, aren't we? Ramblers and gamblers. We unnerve people with our rejection of conventional values, our drop-out lifestyle ethic, our liberated sexual politics, and our drug-crazed mentality. We threaten the very fabric of organised society".

"Oh yeah", I said. "Sorry, I forgot".

He lifted me though and I found myself feeling defiant again – well just a little. I have to admit that at that particular moment, my sense of defiance was quite weak actually, probably equivalent to the time when I once asked for coffee at Auntie Pat's when everyone else was having tea - but I was working on it.

Meanwhile Mike was still banging on. Now he was having a rant about 'rubber-necks' and their empty lives. Technically of course, a rubber-neck is just a tourist, or sight-seer (and that's what we were ourselves, ironically enough), but Mike used it as a generic term of abuse for anyone who was even remotely living a conventional lifestyle. He'd got his energy back though, and he'd reminded me why we were here – to embrace the freedom that came with abandoning a life of convention, to feel the romance of the open road, and to exercise the sheer don't-give-a-toss-ness of our restless spirits. Then the thought hit me that it was actually got quite dark outside and we didn't have anywhere to sleep.

We remembered seeing a hay barn not far from where the farmer originally dropped us so we headed off to find it again. We then spent quite a comfortable night as the barn had a lot going for it in that it was dry and enclosed, and the hay made quite a soft bed. We left fairly early to avoid discovery, not wishing to be seen as ungrateful and intrusive tramps, plus there was the chance that Stalin already had his secret police out searching for us.

Back on the N20, because it was still quite early there wasn't that much traffic, and now that an hour or so had dragged by we were both feeling pretty pissed off – again. Then, apparently out of nowhere, a car drew up and to my surprise it was Stalin's pal, the Mexican, who grinned at us in a mindless sort of way.

"Ah, les beet-e-neeks anglais!" he said. "Allez! Allez! Je vous ......", and I thought he said something about helping us on our way. It crossed my mind that he might actually be saying that he had been ordered to arrest us and have us both shot, but on the other hand, it was still the best offer we'd had all morning, so we got in. In a little while we arrived at a medium-size sort of town where he pulled up at a railway station and invited us to *descendez*. He then looked out of his window and through clenched teeth which was somewhere between a smile and a leer, he said:

"'Ev a nice treeep", before he sped away. I said to Mike that he was like the guys in the old cowboy films who want to "speeet" on things all the time. "I speeet on your gringo treeep" kind-of-thing, and I guess what we were experiencing was somewhat close to being run out of town.

Being a hobo-hero was sometimes a difficult path to tread. Whilst the easy option would have been to have just caught a train as our new pal had kindly suggested, we both agreed that we had to make a stand and refuse to be intimidated. In other words, have another go at hitching a ride. So we walked out to good old N20 and tried our luck.

The thing about being pissed off is the effect it has on one's enthusiasm. Having had four hours of fruitless hitching the day before, and a further couple of similar hours this morning, plus the way we always seemed to spur people into spontaneous acts of hostility, I was not really in the mood for a further spell of standing by the roadside. As ramblin' down the highway goes, a few hours in the rain were probably neither here nor there, but I was only a beginner after all, and our lack of progress was getting to me. I even caught myself feeling nostalgic for Rooney-the-Loony and his Dad's Cortina. After three and a half days I thought we might have at least set foot on the N7, even if we hadn't travelled very far down it. Now, in-between unsuccessful hitching spells Mike seemed to think it was O.K to get out his guitar and pick off a few tunes. I could feel my mood turning darker all the time, so rather than the hypnotic effect *Angie* had on me in Gif, now she was just getting right up my nose.

"For God's sake! Do you have to? How the hell were we gonna get a lift with you looking like a bloody, bloody....busking.... beggar!"

"Ha!" said Mike in his best Mexican drawl, "I speeet on your gringo moozik … pah!"

So we gave in graciously and trudged back to the station where the first thing we did was to buy a map. The town we were in was called Etampes, and it seemed that we had been wending our way from Paris in a general southerly direction towards Orléans. This turned out to be just a few stops down the line, and a single fare was a mere 9F20. Apart from having a hip and bluesy name ('The House of the Rising Sun' was after all *in* Orleans – well alright then, *New* Orleans), we could see from the map that it also seemed to be a promising route centre. So, feeling we were committing some sort of blasphemous act, we bought our tickets, boarded a train, and headed off to Orléans.

When we got there we worked out that, from Calais, we'd actually travelled about 250 miles towards the south. So much for ramblin' down the highway though – we'd travelled 230 of those miles by public transport, and hadn't yet had a single sighting of the mythical old National Seven.

3

We walked out of the station at Orléans and were confronted by a large open square. A huge cathedral, almost as big as the Notre Dame in Paris, loomed up close by. In the distance noisy traffic busied itself up and down a wide street. I felt my heart sink. Another big city. And we were stuck in the middle of it without a clue how to get to the outskirts, where there was the possibility of lifts, the road south, or even access to National Seven. We unfurled the map, which was actually like opening up a bed sheet and it flapped angrily in the breeze threatening to tear itself out of our hands. With a complex mixture of physical contortion and manual dexterity we were finally able to tame it and assess our position. There was however a curious phenomenon at work, which I noticed on the train coming down - whenever and however I opened it, it always seemed to be upside down.

The south of France looked a million miles away, but we were able to deduce that we were about 75 Km from the nearest intersection with National Seven. Pushing back the boundaries of our O-Level French we asked for directions to get us on the right road, but since we tended to get too much 'à droite' and 'à gauche', in the end we just settled for a 'tout droite', and headed in that direction until we felt a need to ask again.

Being pre-occupied with my anxieties and general discomfort at our rate of progress, I hadn't made a connection between Orléans and its famous 'Maid' – Joan of Arc – or Jeanne d'Arc as they say *en France*. Walking through the town however, the casual traveller was forcibly reminded of the connection at every turn. There were cafés named after her, avenues bearing her name, and of course stone statues bearing her likeness. We made our way to another big square via a long avenue, and peered up at a statue of Joan astride her horse, rampant.

"What's she famous for?" I asked Mike.

It was like switching on the radio. "Freeing the city", he began, "from the English. At one point they had totally taken it over and everyone in Orléans was trapped. Joan felt she had a call from God to help free the city, throw the English out of France, and get the Dauphin to claim his crown. She used her passion and conviction to persuade him to give her an army, and basically wouldn't take no for an answer. Anyway, she ended up leading them all to a great victory. It was a turning point type of thing."

He said all this with great authority, as if he'd suddenly transformed into a tour guide. He sometimes took me by surprise like that, with outbursts of apparently wide-ranging general knowledge. I just wished he didn't sound so pompous.

"How do you know all that?" I said.

"Are you kidding?" he said. "I had to write a whole essay about her last year. They burnt her at the stake in Rouen".

"Yes I know that," I said, feeling somewhat peeved. "But why burn her if she did all that for them?"

"That's the French for you. No - I dunno – she got too big for her boots I suppose. She lost favour with the King cos of banging on too much about God's will and all that. Anyway they handed her over to the English in the end, and it was us who arranged for her cremation."

"Her cremation?"

"Yeah."

"But hadn't she just been burnt at the stake? Why would they give her back to be cremated? Sounds a bit excessive doesn't it?"

"No, you pratt. The English had her burnt at the stake – they *cremated* her, when she was still alive. That's why the French still hate us so much – well, one of the reasons."

I wondered if it was worthwhile trying to explain that I was in fact joking, but decided that would only make it worse. So, in a feeble effort to salvage the moment, I just said wistfully, "Well I'd hate anything like that to happen to me."

We lumbered on through the town. As well as the 'tout droite' rule, we also deduced that the road signs were operating a sort of filtering system. It operated by indicating one main route, which was always accompanied by another sign which said *"toutes directions"*. All directions! We translated this as meaning 'anywhere you like' and this was the suggestion we usually took up. But I found that, just as I was losing confidence in it as a way-finding system, the streets started to get quieter and open up to a more rural landscape, and we arrived at a road which offered distinct hitching possibilities. Not only that, there was a sign pointing to a place called Briare which, we knew from the map, intersected with the N7. It was only 72 Km. We were on course again.

Two hours later we were still on course, mainly because we hadn't actually moved. If it wasn't for the occasional car tooting playfully at us, I would have thought we had turned invisible. Why *was* it so hard to get lifts in this country? I suppose it wasn't difficult to work out really. We were hardly the ideal travelling companions – two scruffy blokes, two fairly big rucksacks, and two guitars. Many of the cars looked like upside-down prams rather than motor vehicles – not really built to cope with us and all our gear. Plus, as Mike had pointed out, what we had done to Joan clearly still rankled.

Then, wonder of wonders, a car approached and slowed to a stop. Mike ran towards it whilst I started to bundle our gear together. When I next looked up the car was pulling away, having apparently deposited two of its passengers on the roadside. Two girls. One was short and blonde, but the other particularly caught my eye. She was taller, and dark, with long hair and a fringe, styled in a Marianne Faithfull kind of way. I was also struck by the rather jazzy black-and-white patterned jumper she was wearing which, in an odd way, seemed to reflect something of the slightly agitated impact she was having on me. Both were carrying rucksacks, and I wondered if they might be English too, but as I rushed up the blonde one turned and said:

"Ça va?"

"Oui, ça va?" I said. It was only three words, but apparently enough to give my nationality away. However hard I tried I could never seem to master the art of actually sounding French.

"Ah, Anglais!" she said. "Where do you go?"

"Vers le sud," I said, still trying to sound French.

They both giggled. That phrase – why did it always amuse people so? "We also", said the dark one this time. "We go to the south too. St Trop."

"Yes, St Trop!" I said excitedly. "We are going there!" I started to develop a fantasy about strolling down the highway with them, all of us arm in arm and laughing. The spirit of Joan was with us after all. Rescue was forthcoming again from a French girl (and her friend) for two poor souls besieged and trapped in Orléans.

"You .. er … *faîtes l'autostop?*" she continued, and mimed with her thumb.

"Yes," I said, "but –" and then Mike cut in, proudly announcing that we had just hitched down from Paris. I gawped at him.

"We too," she said. "You are having the success?"

"Oh yes," he said. "We only left this morning."

27

I was both horrified and grateful that he could produce such a lie. But, with our guitars and all, these girls had clearly already formed an image of us as cool folk-singing hobo types, the kind of alienated loners they had probably read about, who drifted and rambled through towns like Orléans before restlessly moving on. Obviously it would have been cruel to destroy their fantasy.

"We have come from near Paris," the dark one said. "Now we go down this road to meet the National Seven. It goes all the way to St Trop, you know?"

Does it? does it really? I thought to myself.

"Yes," said Mike. "Perhaps we could go together..." I held my breath. They looked at each other.

"Ah no, it is not possible," she said at last. " *Je suis désolée*. We have too many bags. It would be very difficult to get the ride for all of us together. But perhaps we could meet you when you arrive!"

Better than nothing I suppose.

"I hope so. Do you know of any places to stay?"

"We are camping. We have some friends who are there and who we go to meet. They sleep on the beach. When you arrive, you come to the beach, yes? My name is Bobbi, and this is Jeanne."

We shook hands and introduced ourselves. I was relieved at last to be on first name terms, especially when Jeanne repeated my name in the most deliciously sensual way I had ever heard – "Ah, Nee-jjelle". I never knew my name could be so .. well .. damn sexy. Eat your heart out Rooney! And *she* was called Jeanne! The Maid of Orléans! She really had been sent to rescue us.

Jeanne was the dark one and I found her very attractive, with her pretty face framed by her long brown hair, complementing her big brown eyes. Bobbi was attractive too, although was the more petite, and looked a bit more world-weary and care-worn than Jeanne. Then, as if she could read my thoughts, Jeanne said, "I have my boyfriend in St Trop. I am going to meet him there. Then we go to Nice where he has – how do you say it - *un apartement.*" I was immediately suspicious of him. An apartment? In Nice?

"Are you going to play at the cafés?" she asked.

I felt pleased she had at last referred to our guitars and I geared up for a detailed conversation about our folksy drift-along lifestyle. In fact I'm sure we would have gone on exploring our new relationship in some depth, and continuing to find more and more things we had in common, had not Bobbi then suggested that they should get going.

"We will walk down the road a little way," she said, "so if a car comes he will stop for you at first. It is easier for girls ... you know ... *l'autostop*. We will not wait long after you have gone." Then, quite unhelpfully, she added, "We could have a race!"

"Good idea," said Mike, equally unhelpfully. "We will see you in St Trop."

I knew the French like some sort of physical contact on greeting and parting, but was disappointed to find that our relationship had not yet developed to the kiss-on-both-cheeks stage. So we just shook hands again as Jeanne said, "Alors ... au'voir Mike ... au'voir Nee-jjelle." My knees went sort of weak, but I just about managed to croak out an "Au'voir" in reply as they walked off down the road.

Mike and I took up our place again by the roadside and we watched them walking into the distance and getting smaller with every step. Then they stopped and started to hitch. After about 10 minutes a car sped past us and pulled to a stop opposite them. I saw them talk briefly to the driver, and then they got in. Bobbi turned towards us as she did so, shrugged her shoulders and waved at us. It only confirmed my feeling that I liked Jeanne better. I also remember feeling a weird sort of certainty that I would definitely see her again.

After about another 15 minutes or so we were both feeling pretty fed up. By then it had even started to drizzle with rain, which only compounded our misery. We were anxiously looking round for a place to shelter when a car pulled up on the opposite side of the road, and a man stuck his head out.

"Allo, allo," he said.

"Allo?" I said.

"Ah, engleesh!" he said immediately. How did they do it? Just one word this time and he could tell! He went on: "I go past an hour before, and I see you. Now you are still here! You have no luck today, ah? And now it rains. I can take you to the railway station, my friends. Come, come."

"Thank you very much," I said, "but –"

I noticed Mike was already crossing the road. I shouted to him and he turned. "Come on you pratt," he said. "We're not going to get a better offer are we?"

Our driver seemed like a good, jovial sort. I thought he was dressed a bit funny though, and wondered if he might have just come from a fancy dress party or something when I realised that he was actually a priest. As we drove along he chatted in a way that wasn't always easy to understand, but there was quite a bit about *l'autostop* and its dangers. He was clearly keen to be of help to us, and even gave us some bread and cheese. We ate it gratefully, although I did think it tasted a bit dodgy for some reason. Mike only took one bite in fact, but I munched on, not wanting to seem ungrateful. When we got to the station he took out his wallet and offered us a 10 franc note.

"This will help with the ticket. Good luck, my friends," he said. "Adieu, et bon courage, ah?"

Of course one shouldn't look a gift horse in the mouth and all that, but for the first time we had accepted a lift from a man who had actually taken us backwards instead of forwards. We left this station about 5 hours ago, and now here we were back again!

"It's what's called *déjà vu*," Mike offered.

But at least we were dry, and by now it was getting late. And perhaps the train was a good idea. After all, it seemed to be God's will in a kind of way.

We looked again at the map. Half-way between Orléans and St Tropez was the major town of Lyon. From there, a thick red line went down the map, almost perpendicularly, to Marseille. Yes, it was the good old National Seven. We could join it at Lyon and be well on our way to our final destination. I felt we could take comfort in the knowledge that we'd given it a good shot so far, what with our attempts at hitching and all, and we'd had a good old ramble through the town. A train ride was allowed when such long distances were involved surely. So we bought the tickets – 42F50 each. Then, having bought the tickets, we looked for the departure time of the next train – 7 am tomorrow!

But by now we were feeling fairly hungry anyway, so decided to go to a nearby café and blow our new found wealth on a decent hot meal. We packed all the bags into a Left Luggage locker, except that Mike insisted in bringing his guitar with him.

"You never know", he said.

I couldn't see the point myself, but neither could I be bothered to make an issue of it. Soon we were in Café Mazarin hungrily munching into *bifteck and frites,* and swilling it down with draught lager. We found the measures a bit of a puzzle at first, but in the end we plumped for the *formidable*, which turned out to be like a tall heavy flower vase. The reception here was also much more friendly than our experience to date, and a tall leggy mademoiselle (who kept smiling seductively at Mike) took our order. She stood in quite a provocative way actually, legs slightly apart and hands on her hips. I got a strange sense of something familiar, but then remembered the scene in that Gene Kelly film where he does an extremely sexy dance with the waitress, Lesley Caron and I thought it must be that. I felt quite pleased with this clever association so I said to Mike, "Do you know that film with Gene Kelly and Lesley Caron?"

"What?"

"The one where he's a sailor in a bar, and she's the voluptuous waitress. *An American in Paris!* Yeah, that's it. She comes over and stands next to his table in a sexually provocative way, so he gets up and grabs her. Then they do this dance where he throws her around the tables and that. This place reminds me of that".

Mike considered this for a moment or two, then said, "It was Cyd Charisse. And it was in *Singing in the Rain*".

"Are you sure?"

"Yeah, definitely. She's a gangster's moll or something, and he's sitting at his table, eyeing her up. She comes over seductively, whips off his hat with her lovely long leg, and then they have this highly sexually-charged dance. It's called the Apache dance actually".

I wasn't convinced, and I particularly didn't like his pompous tone again, and the sneering way he seemed to be putting me down. He sounded so sure of himself, and smug.

"Clever bastard aren't you?" I said, and went into a sulk for a bit. He leant over and ruffled my hair and I felt like throwing my formidable over his stupid grinning face.

Perhaps I was just feeling weary and hungry. My mood certainly brightened as I ate the hot food. Then when we'd eaten Lesley Caron came over to clear away the plates. She nodded vaguely at Mike's guitar case and said: "You are *musicien?*"

"Oui", said Mike, trying to be cool. *"Le violon"*.

"Le violon?" she said.

Not wishing to be left out, I tried to join in the fun. "He's not very good though. Can't seem to get it under his chin".

"P'raps you should try *la trompette,* ah?" she said. "You have – how you say – a big mouth, ah?"

It sounded playful, and I guess this was what the French call *repartie,* but just in case she was feeling a bit offended and before anything apache-like kicked off, I said, "Actually, he's very good. Do you want to hear something?"

"O.K." she said, as if she couldn't care. "What do you play?"

Mike was already unclicking his guitar case as she shouted something over to the guy behind the bar who laughed, gave a few strums on his air guitar, and went back to wiping the counter. She stood at the table expectantly, hands on hips again.

Mike played *Angie.* I watched with envy as Lesley Caron softened and melted into a chair, resting her head on her arms. There were only a few tables occupied, but a quietness descended as the other diners all stopped to listen too. When he finished she clapped, as indeed did the others around and there were shouts of 'Bravo'. The guy behind the bar even shouted, 'Encore!' So he went into *Running from Home,* another Bert classic. This went down a storm too, so he followed that up with John Renbourn's version of *Candy Man.* I was feeling a bit spare by this time and felt myself disappearing yet again into the dark of Mike's shadow. I wasn't sure what to do. Then the lovely Lesley said, "Do you play too?" and I could have kissed her.

I dashed over to the Station and rescued my guitar from the Left Luggage. Since I didn't have any spare coins to secure the rucksacks again, I had to take them with me as well, so I stumbled back looking a bit like a walking jumble sale as I crossed the road back to the café. Meanwhile two more formidables had arrived, courteously of the Management. I'd already exceeded my capacity for liquid intake with the first one, but I could see that Mike was in his element. He was also smoking a Gauloise, which I assumed someone had given him and, as us folkies do, he had coolly stuck it between the strings on the headstock of his guitar. We did a selection of our old standards together, like *Blowin' Down the Road, Hard Ain't it Hard* and *Deep Blue Sea,* and then I played *The Times They are A-changing* whilst he went for a pee. And on it went. People did get a bit restive, particularly as our repertoire didn't stretch to any French songs, but when someone started a French song going, others joined in, and we added some nominal accompaniment. The worst thing was trying to keep up with the flow of lager that kept coming.

By closing time, which was pretty late, we were both feeling fairly well pissed as we staggered back to the Station. Sadly we hadn't entranced anyone enough that they wanted to take us home with them. Even Lesley dashed our hopes when she allowed herself to be collected by some seedy Tony Curtis look-alike, who was presumably her boyfriend. But everyone shook us warmly by the hand and patted us on the back as we left. The barman even invited us back again the next night, but it was with great regret we had to decline. If only we hadn't bought those tickets! But wasn't that always the way. You wait for ages for a stroke of luck to come along, then three come along at once – in the space of a few hours we'd set up a date with two lovely French girls in St Tropez, received a generous donation from Zadok the Priest, and our Official Fan Club had now been established at Café Mazarin, Orléans, France.

As we climbed to the top of the steps leading to the Station Mike suddenly span around, flung his arms out wide and shouted, "I LOVE THIS TOWN!" before sitting flat down on his back-side. I could hear the flutter of startled birds and somewhere in the distance a dog barked. I went and sat next to him and said:

"Sorry about … y'know, b'fore".

"Wassat then?" he said.

"Y'know, the whole Shyd …. Shyd…." I'll need to take a run at this …….. " … ShydSharishIishoo …", and I started to giggle in an uncontrollable sort of way.

"Shyd Sharishhhhhh?", he said. "Shyd Sh……sh…sh…. S'all forgotten, mate", and he slapped me on the shoulder. "Anyway, I'm shhhhhorry too", and we collapsed on the steps.

We spent the rest of the night stretched out on wooden benches on the station platform. We were awoken twice – once by a porter and once by a gendarme, but they moved on apparently satisfied when we were able to show them our tickets to Lyon. The night was unending though, and I felt extremely dizzy and very ill. I tried to fix an image of Jeanne in my mind as a source of comfort and distraction.

When I did drift off I found myself dreaming that I was being burnt at the stake. It wouldn't have been so bad if I could have felt some corresponding warmth from the flames, but it was when I realised that the flames weren't actually touching me and that all I felt was icy cold, that I woke up. Then, suddenly and violently, I threw up.

I stumbled into the washroom and tried to sip some water from my cupped hands. I felt ghastly and considered dying. In the end the thought that I wouldn't then get to see Jeanne again revived me a bit, and I struggled back to the bench. Mike asked me if I was alright.

"Bad pint", I said.

"I don't feel so good myself actually", he murmured. "But I don't think it's the beer. I thought that sandwich we got off the priest tasted a bit off at the time".

This did help me to feel less of a light-weight it's true, but the thought of this made me go rushing off to the washroom again. In the morning I still felt very queasy, but luckily I could just about remember how to walk sufficiently to get myself on the train. Mike seemed fragile too, but had enough strength to take general control of things.

Not many others had luggage which was fortunate as Mike pretty well managed to fill the entire luggage bay with our gear. I spent most of the first 30 minutes or so in the tiny toilet, just in case, but I also found that the gentle rocking of the train was strangely soothing and, as I got used to this, I felt myself starting to recover. Back in my seat I was vaguely aware of swathes of flat countryside whipping past. For a time we trundled along by a wide river when we slowed down. From the scruffy look of it though, I doubt this was to enable passengers to delight at the pastoral beauty of it all. We stopped fairly frequently and I watched all manner of people shambling up and down the corridor as they either got on or off. Some could manage this task in silence and without difficulty, whereas others tended to huff and puff and cause great disturbance. In fact few seemed capable of moving without making some sort of noise, even if it was just a vague sigh of relief. Then to my dismay I realised I was one of them too.

After a couple of hours or so we drew into Nevers, yet another place where the N7 passed through. I found myself thinking wistfully about Jeanne and Bobbi standing on it, hitching their way south. Then I remembered that we were now a day behind them, so Nevers would by now probably be nothing more than a distant memory to them. Mike decided he would nip off and buy some cigarettes. Our train was a through train to Lyon, but the stop here was scheduled for about 20 minutes.

"Don't be long," I said.

"Oh relax. I'm not going to miss it am I?"

Famous last words, I thought to myself. I then spent all the time he was away peering up and down the platform looking for him coming back. There was no sign. As the 20 minutes ticked by I could feel myself getting hotter, and my heart rate getting faster. I got out on to the platform once or twice for a better view, but it didn't help. I was back in my seat, still looking fruitlessly up the platform when I heard the guard's whistle blow. I was on my feet in a flash, much to the consternation of the poor old lady opposite whose foot I trod on heavily in the process.

"A-ï-e-e-e-!", she howled. "Attention!!"

"Pardon, pardon," I jabbered. "Excusez-moi." And I started to bundle the gear out of the luggage bay.

"Going somewhere?"

It was Mike, who appeared behind me, as if from nowhere, cigarette in his mouth, and carrying a white paper bag and a couple of cups of coffee.

"You pillock!" I snorted. "Where the hell have you been? I was about to throw all our stuff off! I didn't see you coming."

"As the short-sighted prostitute said to the bishop ..."

"Oh, ha bloody ha. I've been going mental here."

"For God's sake. I told you, relax. I got on further up when miladdo blew his whistle".

We went back to our seats and the old lady, startled as if by an electric shock at my re-appearance, went into a kind of paroxysm of activity to get her feet under her seat and out of my reach. She eyed me very suspiciously as I sat down again. I smiled pathetically.

I scrunched up my shoulders and tried to melt back into my seat, still fuming at Mike's laid-back attitude.

"Don't do that again", I moaned. "You scared the shit out of me."

"You should have more faith", he said.

Of course he was right. I was over-reacting. Was I so poor a rambling boy that I couldn't bear to be left on my own? He told me that he'd gone to get us something to eat. He hadn't liked the prices in the station so had gone into the town to find something cheaper. He'd brought back bread, cheese, a carton of milk and some soft fruit. Despite the fragility of my internal organs it went down very easily and felt like just what I needed. I reproached myself for acting like a jerk, imagining Mike was abandoning me when clearly he had my interests at heart all along.

From there the journey to Lyon was fairly uneventful, but the countryside we were passing through was a delight. It felt wasteful that we were just speeding through and not taking more advantage of it. We passed close to the river again for a while, so I got out the map to check on our progress. The river was the Loire and we were heading towards

Moulins, and then on to Roanne and Lyon. What was particularly distressing was that we were, mile by mile, following the path of the National Seven. Life could be cruel sometimes.

Travelling by rail has a lot going for it. For a start, there's a serene simplicity about it, that sense of powerful and free movement through the world as you speed along - 'I'm coming and I ain't stopping for no-one' kind of thing - like a single belief that goes on indefinitely. I can see why people have been moved to write so many songs about trains, and I found myself thinking of all those that had been thus immortalised: *Midnight Special, Freight Train, Last Train to San Fernando, The Wabash Cannonball*. And of course, there's all that sexual symbolism bound up in trains. If you're watching a film for example, and you see a couple kissing passionately followed bafflingly by an image of a train speeding into a tunnel, what it really means is …. *and then they have sex*. I remember Johnny Biggins, the Biology teacher at school, carefully explaining this to us one time in a tone of great seriousness. And as our train rocked and rolled along, I started thinking about something else Johnny Biggins had said - that, generally speaking, *all* train songs were really songs about sex, only in code. And oddly enough, I discovered that the more I thought about this, the more evidence I found. *Midnight Special,* for example, and *On Top of Old Smokey* – self-explanatory, clearly about sexual intercourse; *The Wabash Cannonball* – possibly someone celebrating their sexual prowess; *Pardon me boy, is that the Chattanooga-Choo-Choo?* – well clearly a song about exhibitionism; *The Wreck of the Old 97* – it has to be about impotence. I got a bit stuck with *The Runaway Train,* but finally settled on it being a song about premature ejaculation. Then I wasn't quite sure what to do with *Rock Island Line,* but it didn't really matter – as I sang it over to myself, by the time I got to the part where you *'got to ride it like you find it, get your ticket at the station'* I had drifted off to sleep.

We arrived at Lyon in the late afternoon. We sat on a bench on the platform and consulted the map again. Once we'd turned it the right way up, St Tropez didn't seem so far. Well actually, it did, but at least I only had to open up the map by two folds now, and for the first time I could see both where we were and where we were going without intricate manoeuvres of folding and unfolding. I calculated though that we were still about 400 Km from our destination. As we looked at the map, I glanced absent-mindedly up at the arrivals and departures board. My heart skipped a beat and I felt a mild pain in my chest. There was a train leaving in an hour for Marseille which, as we could see from the map, was actually *on* the south coast.

We looked at each other.

"Well, perhaps we could just see how much it is ...."

"Hitching's gonna take an age, going by our past record."

"Aye."

We bought the tickets and handed over another 82F - 41F each - but, in truth, I think we both knew it wouldn't have mattered how much it cost. We just wanted to get to the South. Soon we were rumbling down the line again bound for Marseille, although first we had to get to Avignon, where we were due to change trains. There were fewer people on this train and it sped along with that same rocking soothing motion that I found so comforting, and stopped rarely. It wasn't long before I'd drifted off into a deep and peaceful sleep again.

The next thing I was aware of was a sudden lurch, and then Mike shaking me on the shoulder. The compartment was in darkness, except for the dim cast of moonlight coming through the window. Outside I could hear a distant sound of metal scraping against metal, and the occasional shout of men's voices. We were in the sidings – somewhere.

"Shit!" said Mike. "Why didn't somebody wake us?"

"Where are we?" I said, rubbing my eyes, and straining to peer out of the window.

"God knows."

"I think I can see lights down the track," I said. "I suppose it might be a station."

We collected our bags, opened up the carriage door, and climbed down from the train on to the gravel below. Then we walked in the direction of the lights. All around us had gone eerily quiet now, and there was apparently no-one around to challenge us. We got to the platform and climbed up. A big red sign informed us we had arrived – at Avignon. Goodness knows how long we'd been asleep on the deserted train. We presumed we'd missed our connection hours ago. I looked at my watch – 11.30 pm.- and decided we had come to the end of our journey, at least for that particular day.

We sat on the station platform feeling cold, and rather stupid. But neither of us said anything since we knew we were both to blame.

In the gloomy darkness and chill of our surroundings, it suddenly occurred to me that I was now quite a long way from home. I felt a pang of anxiety and for the first time I was aware of missing my family.

"What did you agree with your folks – you know, about keeping in touch with them?" I asked Mike, but then immediately worried that he might think I was trying to entice him into risky territory again, so I added quickly, "Were you just going to send post-cards or something?" But sitting in the dark, he had gone pensive too, and he didn't appear to flinch.

"Yeah .. happy-hols-postcards-type-thing. Other than that, my Dad said that if he wanted to get in touch he'd write to me care of *Poste Restante*".

"What's that?"

"*Poste Restante?* Basically you send a letter to a Post Office in some big town, and they hold it in *Poste Restante* till someone collects it. But since we don't know which towns we're ever going to be in, I told him not to bother".

"But he knows we're heading for St Tropez ..."

"Yeah, but I think it might only work with the big cities. I don't know".

"What, like Nice?"

"Aye ... if you like".

"Well, don't you want to hear from him then?"

"Look, just shut up about it will you .... sodding *Poste Restante* ... bollocks to it".

I didn't know why he'd gone all testy, but I thought it was best to leave it. Still, I felt reassured to know there was a system and wondered why I hadn't found out about it myself before we left. I suppose I just selfishly thought I'd get on with it and there wouldn't be any need for anyone to contact me. And stuff from home can be a bit of an intrusion when you're away from it all – especially if it's your Uncle Fred telling you what to think and do all the time. *'You want to go to college and get a good job.'* *'You want to get your hair cut.'* *'You want to ask that nice little Sheila Johnson out.'* *'You can get plenty of grape-picking jobs in France.'* *'You don't want to go to Paris.'*

Mike had set me thinking though, and I realised that as much as I was tired of being organised by Uncle Fred, the further I got from home the more scared I was feeling. Uncle Fred would never have let me sleep past my station. Then Aunt Doris' words came whispering at me across the miles. *You're just like your father, wandering off to who-knows-where.* I shuddered as something gave my insides a squeeze. Was I really behaving just like him? Had she been right after all? I resolved to send another post-card home soon, to supplement the one I scribbled to them in Paris, and to tell them about *Poste Restante*. Then I lay down on the bench and gave in to the night.

Next morning we made progress fairly quickly. It didn't take us long to get down to Marseille, and there we discovered a local train that went a bit further up the line to Toulon. We had a meeting, a collective think, and came to the joint conclusion of 'bugger it'. Mike had long since given up on the N7, and as we stood on the platform waiting for the Toulon train and looking out at the pouring rain, I was feeling the same way. We'd arrived at the south coast without setting foot on the N7 once. But what did it matter really? And we hadn't even hitched either, not really. We'd bought rail tickets. We could have done that in the first place and saved ourselves a lot of hassle. I was a bit shocked though when I consulted the map again and found that the N7 actually passed right through Avignon. Destiny had stranded us there one night as if we were being directed to get on it there, but as Mike succinctly put it: "Destiny, schm-estiny. It's just a bloody fantasy. It would have been cool to travel down on it, but what the hell".

In any case the journey had lost its adventurous quality by now, and our aim of making real contact with the country by getting in touch with its culture and colourful characters via begging lifts and drifting through its towns, had long since gone by the board. We just wanted to get to St Tropez.

When we got to Toulon we made a brief foray into the town and sat in a little square for a while to ponder our next move. Our researches had uncovered two important findings: firstly, there was a Bus Station nearby from where there was a service running directly to St Tropez, and secondly, pretty much like most French cities we had found ourselves trapped in up to then, it was a mighty long way to the edge of town.

So we caught the bus.

PART TWO

FREEWHEELIN'

4

St Tropez – sun, sex, and celebrities. Yes, there was certainly a hot glare from the midday sun as we stepped off the bus. As for the sex, I imagined that I'd see at least one bare-chested female at some point, and if I got lucky I might even get tangled up in the sexual permissiveness of the area. Sightings of various celebrities were also a distinct possibility, if not the famous B.B. herself.

We walked through the streets and made our way down to the sea front. There weren't many bare-chested females to be seen in what I took to be the town square. A lot of old men sat underneath neatly arranged trees, whilst others threw silver balls along the dusty ground. Their eyes followed us suspiciously as we walked past. We walked further on through the streets, but there was no sign of anyone famous. There were a few rich-looking elderly women who I suppose could have been one-time film starlets, but all they were doing now was walking their scrawny-looking dogs. One yapped angrily at Mike as we passed. The woman stopped and gave him an abject look of contempt as if he'd just pee'ed on it. Then she stuck her haughty nose in the air and moved away. But at least it was sunny – one out of three wasn't bad. Who needs sex and celebrities anyway? I imagined the scene would be different when we got down to the harbour.

The harbour itself was very pretty. Various sizes of boats and yachts bobbed up and down on their moorings, whilst opposite stood a long terrace of buildings comprised of any number of restaurants and shops. We strolled through and past the many people mingling about on the harbour side, and made our way down to the beach. I was expecting swathes of golden sand melting into a translucent blue Mediterranean sea. Stretched out on the sand would be Jeanne and Bobbi sunbathing, topless of course. They'd be so pleased to see us they'd run to greet us inviting us to throw off our clothes and join them in spontaneous love-making.

In fact the sea was more of a bluey-green colour, and the beach was a thin strip of sandy shingle which quickly turned into untidy grassy banks which rose up steeply. Here and there clusters of sharp rocks jutted out of the sea. The beach only extended a short way before it curved away into another cove, hidden by the outcrop of one of the banks. There was no sign of Jeanne and Bobbi, or anyone else for that matter. We laid down our gear, which by now was feeling quite heavy, sat down and gazed out to sea.

We hadn't been there long when a geeky-looking chap emerged from behind the bank in the distance, and approached us.

"Hullo," he said brightly. "Hey, are you English?"

God, I thought, now we don't even have to speak before we're sussed.

"Yeah," said Mike. "We've just got into town."

"Well hey, welcome to St Tropez," he said. "I'm Brian. I'm with some other guys just up the beach." And he nodded back in the direction from which he'd come. Mike introduced us and asked him where he was from.

"Manchester. Been here about a week now. I noticed your guitars - hey, are you figuring on busking?"

"Yeah, that's the idea."

"Aw, great. Hey, what do you play?"

"Oh you know, folksy-stuff. American. Some blues, some Dylan. Do you play?"

He ignored my question, his eyes fixed with a sort of boyish wonder on our guitar cases. He looked so geeky I was imagining all this was part of some other world for him, especially with this strange affliction he seemed to have for starting every sentence with 'hey'. But to my surprise, when Mike unclicked his case and got it out Brian said, "Wow, you've got a Gibson. Hey, can I have a go?"

He took hold of the guitar, and tenderly tucked it under his arm as if he was handling something very precious. I was thinking he was probably about to treat us to a quick strum, perhaps some amateurish three-chord crap like *Bobby Shafto* or something. He paused for a minute as if admiring the guitar's shape and form, wriggled his fingers a bit, and then started to pick delicately at the strings. My smug little bubble burst as quickly as I recognised the tune he was playing. It was *Angie!*

"That's the Bert Jansch version!" said Mike.

"Yeah, I do a lot of his stuff," said Brian. "Hey, have you heard the latest stuff he's done with John Renbourn?"

And in no time they were discussing the finer points of guitar playing technique. "I wondered how he did that. Yeah, that's a B string bent on a D note. He damps down there, and pulls off doesn't he?"

Then Brian turned to me. "Hey, what about you? What do you play?"

I felt myself cringing, in case he asked me to demonstrate. Under his clearly expert eye I suddenly felt that I might only be able to manage some amateurish three-chord crap like *Bobby Shafto* or something. "Oh bits and pieces. American folksy stuff. Some Dylan".

"Do you know this one?"

"It's not *Hey…. Mr Tambourine Man* by any chance is it?"

"No, no. It's this …."

And he played and sang a verse of a song which appeared to be called *Mama, You've Been on my Mind* and hey, guess what, I didn't know it at all.

"I picked it up just before I left", he said. "Hey, I'll show you the chords sometime, if you like".

"Thanks", I said hoping he wouldn't.

Now he was getting into his stride. "Hey, what about a guy called Jackson C Frank? Have you heard any of his stuff? … American guy … came over and did some stuff with Bert and John recently".

Naturally I hadn't.

"No," I said glumly.

"Oh hey …. Here's one he does – it's fantastic. Easy chords, G and C mostly, you could get this one off no bother." And he started to play, and then sing something about 'blues running the game.' I had to admit he sounded very good but, hey, I wasn't sure I wanted to endure further humiliation by having him run through his entire songbook. Mercifully, he broke off after a couple of verses and said, "Hey, why don't you come over and join us? We're sleeping on the beach in the next cove. Hey, there's a whole group of us."

I quailed at the thought of being in the midst of more Bert and John virtuosos, so I said, "Thanks, but we did say we'd meet a couple of girls here." I thought that sounded quite good actually so added, trying to restore some dignity, "We met them on the road, as we were hitching down. … you know, from Paris."

"Hey, not Jeanne and Bobbi?"

God, was there nothing I had on this geek?

"Wow, that's amazing. They *said* they'd met a couple of English guys! Hey, they're just along the beach. Come on. We've got quite a little camp over there, and there's plenty of room."

So, with the prospect of seeing Jeanne again causing my heart to flutter, we gathered up our gear and followed him. Heigh-ho.

The group consisted of Brian, two other guys called Tim and Simon, and Pip, the guy Jeanne had come down to meet. As it happened, Jeanne and Pip had gone into the town so weren't there when we strolled up, but Bobbi came rushing over and this time embraced us both warmly.

"Allo, Ni-jjell. Allo Mike. It is so good to see you again. We were so worried that you do not arrive. We are here since yesterday. But we have good chance with our rides. And you?"

We mumbled some sort of excuse to her, but luckily we didn't have to say much, as we were then introduced to Tim and Simon. Tim was a tall, curly-headed chap with warm, dark eyes and fair skin. I noticed that, when he moved, it was with a silent flowing motion, almost like a dancer. He also spoke softly with a cultured, middle-class accent. Simon's prominent feature was his long blond hair, which spilled out from under a battered felt hat, his face framed by a contrasting dark beard.

There is a customary uniform for the well-dressed Rambling Boy, with important associated rules. Jeans should be denim of course. You have a choice of shades although ice-blue denim is especially cool. It is also particularly important that the hems of said jeans have been severed off and the material allowed to fray. Generally speaking, there is an added coolness to be gained from a particularly wide fraying, but one must take care not to overdo it. If it's too wide people will just think you're being pretentious. (You also have to be careful about dungarees by the way. They can be an image-maker, but you can also give out the sorry message that really, you've missed the point and have gone too far).

It goes without saying that, whatever pants you choose, they must always look well-worn, so rips and stains are also necessary accessories to the overall look. With regard to shirts, the choice is mainly between standard denim, or the slightly more fashionable collarless 'granddad' style – i.e. made of heavy-duty cotton, and usually striped. Short sleeves are frowned upon as veering too far into rubber-neck territory, so sleeves should be long and then rolled up if need be. T-shirts are allowed, but are only usually worn under the shirt. If extra warmth is needed, articles made of corduroy or suede are O.K. but these really are more high-end. A heavy duty woollen jacket is more customary. Basically you're going for a look which indicates that you hail from a long tradition of manual labour.

To cut a long story short, this is how Tim and Simon were both dressed. Tim's jeans were of the dusty pale denim sort and were not only ripped, but shredded and heavily patched. His off-white T-shirt was covered by a thin denim shirt which seemed to flap about artistically as he

45

moved about. We found out later that one of his claims to fame was that he had been in Trafalgar Square during a CND rally, and apparently there is some film footage of him knocking a policeman's hat off. I could well imagine that the rips and stains in his pants were acquired on that very occasion. Simon was dressed in a strikingly similar way although, oddly given the heat, he was also wearing a brown corduroy jacket. I also noticed that he wore a leather bracelet, braided in an intricate sort of Celtic design. I smiled as I thought of Uncle Fred and what he would have made of a bloke with long blond hair wearing jewellery.

As with Brian the focus of their initial interest was our guitars which evoked the usual questions about the kind of stuff we played. On the strength of our recent audition with Hey-it's-Brian Mike rhymed off some Bert & John tunes, and Tim laughed.

"Do you make much?" he asked.

"Well ..er ... we haven't really done much yet."

"And you won't if you stick with those tunes. People aren't going to stop and listen to good guitar technique and melodic singing. Don't you know any busking songs?"

"Er ... *San Francisco Bay Blues?*"

"Yeah, that's more like it. You have to give people a blast with a good strong tune, one with an instant impact. Here, let's show you what we do."

And he went over to a rock and produced a guitar from behind it. It was a battered old thing that also looked like it was a veteran of CND rallies, having lost most of the lustre on its body. He hooked a harmonica frame around his neck into which he inserted both a harmonica and a kazoo. Brian picked up his guitar which had been leaning against his rucksack. It looked more polished but was distinctive for the jet black colour of its body, which was framed by a stylish white edging. Meanwhile Simon produced a heavy brown earthenware pot from somewhere which he then hoisted up to rest on his chest.

"We present Jesse's Juicy-Fruit Jugband!"

And they broke into this thumping tune with Tim and Brian strumming out chords, Simon blowing into the jar to produce a deep resonating bass line, and Tim adding a melody on the harmonica.

I can tell by your nose, you're a monkey in human clothes,
And you're bound to look like a monkey when you get old.
I can tell by your jaw, that a monkey must have been your pa,
And you're bound to look like a monkey when you get old.

And so on. *I can tell by your face, you must be part of the monkey race etc.*

It sounded wonderful. And the guitar chords seemed like an easy progression that even I could manage. Some people walking above us on the dunes stopped to listen and clapped when they'd finished. Bobbi picked up a hat and waved it, miming the dropping of money into it, but they just laughed and walked on.

"You must have been doing good then? Is there a good busking scene here?" Mike asked.

"Oh not so bad. The fuzz are the main problem. Most of the cafés don't give you any hassle unless they get any complaints. We've been here about a week and have been doing O.K. You guys can come around with us if you like, next time we hit the cafés."

We spent the next hour or so playing other songs together or just talking. They had a little fire going, on which a rusty metal pot happily steamed away, and from it they offered us real coffee to accompany bread, cheese, and apples. The coffee tasted slightly metallic, but that only added to the romance. Here we are at last, I thought – sitting around a camp fire on a beach in St Tropez, drinking coffee, playing our guitars with our mates, laughing and talking. I realised it was the first time I'd actually felt properly relaxed since we'd left home. In fact I found myself thinking that this moment was possibly where our journey had been leading all along, and then I wondered if it was exactly this sort of experience Bob was recalling in the song *Bob Dylan's Dream* when he gets all nostalgic and sings about the times he once had with his mates. He conjures up a wistful picture of them all sitting round a stove, drinking beer, joking around with each other and telling stories.

"So are you planning to stay here long?" I said to Simon.

"Probably not", he said. "Perhaps a couple more days, then we'll just move on up the coast."

"Anywhere in particular?"

"No, just where the wind blows us I guess".

I looked out over the bay in front of us and savoured the cool air blowing in from the sea. My feet felt hot and sore so I took off my sandals and peeled off my socks, suddenly becoming aware that this was the first time my feet had tasted fresh air in days. I massaged my toes, and dug my feet in the sand, sighing with the sheer sensual pleasure and pain relief of it all.

"Feet hurt?" asked Simon.

"Yeah, quite stiff and sore actually. Must be all the walking we've done."

"I'm not surprised in those shoes," he said. Then he lay back on the sand and moved his hat over his face to shield his eyes from the sun.

"Yup," he said. "You know, I reckon it's one of the basic facts of life. You can't ever attain true contentment if your feet hurt. You know … there's only two things you'll ever need in life to be truly happy …." he paused meaningfully, then continued ….. "comfortable shoes and a warm place to shit".

I thought it was the most profoundly wise thing I'd ever heard.

Meanwhile I was feeling anxious about seeing Jeanne again, as she and Pip had still not returned. Bobbi however seemed to be attaching herself to Mike. She hung around him and giggled as he played his guitar and demonstrated the new tunes he'd learnt. At one point they took themselves off for a walk – Mike with his hands thrust deep in the pockets of his jeans, with Bobbi clinging tightly on to his arm. A fantasy I'd been nursing for some time came to mind. I'd nursed it ever since I first saw the picture on the sleeve of Bob Dylan's third L.P. – *The Freewheelin' Bob Dylan*. In the picture Bob is walking down a cold, icy street, presumably somewhere in New York. Alongside him is a pretty girl who is clutching his left arm tightly with both hands. She looks blissfully happy as they bear the icy cold together. I'd been somehow absolutely captivated by that picture, and I so wanted to be like him. I wanted to live on that street too, and I wanted to feel that cold, and most of all, I wanted to love that woman. As I watched them, I saw Jeanne and me. We are walking down a dusty road together, her hands are clutched tight to my arm. She has her head on my shoulder and her hair is flowing freely. She looks up at me tenderly, and whispers my name …

"N-ee-jjell …?"

It was Jeanne and Pip. I leapt to my feet and she gave me a warm embrace which cheered me up no end. "It's nice to see you", she said. "I'm glad you have come". She was looking as lovely as I had remembered her. This would have cheered me up even further if she hadn't then asked me where Mike was. I told her he'd just gone off with Bobbi for a walk.

"Oh I have something I must tell to Bobbi", she said and promptly ran off to find them. The picture of Mike and Bobbi reformed in my head, this time with Jeanne on his other arm. I shook my head to chase it away.

48

Pip meanwhile had walked on past us and had sat down on the shingle further up. I thought I'd better go and say hi, plus I wanted to suss out the opposition a bit. There was a certain lean and hungry look about him, and I had to concede he was a fairly good-looking bloke. He had a hippy look with long dark hair and a goatee-type beard, but his clothes betrayed his true nature. He was not a proper Rambling Boy, that much was clear. His jeans looked decidedly unsullied to me, and he was wearing a very odd-looking shirt – a short-sleeved number with a swirly, Paisley sort of pattern! As I approached a tune popped into my head:

I can tell, by your clothes …

"Hi!" I said.

"Yup", he replied, without looking at me.

I tried again. "We've just got into town. Met Brian who invited us along".

"Sure".

Silence.

"We met Bobbi and Jeanne on the way down".

"Yeah".

More silence.

I was just wondering … what's an ill-mannered prick like you doing with a lovely girl like Jeanne? Tim caught my eye just then, and motioned a 'best-leave-him-alone' sort of gesture to me with his hands. It was fine with me. He beckoned me over.

He was crouched on the sand, whittling away at a stick with his penknife. I sat down beside him. "Pip's not very happy at the moment" he said.

"Oh, why's that?" I asked, hoping he would tell me that Pip's relationship with Jeanne was hitting the rocks. "Apparently Nigel, after your chance meeting on the road, she just can't stop thinking about you and knows she can't fight it any longer. She's just broken the news to him, and now she's rushed off to find Bobbi so she can share her excitement with her".

But instead, he just went on to tell me the boring stuff.

"He's half-French, on his mother's side. She lives in Paris most of the time but she has an apartment in Nice. He's on his way there now, cos there was a gas leak or something recently, and she wants someone to keep an eye on the place. He had plans to travel about a bit this summer and is really pissed off. Feels she's just using him as a caretaker or something".

"Why didn't you all go there in the first place?" I asked. Isn't an apartment better than sleeping on the beach?" He looked at me as if I'd just farted loudly.

"Are you kidding? An apartment in noisy smoky Nice as opposed to this sort of freedom? Anyway, it's only one room, and if his mother found out there'd be hell to pay."

He fell silent, and continued with his whittling.

"So how do you all know each other?" I asked.

"Simon and I used to live in the same village and then we boarded at the same school. We met Pip in Paris, then all came down here together."

Since he was filling in this background for me I thought I may as well ask: "So how do Jeanne and Bobbi fit in?"

"We met them in Paris too. Jeanne and Pip had a thing going before we arrived actually. I don't know that she ever intended to come to Nice with him, but his mother got her fixed her up with a job in one of the bars opposite the apartment there. She knows the owner really well apparently. Jeanne's cool about it, but Pip reckons his mother's just trying to make sure he stays put in Nice and doesn't go off travelling somewhere."

"Using Jeanne as a sort of baby-sitter you mean?"

Tim chuckled. "Don't let him hear you say that. But yes, I suppose so. I don't think he fancies Jeanne all that much to be honest."

My heart skipped a beat as I felt a glimmer of hope that I might still be in with a chance. On the other hand it didn't sound like I was going to see much more of her, and the sense of a web being spun around Jeanne was a bit worrying.

"Thanks for telling me. So Bobbi's just tagged along then?"

"Yeah, but she's great. She had some bad scene going with her old man. She ran away from him to stay with Jeanne or something, and wanted to get away from Paris for a while."

Bobbi, Jeanne and Mike weren't away long, and as they came up I was cheered to see Mike walking a pace or two ahead with Jeanne and Bobbi behind, whispering together in a conspiratorial kind of way. When they got back I did then manage to snatch a brief conversation with Jeanne just before Pip stumbled to his feet and said, "Hey baby, let's go for a walk."

"I hear you're going to Nice."

"Yeah. Tomorrow."

Like I said, it was only brief.

That night we had a sort of beach party. When Pip and Jeanne eventually returned he was carrying a dead chicken. Apparently he had seen it wandering around loose on the bank so had chased after it and killed it. It only confirmed my impression of him as a dangerous loony. On the other hand Tim thought he was 'brilliant' and he and Pip set about plucking it, then cutting off bits of flesh which they threw into a metal pot. Brian produced some potatoes and onions from a secret pocket in his rucksack, and it was all set to cook over a low light. Whilst it was cooking Simon, Mike and I went into the town to buy some beer and cheap wine.

On the way we talked about Bobbi. Mike started it by saying that, whilst they'd been on their walk, she'd told him she didn't want to go on to Nice with Jeanne. In fact she'd asked if she could hang around with us for a while. Then Simon commented on how she seemed to have attached herself to Mike very quickly. I wondered if he was about to assert a prior claim or something, and indeed Mike must have had the same thought because he immediately asked Simon if he fancied her himself. Simon just said, "Er .. no .... not really ... no" and was then quiet for a bit.

Then he said, "Bobbi's a strange one anyway".

"How do you mean?" Mike asked him.

"Well she makes out she's had this really tough life with her drunken father, but we've met him and he seemed alright to us, quite different actually from how she described him. I mean he certainly likes a drink or two, but he didn't seem that aggressive. In fact he seemed very caring, protective even, towards Bobbi. They seem to get on fine actually."

I was puzzled. "Tim said Bobbi ran away from him to stay with Jeanne," I said, "so I guess he must have scared her in some way."

"Yeah well, I imagine he's got a temper, but I would have thought that Bobbi could handle that. No, I just think she likes the drama of spinning a yarn, or embellishing the truth anyway. Who knows what really goes on?"

Whatever the reality was, as I listened to Simon talking, I found my attitude to Bobbi softening who, up to now, I'd seen mainly as something of an intrusion to my relationship with Jeanne, and then Mike. Now she sounded like a girl with problems. What I heard also made me feel wistful again about home. I'd come from a safe, caring family but I'd just selfishly abandoned them and buggered off to France. As time went on though I found myself getting more homesick for the security I'd left behind. I resolved again to write home soon.

Back on the beach the Dead Chicken Beach Party gradually got into gear. It was actually a good night. We sat a bit, talked a bit, and sang and played a bit more. The songs got a bit rowdier as the alcohol loosened us all up. But however much I drank I still couldn't persuade myself to eat the chicken. I had a bit to be sociable, but carefully avoided the meat and just chose the vegetables. There was some 'smoking' going on too, the raw materials having been provided by Pip. Something got passed round and I pretended to partake, but I was very pleased to see that both Bobbi and Jeanne declined. I didn't see them eating any of the chicken either.

I did think that by avoiding both the chicken and the Pot, I was being a Big Girl myself and letting down the whole Ramblin' Boy Movement, but my feelings of vague dishonour turned to smugness when, in the early hours of the morning, the Revenge of the Dead Chicken visited the camp and most people threw up. I missed that particular round of illness, but sadly it was the alcohol that did it for me – that, and an image of Pip and Jeanne which I couldn't get out of my mind, sitting together in the orange glow of the fire-light with his head resting on her shoulder. I threw up near to daybreak just as this image came back to me in my dream. It was my second bout of morning sickness in a week.

As I slowly became aware of the morning sun warming me on the outside, I became equally aware of how ghastly I felt on the inside. I lay for a while concentrating on the difficult task of trying to join the scattered bits of myself together again. The others suggested going into the town for refreshment, but it was a few minutes before I felt ready to tackle walking and talking simultaneously again. Then I agreed to join them.

The guys had a morning routine where they trooped off into the town to wash at a water fountain. Before we went Tim showed us where we could stash our gear whenever we went into town. It was a little place that they had christened 'Rookery Nook' and was not far from where we were sleeping. Just behind an outcrop of rocks which in turn nuzzled into one of the grass banks, was a small cave-like opening, and it was here that Tim said it was always safe to leave things, even the guitars. He considered the beach area to be a safe haven anyway, but here stuff could at least be left out of sight. Miraculously I thought, Mike was willing to go along with this.

The fountain in the town was actually a water pump, which had presumably once been a key facility for all the folks in the town. Now we were helping it to relive its glory days. It was freezing cold water but the shock of the cold water, like a million daggers hitting my face at once, was brilliantly effective in reviving me. The cool water slipping down my parched throat was also very soothing.

By this time my hair had also got into a pretty lank state so I took the opportunity to give it a wash. I held my head underneath and tensed every muscle I could think of as Mike prepared to pump the cold water on to my head. I imagined it was how the aristocrats must have felt at the guillotine. My hair dried out later into a complete fuzzy mess, so Tim offered to cut it for me. I wasn't that keen, particularly as I'd witnessed his manual dexterity the night before in dismembering the chicken, but my hair had gone into a horrific spasm of disorder. I looked like 5,000 volts had just passed through me, and this wasn't a good image really, even for a *beet-a-neek*. He was actually very good when it came to it, and had a gentle touch. There was however an unnerving creepiness about the way he kept stroking it and congratulating me on how naturally curly and wavy it was. I was also very aware of Simon scowling at me all through the session.

After our ablutions we wandered round the town a bit, and laughed at the rubber-necks on their boats and sitting in their fancy restaurants, feeling superior in the knowledge that we had bits of a greasy blackened dead bird waiting for us in a rusty pot on the beach.

The worst part of the morning was Jeanne and Pip's departure. I didn't mind waving farewell to Pip – piss off you surly ignorant sod just about covered it – but saying goodbye to Jeanne was more of a torment. What was it she saw in this chicken-killing nutter anyway? And was she safe to be left alone with him? She came over and gave me a warm, tight hug and said,

"It is nice to know you Nigel. I hope we see each other again soon. If you come to Nice, you must come to visit me too. I give Bobbi the address".

For some reason that scene in *Casablanca* came to my mind, where Ingrid Bergman goes off with that dodgy Nazi resistance fighter, leaving her obvious true love Humphrey Bogart standing in the cold. "We'll always have Paris", he tells her manfully.

"I wish I could stay more", she said. "We have all had a good time here".

"Never mind", I said stupidly. "We'll always have Paris".

53

She drew back with a puzzled look. *"Pardon?"*

But before I had the chance to say more Pip called her over, and she was gone. I watched them walk round the cove and out of sight. Still, at least I knew that the last thing I said to her was something completely prattish. That should at least keep me in her mind.

That night we went busking. It was great. Because we were now a five-piece band we were able to stand on the harbour, instead of intruding at café tables, and make a noise that encouraged people to stop and listen. Bobbi was fantastic in working the crowd, passing a hat, and ensuring hardly anyone got away without paying at least some token amount. By the end of the night we'd made 30F. Of course we went off to a bar and blew it all straightaway on slapsies, but it turned out to be the most profitable evening we had.

The next day and the day after was spent in a similar way – bumming round the town in the day, perhaps a spot of sunbathing, then busking at night. We tried to vary our pitch so as not to draw too much attention to ourselves as far as the police were concerned. We also gave each other breaks so that at times Mike and I played, whilst the others went for a drink, or they played whilst Mike and me went for a piss. Bobbi was the constant star at passing the hat. I think the fact that she could speak French helped. Then the police came. I wasn't sure what we'd done, but they seemed pretty upset about something and insisted we all go off to the police station with them. The crowd booed and clapped as we were escorted away. I hoped they were booing the police and clapping us, but I suppose it could have been the other way round. At the police station they kept insisting to see our *papiers*. I had my passport, which they eyed suspiciously, but unaccountably Mike had left his in his rucksack on the beach. They insisted he produce it within the next two days. Tim reckoned it was all part of an intimidation programme but was actually quite harmless and meant nothing.

The next night they pulled us in again – this time before we'd hardly got started. Tim and Simon were particularly pissed off and decided they'd had enough. "Now they've started they're probably not going to leave us alone."

They reckoned they'd seen enough of St Tropez for a while anyway and planned to move on up the coast, maybe across the bay to St Maxime or on to Nice. Then they went off for a drink together whilst we made our way back to the beach.

On the way back, Brian surprised us by saying that he wasn't going to go with them, but was going to head back home.

"But you're part of the Jug Band", I said. "Don't they need you?"

"No, no, I'm not with them", he said. "Hey, I only met up with them the day before you guys came . No, I'm not with them . Hey, I'm not ... you know".

I didn't know actually. And I thought his emphatic denial a bit strange.

"Oh", I said. "I just assumed ... you just looked so ... you know, together ... when we arrived".

"Hey, Tim, and Simon are ... together. I'm not ... you know. Don't get me wrong, they're great blokes, and dead easy to get along with. But anyway, they're not really a Jug Band as such. We just put that together as a sort of joke. Tim's the only busker really. Simon is just ... well, you know, with him. Hey I don't want to tag along and be in the way ... you know what I mean?"

This 'you know' business was starting to sound like another of his verbal tics, but I also noticed that he was talking in a funny nod-and-a-wink kind of way with Mike letting out an occasional snigger in the background. I wondered what he was on about, so I asked him as much. He looked decidedly uncomfortable, then Mike cut in.

"Excuse my friend", he said. "He doesn't get out much". Then he turned to me and, with that irritating, patronising tone of his said, "They are ... you know ... *together*? They're ... a *couple* ... queer boys. Hadn't you noticed?"

"What ... you mean ... homosexual? Give over". I was quite taken aback. Of course I hadn't noticed. How would I? The only homosexual man I'd known up to then was Liberace, and he didn't look a bit like Tim or Simon. "What possible reason could you have for thinking that?"

"Oh come on! They've said as much haven't they? Anyway, there's been enough hints. What about Jesse's, you know *Jesse* ... Juicy Fruit ... that's Juicy *Fruity* .. Jug Band? Didn't that give you a clue?"

"Oh yeah." I said, not having a clue.

"So hey," resumed Brian, "you can see I don't want to get in their way. Anyway, it's time I was getting back to England. Hey, I've been over here six weeks already!"

As we walked back to our little campsite I ruminated further about Tim and Simon, and when they arrived back I looked at them with a new fascination - so much so that I think Simon caught me staring once or twice, and I looked away quickly. Then I remembered the way Tim had sort of fondled my hair when he'd cut it, and Simon's scowling face. That whole session was now cast in a new light.

I'd never met a real 'queer' person before – I just thought of it as a general term of abuse. Now here were two real ones. But what did it mean to be homosexual? What did they actually do? And then I thought that perhaps this was why they wanted to leave so suddenly – did they think the Police were on to them somehow? I felt sorry too that we were now all about to split up - I wouldn't have the opportunity to study them in more detail. Eventually I fell asleep, but not before I'd reminded myself that basically, I was thinking like a naïve sort of jerk – turning perfectly nice, kind and decent people into something freakish.

5

The day started pleasantly enough, with the warmth of the morning sun on my face and the waves lapping gently at my feet. It was a clear day and the vista in front of me was delightful – tiny yachts sailing serenely across the blue water against the background of green hills and the shadowy outline of St Maxime nestled at their base. Gradually the others stirred and the morning routine began. Mike propped himself up in his sleeping bag, lit his first cigarette of the day, and gazed sleepily into the distance whilst, without much conversation passing between us, the others shuffled out of their sleeping bags and blankets and packed them onto their rucksacks. The whole atmosphere was calm and peaceful. I didn't know then that it was to be the beginning of the end – at least as far as St Trop was concerned.

Tim and Simon wanted an early start. We had considered tagging along but, given our dependency on them since our arrival, we really wanted the opportunity to re-assert our independence, and indeed there seemed many more good reasons to stay. For a start we were getting more of a feel for this whole busking thing now, especially with what we had learned from the 'master-buskers' Tim and Simon. They had helped us get an idea of the more lucrative sites, which cafés to avoid, and how best to attract a crowd. We also had our secret weapon in Bobbi who was our star hat-passer. And hey, we didn't want to be in the way. Oh yes, and there was also the small matter of having to report to the Gendarmerie.

So after about 10 minutes or so of general milling about, Tim and Simon said their goodbyes and headed off. Their departure was fairly short and sweet. I don't know what I expected actually, but when it came to it they made no fuss about going. Each just gave me a manly sort of handshake, wished us good luck, and then lumbered off up the beach. I wondered if we'd ever see them again. Then very soon afterwards, Brian packed up and said goodbye too.

"Hey", he said. "It's been real nice to meet you guys. Hope to see you around".

He pushed a piece of paper in my hand. On it was scribbled his home address and, more carefully laid out, the chords for *Mama, You've Been on my Mind*. I thought it was a really nice gesture, and I felt bad that I'd had such ungenerous thoughts about him when we'd first met. Geeks, queer boys – what did I know? These guys had shown us nothing but kindness and friendship. They were all good, decent people, and I felt a pang of sadness that we were now all going our separate ways.

Indeed the beach seemed empty now without them all. Jeanne and Pip, Tim and Simon, and now Brian, all gone. I got maudlin again, and more of *Bob Dylan's Dream* rang through my head. *We thought we could sit forever in fun, But our chances really were a million to one.*

We stashed our rucksacks in Rookery Nook and made for the town. This time Mike insisted on taking his guitar. Although I pointed out that Tim had assured us Rookery Nook was perfectly safe, Mike was having none of it.

"It's a Gibson. I'm not just leaving it lying around on a beach!"

So, remembering the experience in Orleans when I'd had to run back to the station, I took mine as well.

We got to the fountain and splashed the cold water on our faces to wake ourselves up a bit more, before making for the Gendarmerie, a task we thought we'd better get out of the way. As we plodded along Bobbi chattered happily, her arm looped around Mike's. Although I didn't want to listen I could hear she was talking about her life in Paris with her drunken father. There was a gaiety about her chatter though, as if she was talking about a happy day she'd spent at the beach with him. Instead she was actually talking about the delight she took in annoying him by hiding his boots or jacket, and then concealing herself in a cupboard to watch him stomp about. God knows what would have happened if he'd ever caught her, but apparently he never did, and Bobbi was left free to enjoy her triumph as he upended the furniture in his frustration and roared out his rage …. like … like … "what is it in English? …. Comme on dit 'uhrss'?" she suddenly said.

"Uhrss?"

"Oui, 'ow you say 'uhrss'?"

Urhss? Horse? Roaring like a horse didn't sound a very effective way to convey frustration. Anyway, horse was 'cheval' wasn't it?

But we rounded the corner just then and there was the Gendarmerie. Bobbi came in with us as interpreter and we shambled up to the desk. The man behind it was the stereotypical French police-man – black hair plastered to his head and a thin little moustache, like Inspecteur Clouseau in a uniform. There was a ringing noise and I was tempted to remark wittily, "ah, zat will be ze phurrn", but thankfully thought better of it. Bobbi took charge, explained that Mike and I were English and had been asked to bring our 'papiers' in for inspection. He stared fixedly at us as he took the passports from us and fingered them open. He glanced down, then back at us with the same cold, emotionless expression on his face.

"Où restez-vous?" he suddenly said gruffly.

"Sur la plage."

"Ah! Sur la plage, eh?" and a flicker of a smile crossed his lips as if, by skilful manipulation of our weak minds, he had finally out-witted us and wrung an incriminating confession from us.

"C'est interdit!" Then, to press the point home, he locked his gaze on me, leaned forward and spelled it out further, "Not all-ow-wed!"

Bobbi intervened at that point with some A-level French. I couldn't understand what she said but she didn't sound aggressive, just cool and assertive. He answered back in a more blustery way, pointing at us and saying something about 'Angleterre', before thrusting our passports back at us and waving us away. As we turned to go he persisted with a parting "Pas sur la plage, ah?" and then something else which Bobbi later translated as 'have a safe trip back to England'. It was like Monsieur le Mexicain all over again.

Bobbi told us she had politely pointed out to him that we *could* sleep on the beach as long as we were not creating a public nuisance. Where we were was a rocky cove well away from the town, and which was really like open countryside where we had every right to roam – and sleep. She'd clearly taken no nonsense from him and may have even taken the opportunity to hide his boots for all I knew, but all in all it was probably no wonder that he got a bit narked.

Anyway we left the Gendarmerie and walked into the town, aiming to try our luck with the lunch trade in the cafés. It turned out to be one of our poorer ideas as we found the luncheon set much less generous, and actually much less accepting of our music. In fact we only made about 3F in total despite, or perhaps even because of Bobbi's best efforts, so we went back down to the beach. We then spent the rest of the day sitting about, sun-bathing, and generally dossing. At night we hit the town again, re-visiting some of the sites that had already had the benefit of Jesse's Juicy-Fruit Jug Band and were much more successful. There was no doubt about it though –Tim, Simon, and Brian were a big miss.

Two days later, and we'd got into something of a routine. One night, when the "crowd" that had gathered round us in the harbour area started to disperse, Mike just sat on one of the bollards and started to pick out guitar tunes. Naturally, one was *Angie*. A couple stopped to listen, then another, and soon Bobbi was out with the hat and coins were jangling into it. There was a sense of gentle music being nicely appreciated. That was the point when the fuzz arrived – a couple of burly ones with fierce expressions – and they made it very clear that they wanted us to move on. They crashed in and destroyed the atmosphere completely. One of them reminded me a bit of Rooney-the-Loony, and I could well imagine that, just like him, they were probably the sort of blokes that had revelled in pulling the wings off butterflies when they were kids. Still, this was a minor incident, compared to the sequence of events that kicked off the next day.

Bobbi was a bit behind us when the car pulled up. When she wasn't linked to Mike, she often dawdled behind, gazing into the shop windows, and marvelling at the shoes and handbags and their ridiculous prices. I didn't notice it at first – the streets of St Tropez are so narrow and cars move so slowly that they just become part of the landscape. So we didn't pay much attention when this one stopped, and then bounced up on the kerb and reversed back towards Bobbi.

By the time we missed her enough to turn round and walk back towards the car, she was involved in an animated conversation with the driver, who appeared to be a middle-aged fresh-faced sort of chap in a pink open-necked shirt. Mike and I stood and waited on the kerbside. The tone of their conversation seemed relaxed and happy, with both smiling and occasionally laughing as they chatted, so much so that I thought it must be some long-lost relative. I also noticed that there was a woman in the car, about the same age as the chap, who was leaning over and taking a full part in the conversation too. From time to time Bobbi glanced over to us, and nodded to the couple as if she was talking to them about us. Then her expression seemed to change, the tone became less cheery, and the conversation more hushed. Eventually Bobbi ran over to us and said,

"It's O.K. I will explain. But first I must go with them for few moments. They have a good idea for us. Really, it is a good thing. They give you this 10 francs – here – to have a drink in the café, over there, till I come back. It is good. Really, it is. I will explain you soon. Ten minutes".

I was far from convinced that it *was* 'good', partly because she insisted on telling us that it was, and partly because she looked decidedly anxious. Then there was the money – why give 10 francs to a couple of complete strangers? What was that about? But before either of us could frame any meaningful questions she'd run back to the car and hopped in.

As it pulled away the woman turned back and waved with a smug sort of look on her face. Bobbi also turned and waved from the back seat, still smiling but looking more anxious I thought as the car disappeared into the distance.

Mike and I stood in silence for a moment or two, then we went to the café as instructed to wait. I tried to work out what might be going on over our café crème – well, after all we did have 10 francs to spend – but Mike didn't seem too concerned.

"Did you get the number of the car?" I asked him.

"No, all I noticed was that it was big and silver. Anyway, why would we want its number?"

"In case they don't come back. They may have kidnapped her or something."

"What, to sell her in the white slave trade? This is St Tropez, not Bangkok!"

"Well, where've they taken her then?"

"I don't know. Probably just up the road for a chat. This isn't the best street to park a car in. They were causing an obstruction as it was. And anyway she seemed perfectly happy to go with them."

"So what do they want with her then?"

"Oh give it a rest will you? She said they had a good idea for *us*. Perhaps they want us to play somewhere. Look, just stop worrying, it'll be fine".

As optimism goes, this was probably a good stab at it from Mike, I thought. Then again, given that Mike always tended to think people were overcome with an irresistible need to hear him play as soon as they saw his guitar, I remained sceptical.

So we sat and waited .... and waited. You'd think, given the patient example we were setting and what with him being a professional, the waiter himself would have been able to join in and wait along with us. Instead he kept glancing suspiciously at us as he passed, and far from being captivated by the allure of Mike's guitar, gave the impression of a man terrified that we were going to start busking at any minute. When we ordered our second café crème he even asked us to pay for the first one, as if to make sure we did actually have money. After we'd been there an hour the tables were now beginning to fill up, presumably with the lunch crowd, so he came over and, whipping our empty cups away with a flourish, spat out pointedly, "C'est tout?" which, even with my small smattering of French, I knew very well meant, "Isn't it about time you pissed off?"

61

Luckily that was when the silver car finally re-appeared but instead of Bobbi, the smug-looking woman of earlier emerged from the passenger door. She looked pale and a little apprehensive, but broke into a smile as she came over to us and the car drove off with a brash honk of its horn. She flopped down onto a chair next to us and dealt with the waiter crisply by ordering three beers.

"C'est l'heure du déjeuner!" he protested, and miming an eating motion with his fingers up to his mouth he stared at Mike and said, as if to a half-wit, "Il faut manger!"

But Aimée, as we discovered later she was called, clearly had his number. She waved her hand at him imperiously, garbled out some French to him and sent him on his way. She was well into her story when he re-appeared about ten minutes later with two plates of omelette and chips, three beers, and a distinctly sour look on his face.

She told us, in near-perfect English, that she was very pleased to meet us and that, together with her husband Antoine she ran a café on the out skirts of St Tropez. They had noticed our guitars as they had driven past earlier and had stopped to see if we were interested in playing some tunes for their evening customers. When, in talking to Bobbi, they'd discovered we were English and sleeping on the beach they had thought this was even quite a novelty and were even more interested in marketing us as a special travelling English band. Because their café was out of town regular live music was both expensive and hard to sign up, apparently. As long as we were reasonably good, and Bobbi had assured them that we were, they'd give us a chance – and 25 francs for our trouble. And talking of Bobbi, they'd taken her on ahead so she could suss out the place for us and make whatever preparations were needed. That bit did puzzle me a bit, but I was so caught up in our stroke of good fortune, and the fact that I was finding the omelette and chips delectable, that I didn't question it too much at the time.

And then it all got even better. Since we were sleeping on the beach she said, and had no transport out to their café, she and Antoine planned to put us up for the night in a hotel nearby – at their expense! And if all went well, perhaps for the next night too! Bobbi would be waiting for us there, and when we had finished our meal Aimée was going to take us to the hotel, let us settle in, and then come to collect us for our evening performance later on. Mike mentioned our rucksacks back in Rookery Nook. She looked somewhat irritated, but then smiled pleasantly and suggested that we should simply go and collect them and she'd pick us up in an hour.

We really couldn't believe our luck. Perhaps Mike had been right all along, and there was something irresistible about the sight of his guitar. And Aimée, far from being smug, turned out to be a perfectly charming and likeable lady, and fun to be with. She even suggested tunes we might play that evening, amazing us with her knowledge of American folk music. Looking back we really ought to have seen through her, but I guess we were just carried away in the thrill of our good fortune – like finding a wallet bursting with money in the street.

So it was that a little while later we found ourselves being chauffeured into 'L'Hotel Jeanne D'Arc'- how much of a good omen was that! - a plush hotel deep in the countryside. It stood in its own grounds, surrounded by a high ivy-covered wall. Aimée had dropped us off at the desk where she spoke to a pretty girl on reception, before driving off and promising to pick us up again in a couple of hours time, at 6 o'clock. We were shown to a nice big room which was perfectly situated on the ground floor, overlooking the garden and a huge swimming pool. Oddly though, it only had one double bed in it. I wondered how we were going to work that one out. And there was one other thing wrong – there was no sign of Bobbi.

6

Mike remained cheerfully unconcerned. When I expressed my worry, he just laughed it off. He thought she had probably gone for a walk or something, or that she may even be booked into some other room. Bobbi wasn't in any danger, he said, pointing out how nice and friendly Aimée had been with us, and anyway he was sure Bobbi could look after herself. Then he got out his guitar, sat on the bed and started to play.

I thought he was probably right but went for a stroll around the hotel anyway, thinking I might find her at the pool or in a bar or something. I didn't. The pretty receptionist smiled at me as I walked through the lobby, so I stopped and asked her. Luckily she spoke English.

"We were expecting to meet our friend here – Mademoiselle Bobbi ..." and then I seized up, realising I had no idea what her surname was.

But it didn't matter. She knew immediately. "Ah oui, oui, Mlle. Bobbi. She go out with her friends – before you come."

"She's gone?"

"Yes – after she made the reservation for the room – about two hours ago."

Then her phone rang, she excused herself and I wandered off, feeling a little reassured but still puzzled. More questions were framing themselves in my mind when the receptionist called out "Monsieur!", and held the phone out towards me. "C'est votre amie, monsieur. C'est Mademoiselle".

I raced over. "Bobbi?"

"Allo Nigel. It's O.K." She sounded fine, if a little breathless.

"Everything is O.K. Don't worry. I explain you soon. Aimée and Antoine ask me to say there is a...a .... *confusion?*"

"Confusion? Muddle? Mix-up?"

"Oui, oui, *une confusion.* Le chef de cuisine has got sick suddenly, and they have to take him to the hospital. They have to close the restaurant tonight".

"Oh, I'm sorry. So what do we do?"

"Oh you must stay at the hotel this night, and they hope it is all O.K. for tomorrow. I come back very soon".

"When? We've been worried Bobbi ".

"Oh don't worry. Is all O.K …. really. I come back soon …er, later. I don't know. O.K then, bye bye". And she hung up.

I went back to the room and told Mike who was still bent over his guitar, picking out various chords and riffs. Annoyingly he kept on playing as I told him about the phone call. "Well there you are then", he said. "Meantime we've had a nice slapsie and we get a night in this lovely hotel. Ça va bien, n'est-ce pas?" So he just carried on playing and ignored me when I asked why he thought there wasn't some back-up or standby arrangement when a member of staff got ill.

After the phone-call we dossed around for a couple of hours, then went for something to eat in the hotel's Bistro bar. Mike thought it would be cool to just 'charge it to the room', so we did and had a good snigger about our new rubber-neck life-style. We looked a bit incongruous in our denim shirts and jeans, but no-one seemed to take much notice of us. I thought that was odd given our up-market surroundings – especially since we'd already been threatened with being thrown off the beach in St Tropez, just for making it look untidy. Then we noticed it was 9 o'clock, and still no sign of Bobbi. Even Mike was beginning to get a bit worried now.

"What did she say exactly?"

"She said she'd be back soon – she wasn't specific – just 'later on'".

"Well … there's still time then".

"But that was over four hours ago!"

We decided to have a walk along the road, just to see what we could see really. Aimée and Antoine's place was supposed to be nearby (although the receptionist hadn't heard of it when I asked), so we thought we'd just explore a bit and see what we could find. But all we found was a dark road, which led on to another dark road. Apart from a bit of moonlight piercing the general gloom there was otherwise nothing to see – only the lights of a town way in the distance, which we thought was probably St Tropez. Two or three cars sped by, but it was mostly quiet and rather eerie. Then, quite suddenly, somewhere in the distance we heard a lonely wailing sound, like a cat caught in a trap. We both stopped dead in our tracks, then looked at each other and burst out laughing. It was as if we'd strayed into some 1950's horror film with werewolves on the prowl. There was probably a little country Inn up ahead where everyone would look round at us in deathly silence as we went in. Then they'd warn us not

65

to go and explore the eerie gothic mansion up on the hill. Wisely I think, we decided we'd keep one step ahead of the action at that point, and just go back to the hotel. It was good that we did – when we got back we found Bobbi curled up on the bed sobbing her heart out.

For a while all we could get out of her was something that sounded like 'unterrs'. Mike cradled her as she kept on sobbing, murmuring, "I don't want to leave. I don't want to leave."

"It's O.K" said Mike tenderly. "We're not going anywhere. We can stay here till we've sorted all this out. Sssh. Just lie quietly now. You can tell us all about it when you're ready".

I was very impressed. I'd never seen him quite so – well, maternal.

But what was it with these 'hunters'? Had she been frightened by the wolves' howls too, had she perhaps encountered a group of mad hunters who were trying to run the werewolf out of town, but turned their hate on her instead? Had she strayed into the haunted mansion? I felt ashamed. There was Mike giving her tender loving care, and I was just making fun of the poor girl's distress. But 'unterrs'? Well, it wasn't much to go on.

It took us about an hour or so to piece the story together. Words like 'scandaleuse … déshonoré …révoltante' appeared in her tale, then Bobbi's own eventual translation helped us to realise that 'unterrs' was actually 'honteuse' – in other words, she felt deeply ashamed. But whatever had happened to the poor girl? I searched my mind for the French word for rape, but oddly enough we hadn't covered it in French O-level. Anyway, to ask 'have you been raped?' in any language seemed far too direct a question for her fragile emotional state to cope with. So I just whispered to Mike. She understood straight away, shouted 'Non, non, non', and buried her head in her hands.

Aimée and Antoine weren't café owners at all. They were free-lance photographers. They'd eye-balled Bobbi in the town, and when they'd stopped originally their offer had been for a photo-shoot they said they were doing for a newly-opened hotel. They needed attractive people to pose as guests, or whatever, and had offered Bobbi 50 francs for an hour's work. When Mike and I strolled up they had been stunned to find that Bobbi wasn't alone, so had quickly told her we could not be part of the deal, and to tell us to wait in the café whilst she went with them for the shoot. They'd then taken her to a secluded area where woodland led down to a beach area. On the way they had explained that they were actually 'glamour' photographers, and that the assignment was really about Bobbi posing naked in various naturalistic settings – on the beach, on rocks, in the woods. She assured us that the couple had not been menacing at all but in fact very pleasant, even giving her the option of backing out, and promising to return her promptly back to the town if she wasn't interested. But they had also put the pay-off up to 100 francs, and had convinced her that it would all be very tasteful and take no more than a couple of hours at most. So Bobbi had agreed to do it.

We were amazed at that point. Bobbi had seemed a shy type, but hey, she was French so possibly that made her prone to sudden impulses? Come to think of it, maybe that was why she'd got talked into it so quickly, and of course the French attitude to nudity was known to be more permissive than us uptight English. I also remembered how sweet and personable Aimée was, and how safe she made you feel. I thought that even I might have agreed if she'd asked me … well, no, maybe not. Then there was the lure of the money – that must have helped too. Perhaps it did make a bit of sense. Bobbi was now cuddling tightly into Mike and sobbing, and told him again how she didn't want to leave, and how 'dégradée' she felt.

After they'd secured her agreement, Aimée had then come back to us, sold us her story about their restaurant, and after delivering us to the hotel, had gone back to Antoine to help with the photo-shoot. Bobbi didn't go into the details of that but told us how, when it was over, she had suddenly become overwhelmed with shame and distress. They'd taken her to a bar for a drink and something to eat, but it hadn't helped, and then they'd got increasingly impatient with her. She'd pleaded with them to destroy the film but they had just laughed at her. Eventually they'd dumped her at the roadside, about 5 miles from the hotel. How she'd found her way back I'll never know, but she did, and must have arrived very soon after Mike and I had left for our little night-time ramble.

Having recounted her story, in the fits and bursts she told it, she seemed gradually to calm down. Meanwhile I was struggling with alternate feelings of sympathy, anxiety and guilt. The problem was having to constantly dismiss from my mind intrusive fantasy images of what the photos might have been like.

"You do not hate me?" Bobbi asked.

"No, of course not. Why ever should we hate you?"

"Because I am so …." And she started sobbing again. Mike helped her into the en suite and suggested she should soothe herself in a hot bath. Meanwhile we considered what to do.

"It's all a bit demoralising this, isn't it?" Mike said.

"Yeah. Poor Bobbi". I had a quick flash of images again.

Then he said, "Well I was thinking more from our point of view really".

"How's that?"

"You know, the fact that it was her they wanted all along. I thought it was us and the music they were after".

I could hardly believe it. I went for the moral high ground.

"You don't think you're being just a tiny bit of a selfish and unfeeling bastard there, do you?"

"Yeah, I know. Just joking". But he wasn't, and especially when his next mercenary thought was:

"So do you think they're still going to pay for the hotel then?"

"I shouldn't think so. But then, if they don't, they must know we'll just go to the police, and they wouldn't want that".

"Why not? We're the ones who've committed a crime – we're the ones who've booked into a hotel that we can't pay for, remember? All they've done, apparently, is to take some dodgy photos."

My heart sank with a dull thud as I remembered that the room was actually in Bobbi's name.

"But she's in such a state. What if they did rape her?"

"It doesn't sound like they did, does it? I didn't get the impression they had. It was just a photo-shoot".

I figured for a moment that this could well be another of Mike's stabs at unfounded optimism, but on the other hand he did have a point. She was distressed certainly, but it didn't seem like the distress of a rape victim. Not that I'd know what that was like.

"Well, we have to stay here anyway," I said at last. "She keeps saying she doesn't want to leave, and she doesn't seem in any fit state to go anywhere tonight. The 100 francs she got will cover us won't it?"

"Shit that's a point!" Mike gasped, and he looked anxiously over to the bathroom door. "How do you know they actually paid her?" He went over and gently knocked on the door.

"Bobbi? Did they pay you the 100 francs?"

There was a silence and the sound of water moving about stopped. Then there was a howl and a wail, and she started to sob again.

He looked over at me and screwed up his face. "Did you ever get the feeling you've said the wrong thing?"

68

Bobbi emerged about 20 minutes later, still looking shame-faced, but evidently calmer. Mike started talking about how we should pack up and go straightaway – a moonlight flit, out of the window and away. We were on the ground floor after all. But I wasn't at all convinced. Bobbi however was oddly enthusiastic about the idea. I thought she'd been telling us she didn't want to leave.

"Yes we should go. But we do not go back into St Trop. I think we should go to Nice. We can meet with Jeanne again. Perhaps we can stay with her and Pip. They will be happy to see us again. Oh yes, let us go to Nice".

"Are you sure it's the right thing to do?" I said to Mike. "If we go off without any explanation, the police will be after us for sure. Shouldn't we just stay and tell the truth?"

But Mike was insistent. Perhaps the prospect of a new life as a fugitive from justice appealed to him.

"They'll never believe us. And anyway, even if they do and if we get involved in some big investigation, they'll soon find out we have hardly any dosh and we'll end up being sent back to England for sure. Let's take our chances. Look, the beds haven't even been slept in. Apart from messing up the bathroom a bit, we haven't used their facilities, so we're not costing them anything."

I said I didn't think that was how the hotel industry worked, and had he forgotten about our rubber-necking meal in the Bistro?

Then he sort of snapped. "Oh for God's sake Nige! For once in your life, can't you take one lousy fucking risk? Just shut up whingeing and do as you're bloody-well told!"

I was shocked – partly by his venom, but mostly by the fact that he had suddenly turned into my Dad. I hadn't had many dealings with him before he left but that was imprinted in my memory as one of his favourite sayings.

"Do as you're told!"

I fell silent feeling both hurt and resentful. *I would have thought that coming on this bloody stupid trip with you was taking quite a big risk thank you very much. I'm just as much a free-thinking desperado as you any day, you twat.* I resolved to bloody well show him exactly what sort of risks I was prepared to take just as soon as I got the chance.

"O.K." I said. "No need to be so bloody personal."

He relented. "Sorry. Look, all I'm saying is that, if we keep our heads down for a few days we'll be fine. They've got absolutely nothing to go on".

Then Bobbi joined in, clearly having changed her mind about wanting to stay and adding her renewed support to the plan of absconding to Nice, and teaming up again with Jeanne and Pip. That bit was fine with me, although since we'd only said goodbye about three days ago, it did occur to me there was the distinct possibility that Pip might be less happy to see us than Bobbi anticipated, particularly after what Tim had said.

I did like the way she pronounced Pip's name though. I hadn't really noticed before. Now she seemed to give it an extra P-e-e-e-p sort of emphasis, which made his name sound what it was really, vaguely ridiculous. In fact her idea seemed to perk her up nicely but when Mike expressed a doubt about going that far up the coast, a wave of shame and general upset washed over her again.

"Oh I am so unhappy. I don't want to leave!" she wailed.

Mike and I swapped a puzzled look with each other.

"What do you mean Bobbi? We have to leave. We have to go Bobbi. We'll be in real trouble if we stay here."

"Boys, boys," she said, in an exasperated sort of way. "You don't understand me. I want to go, yes. But I don't want to *leeeve*. It means I want to die if I stay here!"

I stifled a snigger, but Bobbi saw me and shot me a startled look. Then she began to laugh too, and then Mike joined in. It's funny how fear makes simple things seem so hysterical.

7

We finally decided to leave at first light. It was about 2am and it seemed silly to leave only to stumble around in the dark. Mike gallantly offered to look after Bobbi in the double bed. I didn't argue. Of all the possible combinations, it was the one that was, from my point of view anyway, the least uninviting. I didn't fancy curling up with Bobbi in her fragile state, and the idea of Mike and me in the bed with Bobbi on the floor was far too much 'Tim-and-Simon' for my liking. So without further fuss I unrolled my sleeping bag on the floor at the end of the bed and, feeling pretty wrecked after all that had happened, went straight to sleep.

I awoke about 4 or 5 hours later when I heard them shuffling about, packing ready to go. I noticed that Bobbi was looking somewhat sheepish again.

"Are you O.K?" I asked. She shot me another of those startled looks of hers.

"Oui, oui. I am fine. Let's go, quickly now".

So we straightened the bed, left everything in the room as tidy as we could, then climbed out of the window, and set off.

Once outside the hotel grounds, we had no idea where we were, although Bobbi said she could remember the general direction away from St Tropez from her experience on her adventure. Her ability to find her way around strange places was truly amazing, as it wasn't long before we came upon a junction where there was a sign-post which read 'St Maxime: 8 km'. The sun was now slowly beginning to rise and the darkness was lifting. We all felt pretty tired, but decided to press on anyway. There was a shortage of traffic as we plodded along, which was good in one way, although it did mean that we were just about on our knees by the time we stumbled into St Maxime about an hour and a half later. The fatigue distracted Bobbi from her sorrow however, and she became focussed on firstly, finding a water fountain for us to have a drink and a wash, and then on finding the bus for Nice. None of us could be bothered with hitching rides, and we thought it probably wasn't a safe option anyway. Mostly we wanted to put distance between us and St Tropez as quickly as possible.

I guess real fugitives think their moves out a bit more carefully than we did – probably travelling by night, or stowing away on lorries and trains, and perhaps even growing beards and wearing disguises. We just stood shiftily at a bus-stop in the bright morning sunshine – two scruffy blokes and a pretty blonde girl, laden with bags of various sizes, looking cold, tired and hungry. I thought we might just as well have been carrying a big sign that said, "Runaways". And I couldn't help thinking this was all a big mistake. Surely it was *more* likely that we'd be sent home if we were caught on the run than if we stayed and faced it out? I'd tried this one on Mike as we'd walked, and he just shrugged and said, "Well we've done it now."

The bus came and took us along a coastal road to the next big town, St Raphael. It was a beautiful ride, with the most gorgeous views across a vibrant blue sea. With the white puffs of cloud overhead I felt transported, at least temporarily, to another world and my worries ceased a little and I started to feel more calm. At St Raphael we quickly transferred to the train for Nice. It was a busy, bustly train although, apart from annoying people with our bags blocking the doorways, I don't think anybody took that much notice of us.

At Nice we decided to put all our stuff in the 'Left Luggage' lockers. Carting it all through the town seemed a bit unwise, particularly as we weren't sure of the welcome awaiting us. If Pip, or Nice in general, proved unkind, we might be back on the train by nightfall. Meanwhile Bobbi went to ask directions to the address Jeanne had given her.

Whilst she was busy with this, of course there had to be a row about the luggage. Mike wanted to take the guitars at least – how could we go busking without them? I asked him if he was completely deranged – surely *busking* was completely out of the question? And wouldn't carrying guitars around Nice just get us a lot of unwanted attention? Had he forgotten we were runaways, and wanted by the police? Then he said to piss off because he was going to take his anyway. So I called him a stupid pratt, and he called me a tosser and a loser – and no doubt our cheery banter would have gone on a while longer in this vein had not Bobbi arrived back at that point and intervened. To my surprise she didn't back me up at all and couldn't see what I was worrying about. So I just gave in, although I did leave my guitar behind just to show Mike that he hadn't won altogether.

Bobbi's news was that the apartment was just off a main street called Boulevard Gambetta. This Boulevard was reasonably near the station, and we had to walk down it towards the sea front. Bobbi remembered that Pip had talked about how the apartment wasn't too far from the beach in fact, and also that it was quite near a market, where you could get cheap food handily. So we set off.

We hadn't walked very far when we heard the unmistakeable wail of a police siren, and Mike and I panicked simultaneously and ducked into the nearest shop. We did it so quickly everyone in the shop stopped and looked at us. "Sorry," Mike announced, "Nous pensez que … que…il commence de pleut." Meanwhile Bobbi remained standing outside the shop looking quite bemused as we backed out. But we all giggled like kids as we walked off, at perhaps a quicker pace, down the street. It was of course more likely that the police car was out to catch bigger fish than us – our little criminal aberration hardly merited sirens and dogs or whatever. But even so, we didn't want to take any chances so when another car, equipped with the same threatening wail, shot past about 10 minutes later Mike and I ducked into a little arcade. Bobbi on the other hand wasn't at all perturbed, but just seemed to think we were playing some kind of silly game.

Then we passed a Boulangerie. The aroma of freshly-baked bread was unbearable. I couldn't even remember when we'd last eaten. As we drooled at the window, to my complete surprise Bobbi suddenly chased after a smartly-dressed man who'd just gone past. We watched her chatting to him for a few minutes, then he took something out of his pocket and gave it to her before proceeding on his way. She came back smiling all over her face, waving a 5 franc note. I don't know what she said to people, but she seemed to have an amazing knack of getting people to part with their money. Whether it was passing the hat or direct begging she certainly had the *savoir faire* – as they say in France. Perhaps there was something about her sweet, waif-like nature that appealed.

The money was enough to buy two sandwiches between us. But these were to be no ordinary sandwiches. They were like soft, squishy bread buns, cradling the most delicious tuna and salad which were in turn swimming in a gorgeous olive oil dressing. They called them *pain bagnat* – and during our stay in Nice over the next few days we were to crave many more of these little culinary masterpieces. Perhaps it was to do with being so hungry, but they were just so delectable. The worst of it, and best of it too I suppose, was that after my share of one of them, I was left wanting more! I think if Aimée and Antoine had happened along at that moment I would have posed naked there and then, if they'd offered me another *pain bagnat* as my wages. But we had to press on.

73

A little further down the Boulevard we finally came across the market, from which it then didn't take us long to find the right street. We were just turning into it when Bobbi suddenly screamed and ran across the road. She'd spotted Jeanne, serving an outside table at a street corner café. They ran to embrace each other, and we followed. I felt my heart skip a beat as we drew close, and I found myself anxiously scanning the tables to check that Pip wasn't lurking nearby. He wasn't. Jeanne meanwhile was as lovely as I'd remembered her – only moreso.

Bobbi became tearful as they gabbled away to each other for a minute or so, and it seemed clear that she was giving Jeanne the edited highlights of her trauma and the reason for our sudden departure from St Tropez. I listened as carefully as I could in case some more details filtered through, but their conversation had the quality of an anxious whispering and neither my hearing nor my French proved equal to the task. All I could do was watch as Jeanne looked increasingly perturbed. She wasn't due to finish work for a couple of hours so she offered us the keys to the apartment, or *studio* as she insisted on calling it, to let ourselves in.

I couldn't bear it anymore. "What about Pip?" I asked anxiously. Why was nobody else worried? In St Tropez I thought he'd made it very clear that we were firmly on his list of 'people he'd least like to share a *beach* with' so it was hardly likely he was going to welcome us warmly into the even smaller confines of an apartment. But to my relief, Jeanne said, "It is no problem. Pip stayed one night here only, and then he go to Greece. I don't even know when he comes back".

"To Greece?"

"Oui, oui. He has left me to look after the *studio*", she said, not sounding in the least bit resentful. "It is good. I have a job here, and I have nice place to stay. Oh but I am so glad you have all come!"

"Why didn't you go with him?" I asked anxiously.

"To Greece? Oh là là", and she laughed. "No, I am happy to stay *en France*. Oh but now I must go. I talk to you later" and she rushed off as someone from the café knocked on the window and beckoned her inside. I felt a surge of hope. She'd chosen waitressing over Greece and Pip!

The apartment, or *studio,* was not far away. We found it on the second floor of a building overlooking a church. I was expecting at least two rooms and a bathroom, and perhaps with this new emphasis on the whole studio thing, I thought maybe there'd even be the odd easel or potter's wheel knocking about, but it actually turned out to be a one-room bed-sit. The bathroom was a shared facility one floor down.

When I walked in the first thing I noticed was a light and delicate aroma in the air, nothing too potent just a subtle hint of something perfumed. It gave the room a clean and fresh feel. Then the thought hit me that this was actually the first time I'd ever been in a Girl's Bedroom. Well actually I have been in my cousin Mandy's bedroom a few times, but I'm not counting that. As Girl's Bedrooms go, my guess was that Mandy's was very untypical. Her two main hobbies were weight-lifting and judo, and whenever I went there were always dumb-bells and chest expander things lying around, and a very pungent stench of liniment hung constantly in the air. Apparently there was some doubt in the family as to whether she even properly qualified as a bona fide Girl, but that was something that never got talked about much.

Compared to Mandy's bedroom, this was like stepping inside a sweet marshmallow. And thankfully, as well as there being no evidence of dumb-bells here, neither was there any evidence of Pip. If he had been here, he certainly hadn't stayed long enough to put down any markers. Instead, all around me was evidence of Jeanne, her bags, her clothes, and most of all, her smell.

But as I looked round I also felt sad to realise that, even with Pip gone, it was clear from the cramped space that Mike and I weren't going to be able to stay any length of time. In fact when Jeanne got back from work this was the first thing we discussed. She was very keen that Bobbi should stay with her for longer, particularly after the trauma in St Tropez, but as for Mike and me we would have to take our chances on the beaches, or maybe in the Old Town. She seemed to know a lot about possible places, and was very sweet in giving us helpful tips. She was happy for us all to stay for one night though.

I was just starting to feel safe and excited at this prospect when Jeanne then came up with the idea that Mike and I should go and try some busking at some of the nearby cafés and bars. As the fantasy evening I had planned fell to bits in my head I tried to fend off her suggestion – for several reasons. Partly of course, I wanted to spend at least some time close to Jeanne, but equally I was worried about the risk of drawing attention to us. To be honest I think I also didn't want Mike to be right about the advantage of having his guitar. But I got no support and it steadily became clear that the idea really was to get Mike and me out of the way so they could have some quiet time together and have a longed-for girly chat. So after Jeanne had kindly fed us some soup, bread and paté, we took ourselves off. Outside neither one of us had much enthusiasm for busking as it happened, so we decided not to bother and just go and have a drink instead. When we went back to the studio a couple of hours later, we found Jeanne and Bobbi curled up together on the bed, fast asleep.

I was awoken next morning by the sweet comforting aroma of fresh coffee. It seemed strange to be waking up in an actual room – apart from the hotel where we'd only stayed for a few hours, I realised this was the first time I'd slept in an actual room since leaving home. I looked up and saw Jeanne over by the gas-ring, fully dressed, stirring hot milk into a cup. She greeted me with that lovely kiss-on-both-cheeks thing, and invited me to come with her to buy bread and stuff for breakfast.

Jeanne was lovely. There was no two ways about it. She had a soft and gentle way with her as she moved, sort of floating between one activity and another. She had tied her hair up loosely now too, and the raggedy, windswept look made her look really cool and all the more attractive. I couldn't fathom what on earth she was doing with a loser like Pip, who just wandered off whenever he liked, following his own selfish whims and making no effort, it seemed to me, to look after her. Perhaps in order to remind her what a pratt he was I ventured to ask, "Why did Pip go off to Greece so fast?"

She just laughed. "Pip does what he wants to do", and that seemed to be that. She was more interested in Bobbi.

"Tell me what happened to Bobbi."

I said I didn't know any more than I presumed she had already been told.

"But what did those people want with such photos?"

I said I had no idea, and we slumped into silence. After a while I said, "Did she say anything to you about what happened exactly?"

She looked puzzled.

"You know ... did they, er, you know, did they 'touch' her?"

"Touch?"

God, why was she making it so difficult, and what the hell was French for 'rape' anyway? "Well, you know, in a sexual way?"

"She looked shocked. "Non, non. Nigel! How could you think that? There was no intention. They were only wanting the photos. Otherwise, Bobbi say to me, they were kind to her. The woman was kind especially. Bobbi is upset because she feels shame to have said yes to take off her clothes, not because of a matter *sexuelle*".

Presumably that's where I'd been going wrong. I'd always assumed that taking off one's clothes was somehow associated with matters sexual, but Jeanne seemed very sure they were separate issues, and at that moment I thought it best not to argue. So, when I could get a word in I just said, "Good, yes, good. Sorry, We just thought …"

But we'd arrived at the Boulangerie by this time and she rushed off inside to buy the bread and stuff. I hung around outside feeling very uncomfortable, as if I had violated this pretty young girl with my dirty ideas. When we got back to the room though, she whispered to me, "Don't worry Nigel. I know you were frightened for Bobbi. But it is O.K. Nothing too bad has happened. I will look after her." And I felt a sudden wave of warm feelings wash over me.

After leaving Jeanne and Bobbi together, we made our way down to the sea front and walked along the Promenade des Anglais. It was a fine bright morning with the lightest of breezes blowing off the sea. We headed for the old town where we found the morning market in full swing. The displays of vegetables, cheeses, and sausages along with cut flowers and potted plants were just gorgeous. By the side of the stalls were boxes of damaged fruit which, according to Jeanne, the stall-holders just threw away. So I tried my luck, held up a banana or an apple and asked confidently, "Combien?" I'd obviously fooled them at last, as this time the old chap behind the stall didn't automatically assume I was English, and gabbled an answer in French. Instinctively I blurted back, 'How much?' and my disguise fell away like a leaf off a tree. Mostly we were waved away with looks of contempt, although we got lucky on our fourth attempt when a cheery, red-faced lady smiled and said, "Ah, c'est gratuit, ça," and threw in a bunch of black-looking bananas for good measure.

"Jeanne reckons Bobbi wasn't raped", I said casually. We were sitting on a bench in a large square on the edge of the old town.

"Course she wasn't, I know that".

"Well, we weren't sure, were we? I mean, she wasn't that clear about exactly what those people had done to her".

"Yes she was. It was just the photos that freaked her". Then he sat thoughtfully for a minute before he turned to me and, smiling in a smug sort of way, he said, "Anyway, if she had been raped …. she wouldn't have let me near her …"

I felt the shiver of a shock-wave. Did he mean what I thought he meant?

"Do you mean …?"

He turned away, still smiling, and bit another chunk off the end of his banana.

"Might do".

"You bastard", I said. "The poor girl was vulnerable, upset and in shock, and you – "

"I offered her the comfort she needed, that's all", he rasped.

I just looked at him. In the past his 'comfort' had come at a high price – ask Sandra Maddison and her family, or his poor mother come to that. But I still couldn't believe it.

"Comfort? You mean you didn't actually …."

"What? Just say what you mean Nige. Don't be so bloody coy. Did I shag her? Is that what you want to know?"

"Well yes, actually".

"Course not. What do you take me for?"

I take you for Mike I thought - the self-sufficient, unfettered wandering minstrel who attaches and commits to no-one. The guy who gets a girl pregnant, then leaves the country. Like moths round a flame, he never had any trouble attracting girls to him. Whether it was on the way to school, or at the old Merry Neet Club, they were always there, and he often bragged about 'getting off' with them. But it was never very clear what 'getting off' with them meant, since he mainly just insinuated or gave you half-truths, never the full story. Certainly he was never to be seen with a regular girl-friend.

As for me, I found the whole business much more difficult. I won't give you a full history, not because it's that long, it's just not that interesting. The edited highlights are: 1) Marie – she fancied me, I didn't fancy her, so I was coy and aloof. 2) Hilary – I fancied her, she didn't fancy me, so she told me to piss off. 3) Susan – I met her at the Merry Neet, and we went out a few times. We snogged and held hands a lot, and went around together for a while. But when I told her I loved her she decided to call it all off. 4) Claire – we got together at a party where we had a marathon sort of snog. By the time I had finally got my hand up her jumper as far as her bra, she had fallen asleep. I went round to her house the next day but she told me, on the doorstep, thanks very much but she didn't want to start anything if it was all the same to me. So I went home.

And that's it really.

So as I sat with Mike on the bench I began to feel, yet again, that I live in a strange world that I haven't got the hang of. I'm not bad-looking, and feel sure I know how to treat a woman well. Mike treats people badly on the whole, he doesn't make commitments, and most likely he'll let you down. Yet girls are much more likely to choose to be with him. Why is that? Depressingly it occurred to me that it was probably for the same reason that Jeanne had chosen to be with Pip.

We walked down to the sea front. On the Promenade, people were just strolling about or wandering down to the beach. Various pockets of people stood by the railings, chatting or looking out to sea. In the distance what looked like a big white cruise ship was heading out to sea and I noticed a young couple pointing at it and giggling. We were now trying to find Ruhl Plage where, according to Jeanne, everyone hung out. Then one of a group of three or four young lads who were walking past stopped and pointed at Mike's guitar, and asked some sort of question.

"Non comprends pas," Mike said. "Anglais."

"Ah, English," he said, "What do you play please?"

Mike seemed to scan his brain in a search for something they might have heard of. He tried Bob Dylan.

"Ah! Monsieur le Tambourin Man! Will you play for us?"

Mike didn't need asking twice, and it wasn't long before he had cast a little spell over the little group. They seemed entranced. It was just like the lads we'd met on the ferry all over again.

"Bella, très belle," one of them said. Then another request came in, and so on, until he had attracted a small group around him. I hung back and walked to lean on the railings, scanning the Promenade for the police, whilst also cursing the fact that I hadn't got my guitar too.

"Shouldn't you be passing the hat around or something man?"

I looked up and saw a young dark-haired chap, with a droopy moustache, dressed in jeans and a black windjammer-type jacket. Beside him, with her arm linked tightly on to his, stood an attractive blonde girl with an odd-looking red beret perched on one side of her head. It was the couple I had seen earlier giggling at the cruise ship.

"I just thought – well since there's quite a little crowd now," he said, nodding in Mike's direction. His accent was distinctly American. "Tell you what," he said, "I'll have a go." And he quickly pulled off his friend's red beret and ran over to the group.

"Sorry about Steve," said the girl, "He's a bit impulsive like that. I'm Sue by the way."

And so began the start of a beautiful friendship. In no time at all Steve had collected a neat little sum. He was amazingly energetic running around the little circle that had gathered, so much so that people seemed to be willing to contribute just to calm him down. Eventually, as the group slowly dispersed Sue and I walked up to them, applauding. Steve then complained of feeling very thirsty so we went to buy some coke and sat by the railings to guzzle it, and to share our stories.

Steve and Sue were on a brief European tour. They'd started off in Greece, and had travelled up by rail through Yugoslavia and Italy to the South of France. Now they were on their way to Paris for their flight home in a few days' time. They were both going to go to 'School', or University as we would say, when they got back, and were having this last trip beforehand. She was clearly the stabling influence in the partnership, and she had to rein him in now and then as he tended to giggle a lot, and to ask lots of staccato-like questions. He also used words like 'scene', 'pad', and 'bread', often punctuating his questions with 'man' – in other words talking and acting like a hippie, even though his haircut actually made him look more like a banker. 'So where are you guys from? Where's your pad, man? Have you been to the States, man? Can you guys play blues? What's the scene like over here, man? Do you make much bread, man?'

Of course the reason for his hyperactivity and giggling soon became evident when he pulled out a tobacco tin and offered us 'a smoke'. Sue very sharply told him to put it away, and he obeyed instantly, shrinking down into himself like a scalded puppy. Mike took it a little further though and asked him where he'd 'scored' and all that, and he became animated again as they laughed and joked together like long-lost buddies.

Sue asked me about our time in France so far, and I told her a little of our stay in St Tropez. I edited out the bit about the dodgy photos, and just told her we were keeping our heads down for a bit as we'd stayed at a hotel and had left without paying. She thought this was hilarious, but couldn't understand why I was so worried about it. She said it was a commonplace occurrence in America, and that they had done the same thing at a hotel in Trieste. She talked about it as if it was a fun sort of game rather than a serious crime, and I found myself liking her style.

She told me that they were currently staying in a small hotel towards the centre of the town, and suggested that we could doss down in their room for a while if we wanted. We'd all seemed to have made a fairly immediate connection, and they were clearly good to be with, so we agreed fairly readily. Also, after due consideration, and prompted largely by Steve and Sue's bravado sort of attitude, we decided to go back to the railway station and pick up our gear. Mike of course didn't need much persuading

– he'd been constantly moaning about why I'd made him leave it all behind in the first place. Of course it now made sense for us to have all our stuff with us, and my guitar was needed especially of course for busking purposes. We also knew that if we could stash everything in their hotel room, it would potentially save us a lot of money. When we put all the gear in the lockers, Bobbi had translated a big red sign for us which basically said that, if you don't collect your stuff by a certain deadline, it gets transferred to a general store place, and if you want it back after that you have to pay a fine as well as the usual storage charges.

So Mike and I trudged back to the station, liberated all our gear, and then called in at Jeanne's to drop off Bobbi's stuff for her. She was delighted, having been on the point of going to collect it herself. It was also clear that Jeanne's influence was having a very positive effect and Bobbi seemed altogether brighter and more lively. I figured that now she could have some clean clothes that would also have a nice calming effect on her so, for some stupid reason, I tried to paraphrase Simon's philosophy for a happy life, substituting 'underwear' for shoes and 'a warm place to sleep' for the toilet thing. Unfortunately Bobbi didn't have a clue what I was talking about and Jeanne just scowled, so I just smiled weakly and inwardly kicked myself on the shins.

For the next few hours or so things then went relatively straight-forwardly. We met up with Steve and Sue as we had arranged, smuggled ourselves and our stuff into their hotel, and then went out for an evening's busking. With their help we got on really well, and got a nice little routine going. Sue would charm some café or restaurant proprietor into letting us mingle amongst their tables, Mike and I played and sang, and Steve took over from Bobbi as star hat-passer. He had a more direct sort of style but the fact that he had an American accent seemed to be a distinct advantage. We finally returned to the hotel at about one in the morning, elated, and with a very good tally of 25F40, 200 pesetas, and a shirt button. Then our problems really began.

Firstly the hotel was locked. Sue knew that she just had to ring for the concierge as apparently she and Steve often came back late and the concierge was used to this. The trouble was he knew them as a couple, and he was certain to identify us as two extra non-paying guests. But Steve had the solution. He said that there was a garden at the back of the hotel – we could sneak in there, and just lie low for a bit till it was safe for him to come and let us in by the patio doors. Flushed as we were with the success of our evening's work, we immediately put our trust in this as a flawless, well thought-out plan, and disappeared round the back. There we were confronted by a firmly locked gate, six-foot high iron railings, and the glare of a particularly bright street lamp. I thought perhaps the plan needed a bit more work.

The gate was topped with sharp-pointed railings but it seemed the best option for climbing, as at least it had a toe-hold halfway up. It was quiet in the street around us too, so I kept watch whilst Mike started to climb. He was able to heave himself to the top of the gate fairly quickly, but I was so busy looking up and down and roundabout that I didn't see what happened next. All I heard was a sickly ripping sort of noise, a howl of pain, and a dull thud as Mike hit the ground in a crumpled heap. He tried to sit up and I saw him reach out to grasp his leg as drops of blood quickly started to appear on the pavement. Then he lurched to one side and was sick in the gutter.

Just as he was spitting and wiping his mouth I heard movement in the garden, and footsteps on the gravel path. Then all went deathly quiet. I froze in a panic, caught between an urge to tend to Mike, shout for help, and legging it. A voice came whispering out of the silence.

"Are you hurt, man?"

It was Steve. He'd been waiting by the door, heard the thud, then the retching, and had come to investigate.

"I think it's O.K," Mike groaned. "I caught my leg on the railings, and I don't think I landed too well. It bloody hurts, I know that."

"Can you get up?"

"Yeah. I think so. Feel a bit woozy though."

I helped him to heave himself to his feet, but he stumbled and grabbed on to me again as soon as he tried to walk. It was clear he couldn't put any weight at all on to his foot.

"Shit, I think it's broken!"

"O.K." Steve said. "I'll go and phone an ambulance", and he bounded back towards the hotel.

"No!" I shouted in an anguished sort of whisper, but he was long gone. "Shit, we can't go to a hospital. It'll all be up for us then."

"I don't think there's much choice, mate", said Mike. And sure enough, there was now an ugly bloodstain on his jeans, and once he'd got up the little pool of blood on the pavement seemed bigger than before. It was likely he'd need stitches as well as a plaster-cast for his ankle.

"Yeah, sorry", I said, suddenly feeling very selfish. If this was the end of the road, it looked like we were just going to have to face it. Shit, and just when it looked like things were picking up.

"No, it's me who should be sorry", he said. "Bastard railings."

I got back to the hotel at about 6 am. I figured it was just about early enough for me to be a legal visitor, although I was still made to wait in the lobby till 7, before I was allowed to go up to the room. Steve and Sue had stayed at the hotel as there didn't seem any need to involve them unnecessarily, no more than we wanted any conflict with the hotel by admitting to an attempted break-in. So when the ambulance came we pretended Mike had just fallen over badly. They said something about "du grille?" which presumably was the railings, but they gave up asking questions when they realised we couldn't speak much French. I guess Mike's pain and injuries spoke for themselves.

Basically Mike hadn't broken anything but his ankle was very badly sprained. The gash to his leg was also not too bad, despite needing a couple of stitches. He had however banged his head in the fall, and the fact that he had been sick seemed of particular concern to the doctor, so they had decided to keep him in for observation. The doctor was also – and this was the heart-sink bit – very keen for him to see the British Consulate, and when I left he was to be summoned to visit Mike later in the day.

Steve and Sue were brilliant. Sue kept giving me hugs, and Steve chipped in with lots of bright, if empty, reassurances in the way Americans do. They took me out for breakfast and insisted that they paid, and that I should hang on to our takings of the night before. Then we all went to the hospital to visit Mike. I half expected that he'd be under armed guard or that at least, by now, he'd be being interrogated by a gendarme or two. As it was he had been put in a little room on his own for some reason, but there were no police, and he seemed chirpy and bemused by the whole situation. He'd been confined to bed-rest he said, and he joked along with Steve and Sue about all the new French words he'd learned, like *blessure* (wound), *vomir* (to vomit), and *"je m'est foulé la cheville* (I have sprained my ankle) ….. "parce que je m'est foolerring about sur les railings…"

I just felt despondent. Was I the only one who saw this as the beginning of the end?

"What about the Consul?" I said. "Has he been?"

Mike shrugged. "Not yet. And apparently I'm not going to be allowed to leave until I've seen him. So if he doesn't come today, they're going to let me stay another night. Good, isn't it? More slapsies!"

"Slapsies? This isn't the NHS", I reminded him. "You'll have to pay for all this stuff you know".

"Oh it's just like the States", Steve chipped in. "You got insurance, man?" We both looked at him.

"Er ..no", Mike said at last. "Well, he'll sort all that out won't he – the Consul chap? I can't pay if I don't have the bread."

I gave up. If he was going to talk like a beatnik, I felt pretty sure we were in 'couldn't-give-a-toss' territory.

Back at the hotel Steve offered me a smoke. Generally I don't, but given the despondent mood I was in, and the fact that I figured we were now fast approaching the end of our stay in France, I accepted. I'd only ever smoked pot once before, when Mike and I had gone to a Bob Dylan concert in Liverpool. We'd stayed with a couple of friends who were at University there, and smoking pot and burning incense were all the rage. All I remember about the experience was a light-headed sensation and the fact that everything that happened was hilariously funny. So I thought it might cheer me up.

I suppose it did have that effect, in that I felt a sudden surge of optimism afterwards, and when Steve suggested we should go out busking again, I didn't even stop to think about it as I thought this was such a wonderful idea. I was wrong of course. The wailing of the police car sirens as they flew about the streets, apparently constantly, should have given me a clue. But it just made me laugh. The irony of it was that we hadn't even started busking and were just innocently walking along the Promenade des Anglais when we were picked up. A kind of police van drove past us at first, and I thought I saw a man in the back holding a machine gun. It stopped up ahead of us, and the chap with the gun leaped out and ran into one of the hotels. We stopped walking and waited to see what would happen next. Soon he led out 2 guys with their hands on top of their heads, and bundled them into the van. Then, seeing us watching, he came over to us.

"Papiers!" he said, gruffly and menacingly.

"Oh, americains et anglais", Sue said brightly. "Nos passeports sont à l'hotel."

With a wave of his gun he signalled for us to get in the van. We protested, but he just growled at us even more menacingly than before, and so far as I could tell, then yelled at us whatever the French is for "Get in the bloody van!"

Looking back I have no idea why, at that particular moment, I chose to do what I then did. I suppose it just seemed like a good idea at the time. I fainted. In my defence, I suppose that technically it wasn't a conscious decision. One moment I was staring at his gun, the next I was flat out on the floor. It was probably the mixture of the pot, the lack of sleep, the excitement of the night, but mostly the sledge-hammer realisation that I had finally fallen into the hands of the police. The game was up. It was all over.

As far as I can recall I've only ever fainted once before, although I've always had a weak stomach. I went through a longish period when I used to get frequent 'spasms', as Aunt Doris called them. It was never very clear what brought them on – stress perhaps. I know they started just after Dad left, but the strange thing is I've never felt that his departure bothered me all that much. It would start off with a mild feeling of tension behind my eyes which would gradually develop into a full-blown pounding head-ache. Then the nausea would come, writhing inside me like undigested phlegm. And then finally, I'd throw up.

My previous fainting episode happened at school, during morning assembly. I remember I'd left home feeling very worried about Mam. I'd found her curled up on the sofa and, when I'd gone to wake her, she'd looked at me through weary sleepless eyes and asked if I'd mind getting my own breakfast. As I left the room I looked back and saw her body shaking and knew that she was crying. I didn't know what to do.

I don't remember much after that. I must have dragged myself to school somehow because the next clear image I have is of being in Mr Chadwick's office with Mam's worried but smiling face looking down at me. She is stroking my cheek. Then she takes me home, tucks me up in bed, and gives me a glass of Lucozade. She sits with me until I drift off to sleep.

Perhaps that's what I was trying to conjure up as I lay prostrate on the *Promenade des Anglais* – Mam's smiling face, and a bottle of Lucozade. I came round fairly quickly. Steve helped me to my feet, Sue got me a glass of water, and the policeman helped us all into the van. He was muttering something all the while, but it didn't sound very soothing. The tone was more of the "for God's sake" variety. I just sat back wearily. Mike was in hospital and I was in the back of a police van on my way to prison. It truly was all over. Where was there to go from here?

Our two travelling companions looked as miserable as I felt, and both just stared at the floor for the first 5 minutes or so. Then one of them seemed to notice the guitar I was carrying and said something like 'musicien?' I nodded and said, 'Oui''. "Ah anglais!" he said with the usual sixth sense. They introduced themselves as Patrick and André, and in their broken English we gathered that they were buskers too, and had been playing in a hotel when the proprietor had phoned the police. They were really pissed off as they had made a point of asking his permission to play, and he'd said it was O.K. Then the police had arrived without warning, and Patrick had even left his guitar behind in the rush. André however still had his harmonica. I think he was about to get it out and start to play, and my mood was just starting to lift a little as we arrived at the Gendarmarie and were all bundled out.

My mood plummeted again as we were led into the building and into a room at the rear. It was a cold, unwelcoming place, with scruffy, cream-coloured walls and a barred window high up on one of them. There was a table in the middle of the room, and a wooden bench along two sides where we were told to sit. I imagined there were probably a line of tumbrels out the back waiting to take us to the guillotine.

After a while someone came in to take basic details from us all. He asked where we were staying and was distinctly impressed when Steve gave him a hotel address. He must have just assumed I was with them as he didn't ask me. At first I felt greatly relieved, and then the anxious thought crossed my mind that he didn't ask me because he already knew – I was one of the notorious hotel skippers they'd had an APB out on for days. But then he went away and, apart from someone coming in to look at us from time to time we were mostly just left to sit.

I assumed they were making the usual checks, and that it could only be a matter of time. Everyone else would be allowed to go, and I would have to stay to have a humiliating interview with someone from the British Consulate and then be told the details of my deportation.

After a pretty miserable couple of hours, there was a sudden surge of noise outside, which sounded like angry voices and scuffling. A gendarme came in, and told us all to 'allez vite' and to wait by the desk in the lobby, as about 8 or so other men were marched past us all protesting loudly. At the desk Patrick and André had their 'papiers' handed back to them and we were told to bring our passports in for inspection the next day. Then we got a speech which, from the general tone of 'non, non', and the shaking of the finger I gathered was probably warning us about vagrancy and loitering and stuff. The most easily understandable word was *identification*, which I think he was suggesting we should carry at all times. Surprisingly the words *hotel* and *non-payer* didn't come up, nor did he single me out for further detention. In fact, with a dismissive wave if his hand we were all told to *allez*.

I was keen to make my escape as quickly as possible but Steve was after an apology, and was on the verge of making a scene. He started to bluster something about his rights as an American tourist, how he took offence to being called a *vagabond*, and how he was staying in a perfectly respectable hotel. Luckily Sue intervened and settled him down – I was greatly relieved, not being at all sure that I wanted 'hotels' to become a topic of conversation.

Patrick and André suggested we went for a drink to share experiences and stuff, so we chose a quiet little bar tucked away in a side-street. They turned out to be seasoned *musiciens ambulants* and knew a lot about the scene in Nice and the Côte d'Azur in general. Mostly they slept on the beaches, and played around Old Nice where buskers were generally welcome, and explained how they were always careful to follow the 'rule' about asking prior permission, and couldn't understand what had gone wrong that night. They figured that perhaps a customer had complained or something. Certainly at the Gendarmarie, none of us (including me!) had been questioned about any crime – all they wanted was to check our identification.

Actually I couldn't puzzle that out. Didn't they realise I was on the 'wanted' list? Didn't they care I had conspired to rip off a hotel in St Tropez? Steve and Sue thought that was exactly it, they didn't care, and reminded me it wasn't actually a capital crime, but just a one-off incident that hotels are used to. "The police don't have time to waste on such things man." It was a fair point I suppose, but I couldn't help thinking that they still found time to waste on picking up innocent buskers and by-standers in the street.

André mentioned a place they sometimes played called 'La Grange', which was owned by two French-Canadians, and where passing musicians were welcomed on to their stage. No collections were allowed, and no payment given, but there was always a free drink in it for the performers, as well as a possible sandwich. It would have been nice to think we could have given this a go, but I still wasn't convinced we had much longer in Nice. There was still the matter of Mike's hospital bill and the visit from the British Consul.

Next day Steve, Sue and I went to the hospital together to find Mike sitting by his bed, fully dressed, waiting for us. His ankle was bandaged but, apart from that, and the ugly blood-stained rip in his jeans, there were no other visible signs of damage. He said he had 8 stitches in his leg, which were to be removed in about 10 day's time, but otherwise he was free to go.

"But what about the Consul?" I asked

"Oh, you mean John?"

"John?"

"Yeah. He was a real nice bloke. Came from Preston as it happened. He just brought a few forms for me to fill in, and all he needed was identification details and an address in England. He's going to arrange for the bill to be sent there. I just had to sign something to guarantee payment".

"What about the hotel thing, in St Trop?" I whispered.

"Not a problem. Well, he never mentioned it anyway".

"Stop worrying man", Steve chipped in. "It's cool."

And indeed it seemed to be. Perhaps the French were true to their motto after all. Certainly *liberté, fraternité, and egalité*, seemed to apply to the hotel trade anyway. Then again, it was all a bit too good to be true, wasn't it?

8

'La Grange' was actually a basement café, in a narrow street off the central square and, were it not for Patrick and André acting as our guides, I doubt whether we ever would have found it. It was now two days after Mike had left the hospital, and we'd mostly spent the time with Steve and Sue at their hotel, occasionally walking round a nearby park, but always ensuring we were safely back in the room before the night concierge came on duty. Mike had been told to exercise as much as he could bear and, although he moved around more slowly, his limp was steadily disappearing.

Steve and Sue also helped out by paying bus fares from time to time and in fact we'd arranged to meet Patrick and André at the bus station. Just as we were getting off, I swore I saw Bobbi about to get on a bus across the way. I shouted and waved, but whoever it was just looked around quickly, then got on the bus, and the bus drove away. I wasn't sure it was her, and I thought it seemed odd anyway that Bobbi would have come up to this part of town on her own.

We walked down the steps and entered the bar of 'La Grange' as a big, bear-like man with wild hair and a huge beard lumbered towards us, holding out his hand and beaming.

"Ah mes braves! Ça va? Welcome, welcome".

This was Hoot. He was extremely warm and welcoming, and ushered us over to an empty table he had apparently been keeping in readiness for us.

"Patrick says you will sing for us tonight. We are delighted. Tonight is very special night. I get you drink. Les bières pour tous ah? Excusez-moi."

The room we were in was actually fairly small. The bar ran down the length of one wall, with small tables and chairs in front. Each table was furnished with a timid little burning candle. In one corner of the room was a raised platform, which was presumably the performance space. The whole place was already fairly full with a motley collection of people milling about. The general atmosphere was dark and smokey and it was difficult to see. It all gave me a good feeling though. I had read about the coffee houses in Greenwich Village where Bob Dylan had first earned his crust, and I liked to think we had now found our way into the French equivalent.

Mike whispered something to Steve and they both looked around and nodded to each other. Then Steve whispered to Sue.

"What's going on?" I asked her.

She leaned towards me and said, "Steve reckons he can smell pot. He always knows".

We later found out that 'La Grange' was actually an important trading-post for drugs of various kinds. Just then Hoot came back with a trayful of beers, accompanied this time by a thin, statuesque sort of woman. She had an explosion of thick wild hair and wore a profusion of beads, which were draped over a sort of Indian smock. This was Annie, Hoot's business partner, and she stopped to talk to us for a while before some-one called her over the bar.

"Patrick tells me you had a run-in with the police the other night", she said. She spoke with a funny sort of accent, presumably a mixture of French and Canadian.

"Yes", I said. "But they just wanted to check our papers".

"Aw, they do that all the time. Every now and then they swoop, then they gather some boys together, and they take them to *le commissariat*. Then …" and she did that 'phrrrutt' thing with her lips, and shrugged.

As reassurance goes, I gave this a pretty low mark. She made the police sound like voracious predators, and what was this 'phrrrutt' thing with the accompanying shrug? In the context of *le commissariat* might she be telling us that usually people were taken out and shot? It just confirmed my feeling that, as far as our unpaid bill was concerned, we still weren't out of the woods.

She came back with some news. She said that tonight was to be special because "nice pictures" were going to be taken of *le cabaret* as she put it.

"We have nice lady come to take nice pictures. We make nice …er … prospectus … it is good for business. We make the tourists to know about La Grange, eh? It is good." Then she shot off.

I felt a little stab of anxiety as the thought struck me that the nice lady with the camera could turn out to be Aimée. No, what were the chances of that? Even so, it had the makings of a very embarrassing encounter – especially if she was in the habit of asking people to take their tops off. Then Hoot jumped on to the little raised platform in the corner of the room and clapped his hands for silence. The cabaret was about to begin.

"Hoot'n'Annie" turned out to be a star turn. They clearly had quite a following, and indeed, as their set got underway, they proved to be an accomplished folk duo. As they sang a young girl with a camera danced round them taking pictures from various angles. To my relief it wasn't Aimée. They also tried to include some comedy into their act, and there was obviously some running joke going on between them and the audience, which had something to do with peas.

"Les poids?" says Hoot to Annie.

"Non, non, les petits-pois!" replies Annie, to roars of laughter from the audience.

We clapped and laughed along with everyone else, without having any clue why peas were so funny. Mike and Steve seemed more convincingly convulsed by the whole thing, but I guessed that the fact they were 'smoking' helped quite a bit.

Then it was Patrick and André's turn. They didn't sing much, but just played together – André on guitar, and Patrick on harmonica. Mostly they played blues tunes, and Patrick's ability to bend notes complemented by André's delicate finger-style guitar made me wonder why anyone would have wanted to complain about their sound. It had a haunting quality, and indeed a hush fell over the whole bar as they played.

After them a pretty young girl got up and sang sweet little songs, accompanying herself on a nylon-stringed guitar. She didn't look as ragged as the rest of us, more doll-like if anything, rather than folkie or bohemian. She got rousing cheers anyway but, when she'd finished I saw her go behind the bar where she was serving drinks. I hadn't noticed she was one of the staff.

Then there was to be a little break, before Mike and I did our little set. During this break the lady with the camera came over and introduced herself. We discovered she was called Mireille, that she was a free-lance photographer from Nice, and that the 'prospectus' Annie had mentioned was actually a leaflet or flyer, which he had commissioned to advertise La Grange. She was very interested in the fact that we were from England and wanted to know what we were doing, why we had come here etc. She was also fascinated by Steve and Sue's accent, particularly as she was intending to go to New York later in the year to seek further outlets for her photography. All in all she was warm and friendly, and easy to talk to. I remembered that Bobbi had said that Aimée and Antoine were like this too, to begin with, before they had turned decidedly sour on her. Perhaps it was partly this wariness, or perhaps just self-interest, that prompted me to ask her if there was any chance we could see the photos that she took. She seemed perfectly happy about this and gave me a little business card with her address. She was working to a tight deadline she said, so we could all call tomorrow if we wished. It was a date.

Then it was our turn to sing. We went down quite well actually, with a selection of our greatest hits – *Mr Tambourine Man, Blowin' Down the Road*, Mike's *Angie* instrumental, and to finish off (partly in homage to Mike's injury) we did a version of *St James Infirmary Blues*. All in all we did well I think, and we were rewarded with a big bear-hug from Hoot, a ham sandwich, and another beer. Vive la France.

Mireille had a little studio above a shoe-shop. It was as cramped and small as Jeanne's studio, but unlike hers it was a real studio with files, paper, and lots of photos and booklets scattered about in an untidy clutter – and, apart from a couple of tables, no unnecessary furnishings like beds and chairs. Mike and I had gone round the night after our set at La Grange, leaving Steve and Sue to go rubber-necking for the day in Monte Carlo.

"You must do a lot of free-lance work," I asked, rather obviously.

"Oh yes. It is very good just now. I work on advertisements, *les calendriers*, or the brochures", and she pointed over to a pile in the corner and invited me to have a look. "It is *le calendrier* for the next year. Toute la Côte d'Azur."

I thumbed through a collection of the most beautiful pictures of translucent seas and gravity-defying rock formations, alongside busy street scenes and compact little harbours and fishing villages.

"Beautiful", I said, "Like paintings".

"Oh no", she said. "A photo is not like a painting at all. A photo can take you right to the heart of the moment, and they have within them the feelings and the reflection of that moment …. *exactement*. The paintings are beautiful of course, but it is a different thing. They … what would you say? …. represent only. They are *subjectif*."

I was sorry I'd spoken, and I certainly wasn't going to argue as she seemed so passionate about her craft.

"And here are the ones from last night," she said, picking up a pile from the table.

There was no doubting she was very good. The photos were all black and white, a lot of them consisting mainly of a complex mixture of dark and shade, but they did indeed re-evoke very successfully the atmosphere of the little basement bar. There were also other more sharply focussed images where it was possible to make out faces and shapes more easily. There was a spectacular shot of Hoot grinning broadly which captured his personality perfectly. There was also one I particularly liked which she had taken of me and Mike from behind. Set against a light, shadowy background there was a black silhouette of Mike sitting on a stool hunched over his guitar, with me standing next to him. Before us were blotches of dark, barely distinct faces. I thought it evoked an atmosphere of intense mystery, mingled with a sort of silent concentration. I made a mental note that if we ever made an L.P. it would be perfect for the sleeve. *The Outsiders - Live at La Grange, featuring Hoot'n'Annie.* Yeah, well the title would need a bit more work obviously.

She was clearly pleased to see us appreciating her work so much.

"But I cannot give you copies", she said, as if reading my mind. "I must take all these today to the ..er ... *editeur* – the man who will publish. Perhaps, after, you can buy if you like. It is how I make my living, you see?"

"How does it all work then, this free-lancing?" Mike asked.

"What do you mean?"

"You sell photos, but how do you know what photos to take, which ones you can sell?"

She explained that she mainly worked to direct commissions. She said she was quite well-known in the area and had built up a reputation so people now came to her with their own particular promotional projects.

"What if you had no particular customer though?" Mike persisted.

"I don't know what you mean".

"Well, could you just take pictures and then try to sell them?"

"Oh yes, of course", she said. "This is what I do to start. Now it is more difficult".

I was fairly certain I could tell where he was going with this, and sure enough he then said to her, "The thing is, we met some people in St Trop. They told us that they took pictures of girls sunbathing on the beaches ... you know ... without –" and he moved his hand across the front of his shirt.

She looked shocked and puzzled for a moment, then she laughed.

"Aux seins nus? Without the shirt?"

93

"Yeah, without the shirt".

"They are naughty, your friends. But this is … *spécialisé*, the pose is very important. You would need professional models. I think it would be very difficult to sell such pictures without to have the commission".

"Oh they're not our friends. We were just talking to them. They were called Aimée and An-twat … sorry, I mean Antoine. Do you know of them?"

No, she had never heard of them. I was partly disappointed, and partly relieved. Mike persisted.

"Apparently, they ask people for their permission first, then take pictures. Maybe they do work to commissions".

"It is possible. But as I say to you, this is a specialism, and a special market. Usually such people will have models, and studios, and special lighting, and so on".

I felt we had heard enough, and I was starting to worry that we were showing too much of an interest in this and that we would alienate her if Mike pursued this any further, so I tried to change the subject.

"So are you taking these to the publisher, did you say?"

"Yes, then someone will chose one for the prospectus".

I checked again.

"One photo?"

"Yes, He has a lot to choose from here, eh? The others I take to *La Grange* and Hoot will try to sell them there".

One lousy photo from the 50 or so she'd taken. What were the chances he'd pick one of me and Mike?

Then Mireille said, "This is my favourite", and she put the one I'd been admiring of me and Mike in silhouette on top of the pile. My heart soared.

Mike decided to go back to the hotel at this point. It was a longish walk to the Publishing Office, his stitches were beginning to throb and it seemed like he'd lost interest anyway. So Mireille and I walked along together and she continued to chat about herself and her work.

Suddenly she said, "Actually it's funny when you talk of the photos … les femmes, without the shirt? Monsieur Mistral, *l'editeur*, where we go, he does buy such photos. He thinks I don't know. It is his – er, *activité secondaire*, do you understand? I am not interested in such work myself. He buys many pictures from me of St Trop and usually he asks if I could please take some of B.B. – you know, Brigitte Bardot?" She seemed to be joking, and we laughed.

Then something amazing happened. I couldn't believe my eyes. A woman who looked somehow very familiar emerged from a doorway up ahead, crossed the road quickly, and disappeared into a side-street. I had been listening closely to Mireille so there was a delay before anything really started to register in my brain. Then it hit me. It was Aimée!

Just as I was recovering from the shock, I realised we were turning into the very door she had exited from. It was the Publishing Office. Mireille immediately excused herself and went off to the Ladies, so I took the opportunity to go to the Gents, and mulled over this supposed sighting. Was Aimée involved in M. Mistral's sideline after all? Had she brought Bobbi's pictures here to sell? But surely it was too much of a coincidence for it to have been her? I considered that the most likely explanation was that she'd just been brought to mind by the conversation I was having with Mireille, and all I'd seen was someone who might have looked a bit like her. I felt reassured at this thought, but the idea that it just might have been her kept niggling at me.

First I met Monsieur Mistral. When we went into his office he had his back to us, apparently hurriedly putting some stuff into the top of a cupboard behind his desk. When he turned round I saw a short, fat, seedy-looking man who looked exactly like someone who would trade in dodgy pictures. Not that I'd much experience – he just struck me as a lecher, and I thought his conversation with Mireille had a definite 'nod and a wink' tone to it. Mireille introduced me as a friend who she had met at *La Grange* and who was interested in the process of publication. He began to talk excitely to me but seemed to lose interest when I said I was from England. Then he rang someone on his intercom who subsequently came to take Mireille off so they could review her work together. M. Mistral gave me a quick and fairly uninspiring tour of the Print room, before taking me back to his office to wait for Mireille. He busied himself with some writing. It seemed unlikely that I'd ever see him again, so I chanced my arm.

"Do you ever buy pictures of St Trop?"

"Oh mais oui, St Trop, Ste-Maxime, Cannes – tout la Côte d'Azur. But I have many pictures, and many people …. I do not want to buy …" I interrupted him. "Oh yes, monsieur. But I do not have pictures myself. I have a friend who takes pictures on the beaches of St Trop … he specialises in females on the beach, when they are sun-bathing, perhaps 'aux seins nus'. He has many such pictures …."

He looked up sharply, and I thought for a minute he was going to throw me out. Then he softened and said, "Mireille, what did she say …."

"Oh non, non, monsieur", I said quickly. "Non. It is nothing to do with Mireille. She doesn't know my friend. She would be angry if she knew I was asking you this. Perhaps this is wrong of me to ask. Please monsieur, I do not want to offend you. I am very sorry …."

He stared at me closely for a moment, then resumed his writing. I was left feeling very uncomfortable for a minute or two as the silence fell between us. I'd dropped the bait – was he going to bite or not? Then he looked up and in a conspiratorial kind of way said, "If he brings pictures, we can see."

Aha! I thought. So it could be true! It *could* have been Aimée, and Bobbi's pictures could *easily* have found their way here. Mireille had said he was a fairly big noise in publishing on the Côte d'Azur, and at that moment not only did it seem probable, it seemed to me *definite* that this was where they had ended up. And here was a golden opportunity to prove once and for all what a hardened, heroic, stout fellow I really was! Danger? Pah! I speeet on-a your gringo danger.

When Mireille came back to join us, I was fully decided on my next move. But I wouldn't involve her. I wouldn't tell her anything about it, then she couldn't be accused in any way if it all went wrong. We left the building with my spirits raised and my confidence running high. It didn't even bother me when she told me they had chosen a picture of Hoot'n'Annie for the prospectus thing. My mind was now focussed on something else entirely, and I felt that both luck and coincidence were finally on our side. It wasn't till I was putting the first stage of the plan into action that the anxiety really hit me.

I said goodbye to Mireille when we got back out into the street and thanked her for the visit. She was very sweet, kissed me on both cheeks and we exchanged good wishes to each other for the future. Then when she was safely out of sight I doubled back into the Publishing Office. The girl at the reception desk gave me a smile of recognition and I said, mainly through mime and hand gestures, that I had left my comb in the Gents. She looked puzzled but just pointed me down the corridor. "La porte seconde à droite." When I'd been in the Gents previously, I'd absent-mindedly noticed a small window high up in the wall, and my intention now was to pop in quickly and take it off its latch. Goodness knows what the girl at reception had understood from my gestures, or thought I was doing, but it only took me a second to nip in, and by standing on one of the sinks, to reach up and unlatch the window, so I guess I didn't look too suspicious. Then I made my way back to the hotel.

Of course I knew it was hardly a fail-safe method of breaking-in. Someone, like the cleaner, might easily spot that the window was off the latch and close it again for the night. It also occurred to me that there may be a night watchman or guard dogs, although it didn't actually look like the sort of building that would be well guarded. I just thought it was worth a shot to create the possibility of getting back in, if we wanted to. I planned to go and consult with the others, who I hoped would either be able to come up with a better plan or, at least, talk me out of mine.

On the contrary, Mike and Steve were all for it although, given the resistance I'd put up towards his house-breaking proposals in Morecambe, Mike's encouragement didn't come across as exactly genuine. He didn't miss the opportunity to scoff for example, saying sarcastically, "What a shame you didn't get some practice in with me when you had the chance. If only it wasn't for my leg, I'd be right there with you mate." I had the distinct feeling that he was mentally rubbing his hands at the prospect of my failure. It was the ever cautious and sensible Sue who was, perhaps predictably, the only one against it.

"I don't understand," she said. "You were so worried about the police when you hadn't really done anything. Now you want to go and knowingly commit a crime!"

"But I'm not actually going to steal anything."

"Yes you are! You're going to steal photos of Bobbi. That's if they're even there. It's a chance in a million he's even got them."

"But there's *every* chance he's got them if that was Aimée I saw!"

"That's the point isn't it? *If* it was her you saw. I mean, come on, what are the chances really? You only saw her from a distance, and you said yourself you were thinking about her at the time, so you most likely conjured her up because you *wanted* it to be her."

There was the ring of truth in that of course, and I had to agree there was the hint of madness attached to the whole scheme. But I was encouraged by Mike and Steve.

"I think Nigel's right. This chap Mistral sounds like 'the man' for this stuff in the area and it's therefore *highly* likely these guys would take their stuff to him. Even if it wasn't Aimée Nigel saw, it could still be the right place."

"O.K" said Sue, clearly exasperated. "Let's imagine this is the right place. Let's imagine that Nigel can get in through this little toilet window – you know, the one he doesn't even know if he can open. Then let's imagine he can find his way to Mistral's office, in the dark – oh, and of course that, as luck would have it, his door isn't locked. Right. Now how are you going to find these photos?"

"Well I'm pretty sure I do know where they are," I said. Sue shot me a withering look. "Well, I think I might know. When we went into his office, he was putting some stuff in a cupboard. If that *was* Aimée leaving, she might have been bringing the very photos that he might have been putting away in that very cupboard!"

Sue groaned. "That's a lot of 'mights'. But O.K., let's proceed and imagine these are the very photos. What then?"

"I nick them."

"And the negatives?"

Shit, yes, what about the negatives. "Well they'll be with the photos," I said, without much conviction.

"Why should they be? Isn't it more likely he's done something with them already?"

Steve then cut in. "Wow, Sue. Stop being so heavy man. You're bringing us down. Let's just give it a go, you know, at least go and see. I think there's good vibes. The river's running with us man."

Even so, Sue's opposition, combined with the practical sense of her arguments did make me hesitate, and I was thinking seriously about calling the whole thing off. But then she said something that made me realise that I just had to give it a go.

"If you're willing to take such a heavy risk on the strength of nothing very much at all, I can only think that Bobbi must be really important to you."

That was it. Well it wasn't quite right actually. I realised that it wasn't Bobbi I was wanting to impress with my heroic act of selfless disregard. It was Jeanne.

When it came to it, both Mike and Steve offered to come and act as look-outs. I was taken aback, but it was clear Mike wasn't up to standing about or indeed legging it if the going got rough, so again I was left wondering if he really meant it. And Sue was most unhappy about

Steve's potential involvement. She made it clear that she thought the whole plan was madness anyway, but also figured it could prove very difficult for Steve to get to do any more European travel if he was caught assisting in a frank criminal act. Sadly it dawned on me that attempting a break-in without any back-up at all really was a huge risk, so we came to an agreement. I would just go by myself and do nothing more than suss things out further. I wouldn't try to enter the building – all I'd do was test the window to see if it did open and was a possible point of entry, and assess what other sorts of dangers there may be to overcome (like dogs, caretakers, or just nosey passers-by). I also promised Sue faithfully that I wouldn't take any unnecessary risks – but, just in case I did, I ducked into a little general dealers on the way and bought a torch.

The street was very quiet, quite a contrast to the hustle and bustle that had been around during the day. Also, as the street mainly consisted of offices and storerooms and such, there were no bars or cafes around to attract a night-time crowd. A narrow little alley ran behind the Publishing House and the neighbouring building, and it was this that I first ducked down in search of the toilet window. I found it fairly quickly, and immediately spotted two obstacles to further progress. Firstly, it was only about 10 or 12 yards along, so if I was to try and climb in, my antics would be easily visible to any stray passer-by. And secondly, it was about 9 foot up the wall, i.e. at least a foot or more out of my reach.

I gingerly walked further down the alley which got steadily blacker, so I stopped for a moment and got out the torch. It just flickered in a reluctant sort of way when I switched it on, but it was enough for me to make out a black shape about 4 or 5 steps in front of me. Three dustbins. Luck really was on my side I thought – not only had I stopped before smashing blindly into them, one of them would be perfect for me to stand on and allow me to reach up to the toilet window. It must have been fairly empty too, as I was relieved to find I could pick it up easily and carry it back to the window. Then a man walked past the top of the alley, whistling. I stopped dead. But he just kept on walking. I didn't move, just stood still, holding the dustbin, with my heart pounding.

'No unnecessary risks!'

I reasoned though that this was a *necessary* risk. I mean, how else was I going to test out the window?

Then a couple went by, laughing together. I thought I saw one of them glance down the alley, but they didn't stop, so I guessed I was sufficiently in the dark so as not to be visible after all.

Cautiously I moved on, placed the bin underneath the window and clambered up. To my initial dismay the window looked as if it was tightly shut, and when I pulled at its side it didn't budge. Game over. But no, as I exerted a bit more pressure its resistance gave way and it opened with a little creak. As my heart leaped with excitement, or maybe fear, I also knew that this was now the time to stop and think.

So I didn't.

I remember that it actually felt as if I was being *invited* to proceed at that point – the window had popped open, and I was being presented with a clear opportunity. I felt I just had to take it. I stopped for a moment, looked around, and listened. There was the vague sound of traffic, some voices shouting in the far distance, but nothing else. I pulled the window open as far as I could, heaved myself up the wall, and poked my head in. Then with a little effort I was able to shuffle my upper body through, reach over and hold on to the top of the cubicle rail to support my weight, and then to pull my legs through and drop gently on to the floor.

Feeling very pleased with myself, I then had a pee. After breaking in to a toilet unlawfully, it seemed the honourable thing to do. Then I really started to get anxious. I was definitely in the forbidden zone now. Looking up at the window I realised that getting out might be a lot more difficult than getting in. Also I realised that I had nicely advertised the fact that I'd broken in by leaving a window open with a big dustbin underneath it. I'd have to work quickly.

The torch flickered lazily to life again and I realised why it had been so cheap. The light it provided was weaker than that of a melancholic glow-worm. Not only that, it was also very temperamental, flickering on and off at a moment's notice. I tip-toed out of the toilet and made my way down the corridor which I knew from my morning visit led to M. Mistral's office. Oh God, I thought, what if it's locked? Surely all his cupboards and filing cabinets will be locked? Why hadn't I thought of that? Well, to be fair, Sue had of course.

What on earth was I doing, breaking in to a building and sneaking around in the dead of night? Rambling boys like Mike and me were supposed to get arrested for being drunk, or for being innocent bums, not for being a stone-cold sober criminal sneak-thief. I found myself thinking about Pretty Boy Floyd. Woody Guthrie had sung about him. He was a sort of Robin-Hood-type figure who was driven to a life of crime for simply insulting a policeman whilst protecting his wife's honour. Yes, that was it. Here I was, a poor innocent boy, driven to commit this noble criminal act in order to protect Bobbi's honour. Once word got round they'd soon be singing ballads about me too.

Then, without warning, the torch flicked off and before I knew it I had smashed my shins against a bucket someone had left by the wall. It was a fire bucket, filled with sand, and it keeled over with a horrendous crash. As I ducked down quickly to catch it I bashed my head against a fire extinguisher hanging on the wall. Instinctively I spat out something like 'shit and bollocks!' and hopped around in pain, alternately grasping my shins and my forehead. Far from being an anti-hero of folkloric fame, I'd now apparently stumbled into a Norman Wisdom film.

I pressed myself up against the wall and waited. All I could hear was my anxious breathing. I slowed it down. More silence. I decided I'd had enough stupid excitement for one night and determined to leave - and fast. I shook the torch back into what dim life it had left and groped my way back to the toilet. By putting one foot on a sink and the other against the door jamb of a cubicle, I found I could hoist myself up to the window again fairly easily. I stuck my head out – all was quiet.

Then I had another think and it occurred to me that, despite my best efforts, I was finally living up to my nick-name - quivering like a jelly-fish. I pulled myself together and gradually felt some of my courage return. All was quiet again, so I told myself that what I had actually been doing was giving my escape route a dry run. Yes, indeed, I had taken a wise precaution here and proved to my satisfaction that I could get out quickly and easily if I needed to. And since I had now climbed back up as well, I could even pull the window to! The river was clearly still running with me, so I decided to give it another go.

Soon I was inching my way down the corridor again, this time hugging the wall. I was also ready for the bucket, and the fire extinguisher, although I was aware of leaving footprints in the sand that was now spilled down the corridor. I made a mental note to brush them away on my way back. I got more aggressive with the torch too which, having viciously made its point, now seemed more willing to cast a reliable light ahead of me. I flashed it around, scanning for any further obstacles.

Eventually I reached M. Mistral's office. Having come this far, and with success now in my sights, I prayed for the door to be open, whilst at the same time secretly hoping it would be locked fast. Then I would be able to leave, secure in the knowledge that I'd made a bold, if sadly thwarted, attempt to retrieve Bobbi's honour. It was not to be – with a little click the door opened, and I stood on the verge of M. Mistral's private domain.

I flashed the torch round the office to gain my bearings. Next to the door, along the side of the wall, were 3 or 4 filing cabinets, each piled high with papers and clutter. In front of me was his desk, with in-trays and out-trays spilling out their contents in another cluttery mess. It looked as if someone had got there before me and done the whole place over. Behind the desk was his big, leather-clad chair. I momentarily pictured him sitting there, glaring at me with a fixed look of hate and contempt at my intrusion. I quickly flicked the torch off his face and the light fell on a tall metal cupboard behind his chair. There! That was where I had seen him hurriedly putting something away when I had come in with Mireille. That was where the photos were! I was convinced.

I crept across the room, eased myself behind the chair, and tried to open the cupboard. Locked! My heart sank. End of the line. But just how far had I expected my luck to run? Still, I thought it was worth a quick look round to see if he'd left the key in any obvious place – like in his desk. No – drawers locked too. Anything obvious on the desk? No. Could I perhaps pick the lock? No. Had I brought a crowbar? No. With a weary sigh I decided it really was time to acknowledge defeat and go home. I was feeling really frustrated – just a quarter of an inch of metal between me and success. Then my gaze fell on the filing cabinets. Could it be ...? Well, now that I was here, it was worth a look.

I moved over to them, scanning the papers on top as I did, but nothing looked at all promising. I moved along the line – locked – locked – locked. Wearily I turned to go - and that's when I saw it. Leaning up against the far end of the desk was a shabby-looking leather brief-case, one of those old concertina types. I leapt on it as a drowning man might leap at a straw – my last hope. As I bent down I noticed M. Mistral's reading lamp on the desk. Since this was to be my last shot, I plucked it off the desk, sat it next to me on the floor, and switched it on. It gave off a dim, eerie light.

The flap of the brief-case unlocked with an easy click and it gave up its contents to me without any resistance at all. Inside were various odd bits of paper, some looking like letters, but mostly the briefcase was packed with a collection of large brown envelopes, about 10 in all. I took them out one by one, each feeling quite heavy and stiff. I could feel my excitement building as slowly and carefully I slid my finger under the flap of the first one. It sprang open willingly, and I pushed my hand slowly inside. I could feel the gloss of photographs under my fingers. I pulled them out to expose them to the light.

They were photos alright – and photos that literally took my breath away. I gazed in wonder at the naked female form. I don't know how long I looked at the first one, but it must have been quite a while as I realised this was the first time I had really seen the beauty of the female body in all its nakedness. Of course I'd had glimpses before, but just odd bits and pieces, like bare breasts or bare backs. I remember someone once brought a pack of 'rude' playing cards to school, but the photos were grainy, black and white, and fairly modest. The ones I had in my hands were in razor sharp focus, and in glorious technicolor. The one I was gazing at was of a beautiful blonde girl, kneeling on the sand, and wearing nothing but a wispy nylon shawl round her shoulders. She was staring seductively ahead, with her hands resting gently on her thighs. The others in the collection were of the same girl, in a similar beach setting, striking different poses with various degrees of eroticism.

I'd hit the jackpot! But Bobbi, Bobbi – I had to struggle to bring my thoughts back on track. Where were Bobbi's pictures? That's what I had come for. I frantically opened all the other envelopes, spilling out the contents on the floor in my excitement. I couldn't help but stop to stare and wonder at the pictures I was uncovering as I went, but I found none of Bobbi.

Then two things happened in very quick succession. Firstly I remember suddenly seeing myself as I was – sitting in a darkened room where I wasn't supposed to be, surrounded by pictures of naked women. Was this the goal I'd been motivated to seek all along? Had I even been driven by the dim possibility that I might get to see Bobbi naked? And then just as I was having these worrying and disconcerting thoughts, I heard a clattering noise outside. Stupidly I thought it was Uncle Fred, come to get me. As it happened, it was to be something far worse than that. The light in the corridor snapped on, and I heard voices, sounds coming towards me. Then the office door opened with a crash, someone switched on the light, and there in all his fury and surprise stood Monsieur Mistral.

I didn't see her immediately. I was so shocked at the sight of M.Mistral, I just jumped to my feet in a panic. Immediately I'd done that I became uncomfortably and embarrassingly aware of a bulge in my trousers so foolishly I tried to duck behind the desk. Meanwhile M. Mistral stormed into the room, exploding all kinds of expletives, and advanced towards me with the look of a man with murder on his mind. Then I saw her follow him into the room. It was Bobbi.

"Nigel?" she said. "C'est toi?"

Mercifully M. Mistral stopped in his tracks and snapped his head round towards her.

"Tu le connais?"

"Oui, oui, je le connais". I didn't catch the rest, but it was something like 'c'est l'anglais qui m'accompagne de St Trop'. They exchanged some more words as I stood there stupefied. M. Mistral's hostility then seemed to veer towards Bobbi and, so far as I could make out, I think he was trying to accuse her of being somehow involved in this botch-up of a robbery. I attempted to intervene with a humble 'Monsieur, je suis trés désolé' but he just spat out 'taisez-vous!' and 'salaud! salaud!' (Bobbi told me later that means 'bastard' or some such). Then he continued to rant at me, his face uncomfortably close to mine, whilst pointing at the photos and gesticulating like a demented windmill (one that performs some kind of key function in the garlic industry.)

When he'd finished with me he turned his attention back to Bobbi and continued his rant at her whilst she, I presumed, protested her innocence. Eventually he seemed to calm down a little and, as they continued to converse in a somewhat quieter tone, I busied myself trying to tidy up the photos and return them to their envelopes. Bobbi then turned to me.

"What are you doing here Nigel? This makes no sense. I do not understand. He thinks you are ... I do not know the word ... a *perverti*".

Perverti? Moi? a pervert? I thought that was rich, coming from the man who collected the pictures I'd just been, well, poring over I suppose. Anyway I thought I'd better just let that go and try to account for myself, at least to her. So I told her about Mireille, and about how I thought I'd seen Aimée leaving when I'd come here that morning. I said I'd thought it likely that Aimée was selling her photos to M. Mistral and that I was simply trying to get them back for her. I thought at least she'd be pleased at that and even impressed at my bravery but strangely, that wasn't her reaction. Instead, it was more on the lines of: "Oh là là. Quelle bêtise! Nigel, tu es fou! Ah merde!"

Then she turned to M. Mistral and said something long and complicated to him. I couldn't catch any of it really, but it must have been something magical because when she had finished he looked hard at me, then said,

"Ah bon. Now you go. Understand? Allez-y! Peese off!! I not see you here again! You understand? I see you here, and I telephone le Police, ah?"

I looked at Bobbi. She simply nodded and told me to go back to find Mike. "I will see you soon chez Jeanne. Then I explain you. Now, you go."

I started to say something, but whatever it was the words didn't come. I just felt wretched - stupid, somewhat bewildered, but mainly swamped with shame. I shuffled out of the building and into the street. I paused for a second and wondered whether I should go back and offer to sweep up the sand I'd spilled in the corridor. But that didn't seem quite appropriate, so instead I trudged off into the night. I knew there was no point going back to the hotel at such a late hour, so I made my way down to the Promenade and on to the beach where I huddled up against the sea wall and waited for the morning.

9

Absorbed as I was in my misery and humiliation, it wasn't until I started to walk back to the hotel that I began to think more clearly about what had actually happened. It all felt confusing and mysterious. Why had Mistral just let me walk away without calling the police? Perhaps his dealings were so dodgy he couldn't afford to. But more importantly what was Bobbi doing there? And why had they both turned up there in the middle of the night? Was she was trying to get her pictures back herself? But how would she know they were there?

I got back to the hotel and prepared to tell Mike, Steve and Sue my story. Although I feared Sue's reaction most of all, she was in fact very soothing and comforting about the whole thing. Perhaps my attempt to be a hero on Bobbi's behalf appealed to her. Mike and Steve thought it was all a big joke.

"You must have thought your end had come when you kicked the bucket." Ha, ha. "When Mistral walked in, why didn't you just tell him you were trying to keep abreast of things?" Ha, ha, ha. "I hope you rose to the occasion". Oh how we laughed.

When we put it all together though, they didn't have any better theories than me about why Bobbi should have turned up. Mike didn't seem to care much about it anyway, and just summed it up wearily,

"The only reason she'd have been there was to do with the photos. She'd found out, like you did, that Mistral's was the most likely outlet, and was trying to do a deal to get them back. Anyway, just think how lucky it was for you she was there – if he'd caught you by himself he might have beaten you up or handed you over to the police. Our luck's still in man."

I thought he did have a point there. We had been very lucky altogether so far. Up till now, we'd been arrested for vagrancy, skipped off from a hotel without paying the bill, tried to break into another hotel, and now I'd been caught in the act of robbing a print works. Yet somehow or other we'd managed to avoid capture and further criminal proceedings.

Sue and Steve then wanted to go out to the Post Office to see if any mail had arrived for them. Since they were moving around a lot they were using Poste Restante as a means of keeping in touch with home. Mike went with them whilst I had a lie down. I was feeling pretty knackered after the exigencies of the night, and general lack of sleep. I couldn't help mulling it all over, reliving all the things I had done wrong.

Suddenly I had an anxious thought. What about Mireille? I didn't have the chance to make it clear to Mistral that she was not involved in my escapade in any way. What if he thought that she had been somehow helping me to case the joint when she'd introduced me to his set-up? Since she'd been so kind I couldn't bear to think I might be dropping her in it.

"I've got to go back to explain," I said to Mike as soon as they all arrived back.

He rounded on me as if I'd just told him I'd pissed on his guitar. *"What?"*

"Mireille. I have to tell Mistral she had nothing to do with us breaking in."

"Us? Go to hell you daft twat. It's nothing to do with me". The humour he had initially found in my predicament had clearly now evaporated. I felt more than a little stung at his riposte, but my anxiety for Mireille propelled me on anyway.

"She took me there, to Mistral's, in the first place. He might think she was part of the plot to break in and steal his stuff. I might have ruined her reputation. I – "

Sue cut in and, in a fed-up exasperated sort of way, said, "Nigel, what is this thing you've got about saving women? First Bobbi, now Mireille. Just leave it alone will you? You said he knows Mireille. He's done business with her for a long time. Why should he suddenly think she's teamed up with you? What would he think was in it for her? Look, no disrespect and all that, but I'm quite sure she can look after herself. And if you really want to know, Bobbi obviously can too! She was trying to get her photos back *herself*, right? Didn't need you, right?"

First Mike, now her. I felt stung again, but it was probably all true. Even so, I still wanted to make sure, so I thought perhaps the best thing was to check it out with Bobbi. She'd know if Mistral did think Mireille was implicated. And anyway, I needed to apologise, and to find out more from her about the whole business of her turning up like that. Mike had by now pulled out his guitar which he was huddled over, and he was idly picking out tunes. I asked him if he was O.K. and at first he ignored me, but then looked up and gave me a pained look which was hard to read, somewhere strange between despair and anger. It was weird to see him in such a black mood, but I put it down chiefly to him feeing pissed off with

107

me and my Mireille neurosis. Anyway I thought it wise not to press him further.

But after a while, I got the feeling that he was softening, as if perhaps his doodling on the guitar was thawing him out a little, so as casually as I could, I ventured to say, "I think I *will* go and see Bobbi – I've got to apologise to her at least. I think I've probably made a complete dick of myself ...." (I heard him mutter "you got that right") " ... and I want to check I haven't totally messed things up for her".

"If you like," he said.

"Do you want to come?"

He lapsed into silence for a minute or so, then just said,

"Yeah, why not?"

"Great. You'll be able to hear Bobbi tell me what a wanker I am." I know it was only a weak attempt at levity, but he didn't even smile.

We walked through the streets not saying much to each other at first. Eventually he said, "You are a stupid tosser, aren't you?"

I was taken aback by the suddenness and bitterness of this. "What do you mean?"

"Getting caught like that," he said. "This whole photo thing is just one big drag man. I mean what's the bloody big deal? A few nudie pictures and we have to leave St Trop. Then we come to this shit-hole, and all you do is bang on and on about that stupid hotel bill. I nearly get my leg ripped off, and then you try your hardest to get yourself busted."

"Shit-hole? Since when? I thought you liked it here? And anyway, you've been up for all this as much as I have – at least up to now. And you were just saying how lucky we'd been."

"Oh sod off", he said. "I've had enough of this town. It's time to move on."

Move on? I didn't know whether to pursue this or not. Was he serious? Move on where exactly? Our trip had only ever been set up as a way of spending the summer. The plan had been to come to the South of France, bum around for a bit, then go back and go to college. We trudged along in silence for a bit, then he said, "I'm pig-sick of Nice. I think I might go to Italy."

I decided to leave it. Although he was often sneery and negative, there was usually some humour and some light in him somewhere to be seen – but his mood now had a much bleaker quality than I'd seen before, and it worried me. But he wasn't going to let it go.

"I mean it you know. I'm not gonna go back."

"O.K. You're not gonna go back. Let's just leave it for now. I don't want to talk about this right now." The truth was I didn't know what to say.

Thankfully we got to the *studio* very soon after this, and I rang the bell. Jeanne answered and after struggling in the darkness of Mike's mood for the past hour or so, seeing her again was like looking out into the light. Bobbi wasn't there, but was expected back soon. I noticed that Jeanne was looking pale and tired.

"Are you alright?" I asked her.

"Yes, I am well", she said, and then began to chide me gently about my escapade, but smiling in an affectionate kind of way as she did so. I felt myself blushing as I wasn't sure how much of the detail Bobbi had shared with her. Did she have a picture of me in her mind sitting amongst photos of naked women? Did she think I was brave or just stupid?

"It was very foolish Nigel", she said eventually, "but very brave". Both then.

I watched her float over to the window and look out into the street. Then she suddenly said, "Oh, I nearly forget" and picked up something from her dressing table. She handed us two envelopes.

"Here. These come in the post for you". She shrugged. "I don't know how, but they come here. It has this address".

"Oh yes", I said. "I hope you don't mind. I wrote to my family and gave this address in case they wanted to write back to me. I should have told you, I'm sorry".

"Its not a problem", she said.

But Mike shot me a quick angry look. "You never said".

"I know. It was when you were in the hospital. I wrote from Steve's hotel".

I'd forgotten Jeanne knew nothing about Mike's accident, and she exclaimed, "You have been in the Hospital...?!" But I was distracted by my letter. I heard Mike filling her in with some brief details of his skirmish with the railings, and making jokes about it such that it must have lifted his mood because soon they were both laughing. I also noticed that he had just quickly stuffed his letter into his pocket, without apparently showing any real interest in it.

Meanwhile I had eagerly ripped mine open, and found two letters inside – one from Doris and one from Fred – *and* a £5 note! I quickly scanned the contents hoping to read them more thoroughly later. Doris's was about the usual stuff – how they'd been really pleased to hear from me, how she hoped we were getting enough to eat, are you still sleeping in the tent (don't know where she got that one from), how they were having the bathroom painted. Then there was Uncle Fred's letter, asking why we hadn't got work yet, followed by some advice about where we should be looking and something irrelevant about work permits. *'And if you can't get a job over there, just come home, there's plenty to do here.'* Then he went on to give me a list of things he'd been doing, a progress bulletin on the building of some new roundabout, and a review of recent Morecambe weather. It was so like him – no real connection to me and what I was interested in – just the desire to see me occupied whilst he carried on with his own stuff. Even so, I thought they were both wonderful letters both by their familiarity and ordinariness, and again it made me realise just how much I was missing my home.

I looked up and found Mike staring at me, his face set in a hostile glare.

"What's the matter?" I said.

He continued to glare for a few more unnerving seconds then said, "Why did you want to go and tell everyone where we are?"

"Sorry?" I said. "What's wrong with that?"

He looked away. "I don't understand," I persisted. "Aren't you even going to open your letter?"

"Oh forget it", he said grimly. "I'll look at it later."

Of course I knew he was in a black mood with me, but I would have thought he would have been pleasantly surprised by news from home. I couldn't understand why he was being so dismissive. I was about to take this up with him further, but just then we heard footsteps running up the stairs, and a few seconds later Bobbi rushed in.

"'Allo Mike, 'allo Nigel", she said, embracing us both. "I am so happy to see you. When did you came, I mean arrive?"

I thought I saw her exchange an anxious glance with Jeanne but Jeanne then started to fuss around her, wanting to make us all coffee and such, so I just dismissed it. Also, I was very keen to talk to Bobbi myself. I looked at her, opened my mouth to speak, but she jumped in first.

"Nigel. You scared me so last night. You are so foolish to come to Mistral!"

"Yes, I know," and making sure Jeanne was listening as I spoke I added, "but I wanted to get your pictures back for you."

"Yes, I know this. But still I explain to Mistral that Nigel is a STUPID IDIOT who is trying to help me." I didn't like the way she pointed her finger and raised her voice on the 'stupid idiot' part, but I let it go. I had a burning question to ask instead.

"Why were you there, Bobbi? It was a big shock for me too, when you walked in."

I noticed she glanced up at Jeanne at this point and, as they caught each other's eye, it was as if some unspoken understanding passed between them. Jeanne then quickly turned away and gazed distractedly out of the window.

"O.K", said Bobbi. "I explain you. I meet man in Jeanne's bar. He is photographer. He has studio in Nice and he knows *tous les photographes indépendents* who work on the Côte d'Azur, so I wonder if he perhaps knows who might buy my photos. He tells me about Mistral so I go to see him. At first he is not happy to give them to me."

"He had them then!" I gasped. "He did have your photos!"

Jeanne turned around quickly.

"Bobbi!"

Bobbi shot her a glance, then took my hands and said, "Yes Nigel, yes he has them. He knows Aimée and Antoine very well I think. Anyway, eventually I persuade him to give them me. So I go with him to his place, and *voilà,* you are there! He is very mad, and at first he says no, he will not give me. But after you have gone, and he becomes *calme,* it is O.K. again. He give them me, and now I burn them."

So we had got it all pretty much right! I marvelled at Bobbi's initiative and persistence – I didn't know she had it in her, as this was a side of her I hadn't seen before. I still wanted to ask her why all this had to be done in the middle of the night, but I needed reassurance on a couple of points more urgently.

"He's not going to the police?"

"No, he says there is no need. Nothing was taken, and there was no damage. He thinks it is funny that we caught you with the pictures all on the floor, and he says it is good how you protect my honour. He likes that. You are like a Frenchman he say!"

I wasn't sure how to take this but Jeanne laughed and said, "Oh là là", and that made me feel a whole lot better.

"And Mireille?"

"Who is Mireille?"

111

"The photographer I told you about. The one who first took me there. He doesn't think she was involved?"

"No, no. It's O.K. He knows it is just you and me, no other *personne*."

"Are you sure?"

"Yes, yes I am sure. He does not even think of her. He thinks it is me who has told you to get the photos. But I explain him, and it is O.K. No more photos. C'est fini".

"But why did he take you to his office so late? It was the middle of the night".

She hunched up her shoulders in a testy sort of way. "*Les questions, trop de questions!* It is all O.K. now, ah? C'est fini". So I backed off.

Jeanne then offered some more coffee and she and Bobbi, after excusing themselves, went over to the gas-ring to boil up some more water. They talked together in a whisper, and although I couldn't understand what they were saying, the tone of their conversation was mainly serious and intense. Even so, I didn't like the way that they kept looking at me occasionally and giggling. I was tempted to remind Bobbi that it was *fini*, and could we leave it alone now please. But then Jeanne came over and kissed me.

"Bravo, Nigel," she said. My heart leapt, and I was glad it wasn't *fini* after all.

By the time we left I was feeling very reassured, and fairly high in spirits. I even allowed myself an optimistic moment, and thought that perhaps everything was finally starting to come together. What I didn't know was that, far from coming together, everything was about to start seriously falling apart.

10

The dark mood that had descended on Mike, and his attitude to the letter from home were actually the first clues that things were going wrong. On the way back I asked him why he wasn't going to read it.

"Because I already know what it says", he said mysteriously. "At least I'm pretty sure I do."

"How can you possibly know?"

"I just do. Leave it will you?"

Had I missed something? What did he mean, he 'already knew' what was in his letter? Was he expecting bad news about his Mum maybe? I recalled how he had been worried about her shortly after we set off. Perhaps it wasn't from his parents at all? But no, they'd be the only ones who knew Jeanne's address - I assumed they'd got it off my mother. In short, I was confused.

Then the thought hit me that he was probably expecting some reaction to the fact that he had redirected all his Hospital bills to them.

"Oh, it's about the Hospital isn't it? You think they're pissed off with you for that".

"No. It's not about that."

I guess he could sense me trying to puzzle it all out so he added, presumably to fend off any further questions, "Look. When I went out with Sue and Steve this morning to the Post Office, I thought I might as well check with Poste Restante – just for interest y'know? And there was a letter from my Dad. He just said he'd written to me at Jeanne's and to be sure to collect it. O.K?"

"That's odd. Why didn't he just tell you what he wanted in that letter?"

No answer.

"Why did he write you two letters? Why bother writing to Jeanne's?"

"Christ, I don't bloody know, do I? He works for the Post Office doesn't he? He likes all this Poste Restante crap. He was just being doubly sure."

"So how do you ..."

"Look, you're getting right on my tits about this! Just leave it man. It's no big bloody deal." And then he went over it again in a slow, words-of-one-syllable kind of way as if he was explaining it to a half-wit. "He writes to me at Poste Restante, and says there's a letter at Jeanne's, don't miss it – that's all, plain and simple. I've now *got* the letter he sent to Jeanne's, but I haven't read it yet. And the reason I know what's in it is because it's just the usual bollocks from home. I'll read it later on – that's if it's alright with you …"

"Yeah, fine," I said, feeling more irritated than usual about the aggressive tone he was taking with me. Something still wasn't right. If it was just 'bollocks from home' and 'no big deal', he seemed to be making an awfully big deal of it. My guess was that they were worried about his accident, in addition to being totally pissed off with him about the Hospital bills, and wanted him to come home.

Then we lost Sue and Steve. When we got back they told us that they had decided to stay just one more night, and were then going to head on up to Paris. They had never really planned to stay in Nice as long as they had done, and they wanted to do the sight-seeing thing in Paris before finally getting their flight home.

Our last night with them was pretty grim. We thought we might go back to *La Grange* at first, but none of us really had the energy. Then Steve suggested going down to the sea-front to do a last bit of open-air busking, 'for old time's sake'. It wasn't a big success. It was fairly breezy and, when we set up, our music tended to be carried off in the wind, so we never managed to get enough attention to attract a crowd, even a small one. Steve and Sue pretended to be passers-by themselves, in the hope of encouraging others to stop, but they were very half-hearted in their technique and mostly everyone just hurried on by. It was all very different to our first meeting when Steve had been so lively and full of energy in working the crowd. Now, given Mike's change of mood and their imminent departure, the whole experience was like an echo of the feeling I had inside, that the life and energy of our stay in Nice was slowly evaporating.

Eventually we gave up and went for a final drink in one of the bars. We all sat in something of a mournful silence for a bit, then Sue asked what our plans now were. I told her that we hadn't really decided, but Mike had the idea that we should go on to Italy.

"Do you have enough time? You know, before you have to be back for college?" she asked.

"Yeah," Mike said with a sigh. "Anyway, even if I'm not back in time, I'll just put it off for a year or so … maybe bum around for a while longer."

If you say so Mike, I thought, but I knew it wasn't that simple.

"Wow," Steve said. "You guys are so lucky. I have to go to college right away – if I didn't I'd get scooped up into the Army – real quick. Can you imagine that? To go home, and find yourself just thrown into the middle of someone else's war."

"Funnily enough, I can," said Mike.

Next morning, we said a very awkward sort of goodbye outside their hotel. It was as if they were just going away for the day rather than forever. We had exchanged addresses but I guess we all knew we were probably never going to meet again. We had shared such a lot in a few short days and I had grown very fond of them both – Steve was fun to be with, and sort of wacky and exciting with his sudden impulses, and I had grown attached to the warmth of Sue's personality and her practical approach to things. She had looked after Mike, Steve and me like three wayward children, affectionately tolerating our risk-taking whilst simultaneously making it clear where lines should be drawn. I wanted to give her a hug but I was overcome by a curious sense of shame, so when I shook her hand I avoided even looking at her.

"Oh Nigel," she said. "Take care, won't you? No unnecessary risks remember?"

I thought I heard a tremble in her voice and then, as she gave me a big hug and a peck on the cheek, I got scared I was going to become emotional myself. Quickly, I shook hands with Steve and thanked him for putting us up in the Hotel.

"No problem man", he said. "I've had a ball. And thank *you* for the show".

I wasn't sure what he meant by that, but it sounded good. Mike was more pragmatic about the whole thing. "Thanks for the use of the pad. See you around!"

So now we were homeless again. Given our circumstances, Sue and Steve's departure, and the apparent conclusion of our adventures in Nice, it did seem logical to think about moving on, but we clearly didn't agree where to move on to. I wanted to go back to St Tropez. We both thought of Nice as big and bustly, and although I didn't share in Mike's assessment of it as a 'shit-hole' it did feel more threatening and unwelcoming than St Tropez had done. I'd never really got used to the sight of police vehicles flying about with their sirens blaring. It was like someone somewhere was constantly committing a crime. Mike however was adamant about moving south, first to Monte Carlo and then on down to Italy. This was a completely new addition to our original plan, and I was not at all keen. Our situation was still insecure, and I wanted to hold on to what familiarity we now had – at least for a while.

"What's to lose?" he said. "We're rambling boys aren't we? Freedom of the open road and all that. We've gotta keep movin' on down the line." His tone was sneery and sarcastic.

"We're OK here aren't we? Things are working out now. I want to stay in France. At least we know what it's like here."

"Well, you can please yourself. I'm moving on".

I'd had enough. "Look, just tell me what's wrong, will you? You've been a pain in the arse since yesterday ... ever since you got those bloody letters. Are you pissed off with me for giving them Jeanne's address?"

"No, it's not that," he said quietly,

"Well, what then?"

I thought he was about to tell me something, but then he suddenly jumped to his feet and said, "Oh come on. To hell with the letters. Let's go and see Bobbi. If you're not coming with me, I need to check out if she wants to come to Italy with me instead."

There was no-one around when we got there. We thought perhaps Jeanne was at work, so we went round to the bar to see if we could find her there. There was no sign, so we went inside to check with the bar-owner. As we approached him he seemed to bristle as if we were two bits of debris that had blown in off the street.

"Messieurs?"

"Nous cherchons notre amie, Jeanne." Mike said.

His half-smile turned quickly into a frown, and then he glared at us in a more hostile way.

"Elle n'est pas ici."

"Does she come later? A quelle heure ..."

" ... Non, non, pas ici ..." and then he started to gesticulate at us, directing us towards the door ... "allez! allez! ..."

I instinctively turned to go, but Mike bravely stood his ground and tried to ask him what was wrong. The café-owner glared at him for a moment, then spat out something which sounded like, "Fetch me the can!" (When we later ran this past Jeanne she thought he was probably trying to tell us to 'fiche-moi le camp' which loosely translates to 'bugger off!') Meanwhile, Mike persisted.

"Nous cherchons notre amie, Jeanne."

By now however, his insistence that we leave was pretty clear, so to avoid any further bloodshed we left graciously, and went and had a drink in a café nearby.

"Perhaps Jeanne doesn't work there anymore?" I ventured.

"Course she doesn't, you twat!" said Mike. "I would have thought that was obvious!"

And so we sat in silence, each nursing our various feelings of hurt, resentment, and general puzzlement. We sat for what felt like an hour or so, our reverie broken only on two occasions – firstly when Mike, ill-advisedly I thought, went over to another table to bum a cigarette, and secondly when the waiter came and virtually insisted that we bought another drink. I tentatively suggested we should try the apartment again. Mike said nothing, gave me a look of contempt, and gathered up his bags.

We walked back to the apartment in a gloomy silence, amid angry city noises and a darkening sky. When we arrived there was still nobody in, so we just sat on the steps in a miserable heap. Mike got out his penknife and started picking at his nails. I couldn't bear the silence any longer.

"For God's sake Mike, what did I do?" I asked.

But he didn't even look up. He just carried on fiddling with his nails as if I hadn't spoken. Mercifully Jeanne then arrived, carrying a bag of shopping with a baguette sticking out of the top. The sight of her, coupled I suppose with the prospect of food, cheered me no end. Even Mike managed a smile and in no time we were all sitting in the studio, each cradling a warm cup of milky coffee, and munching into bread and paté.

As we ate, Jeanne told us the sorry tale of her falling out with the café-owner, and the loss of her job. It had only been a couple of nights ago. One of the regulars, a guy called Pascal, had got more than a little drunk and had made a pass at Jeanne. At first this had seemed harmless enough, and she had taken it in fun as something she was used to. Then he had pulled her on to his knee and was singing to her. She'd tried to pull away but he wouldn't let her go, nor could she get him to relax his grip on her thigh. His hand movements became increasingly inappropriate, so in the end she had picked up his drink and poured it all over his face. I almost applauded. I loved the idea of her as a feisty independent woman, and the image of her standing up for herself like that and brooking no nonsense struck me as very Joan of Arc-ish.

The café-owner had of course sided with Pascal – waitresses were easily disposable, so he had told her to 'fetch the can' in a similar tone to the one he had used with us. Up to now, she explained, she hadn't been able to get another job and suspected in fact that he had spread the word that she was troublesome and not to be trusted. She'd been out searching all that day she said.

"And where's Bobbi?" Mike asked.

"Oh, she … she… has moved out to stay with a friend."

"What friend? I didn't know she knew anyone here."

"No, it is someone she has just met."

"That's a bit sudden isn't it?"

"Sudden? What is 'sudden'?"

"You know, quick, *vite*, unexpected …"

"Ah no. She meet him one night, in a bar."

She meets someone in a bar and moves in with them? I don't know why I should have been so surprised, yet I felt very uneasy. I knew Bobbi had a happy knack of meeting people and making swift connections, but I thought she was more like Mike – happy to avoid attachments. I also thought it was strange that she should be making such a move so soon after all the business with the photos and M. Mistral. Was she plunging herself into another risky situation? And I was miffed that she had moved in with someone without consulting Mike and me.

We explained to Jeanne that we had now lost our American friends and were thinking of leaving Nice. I watched carefully for her reaction to this news but, if she was appalled at the thought of my being torn away from her, she hid her feelings very well. She merely offered to take us round to see Bobbi the next day. Meanwhile, since we had nowhere else to go and it was just for one night, she suggested that we could doss down on her floor.

We spent the rest of the evening in the warmth of the studio, and Jeanne's company. Inevitably Mike produced his guitar and at first played delicate tunes whilst Jeanne and I listened. Then I got out my guitar and we played and sang some songs together. How music does soothe the savage breast! Outside there was the rumble of thunder and it had started to rain heavily, but inside the atmosphere between us all warmed as we laughed and sang together, and Mike became much more like his old self. It was sometime after 2.00 am before we all finally drifted off to sleep. I didn't know it then, but that was to be the last time we ever played and sang together.

Very early next morning we were awoken abruptly by the sound of the door crashing open. There in the doorway, ruck-sack on his back and looking like the proverbial drowned rat, stood Pip. His eyes, again rat-like, scanned the room, and after a heavy silence he spoke. It was the sort of welcome Mike and I were familiar with when we took people by surprise. "What the fuck are you two tossers doing here?"

Jeanne ran over to him as if to offer him a welcoming hug. He didn't respond, but just stood immobile. Jeanne shrank back fearfully, as if she'd just received an electric shock.

"*Qu'est-ce qu'il y a?*"

"I asked what these two tossers are doing here!" he growled, even more menacingly than before.

"Steady on mate", Mike began. "It's us. We …"

"I know who you are!" He was shouting now, and the atmosphere in the room had turned distinctly chilly. Jeanne then took up the challenge, adopting a calm sort of tone, but speaking firmly and clearly she said, "They are here only one night. We are having a bad time, these past days. Mike and Nigel, they have nowhere to sleep last night, and …"

Her voice trailed away as Pip's head slowly turned towards her with a cold look of contempt in his eyes.

"Oh, you've had a bad few days have you? My heart bleeds. I haven't exactly been rolling in clover myself as it happens. I spent most of last week in a fucking Greek jail if you want to know. I haven't eaten since Tuesday, I had my arse kicked and my money nicked on the way back here, and it pissed on me all last night!!"

I mustn't laugh I thought to myself. I must not laugh.

"*Ah mon pauvre,*" said Jeanne tenderly and took a step towards him. He then breathed in deeply and exhaled, allowing his shoulders to relax as he did so. He suddenly seemed weak and spent, and I thought for a brief moment that we were entering the calm after the storm, that his initial shock and bluster at seeing us was starting to pass. I looked away momentarily and started to get out of my sleeping bag. The next thing I knew Jeanne had landed on top of me apparently having stumbled backwards following a particularly violent push from Pip. Our heads clashed together as she reached out to break her fall and we each let out a howl of pain. Mike was on his feet in an instant.

"Look, you mad bastard, just calm down, for God's sake. There's no need for that. We're going. Jeanne was only doing us a favour for one night!"

"Doing you a favour!! Been shagging you both then has she?"

I had no idea Pip had such a temper. I'd certainly never heard him string so many words together before. He had been fairly quiet in St Tropez and, although unfriendly, was never as frankly menacing as this. Now, standing there water-logged and growling, he was doing a passable impression of the Creature from the Black Lagoon.

By now Jeanne had stumbled to her feet and had moved across the room to sit on the end of her bed, nursing her bruised head in her hands. I got up and went to sit next to her and to check she was alright. I put my arm round her.

"Get off her!" Pip yelled as he rushed over, grabbed me by the collar, and yanked me to my feet. Now I was at close range I could see that his eyes were bloodshot and his breath smelled of stale beer and smoke. I struggled to get away as Jeanne tried to get between us and to prise us apart. He somehow elbowed her away, then swung me round and pushed me to the floor. I toppled backwards in an instant and fell into the corner. There was a sickening, dull cracking sound accompanied by a discordant twang as I crushed against my guitar, which had been resting against the wall where I had lain it the night before. Its neck was completely snapped, and most of its body flattened. I sat amongst the ruins in shock and disbelief.

The next thing I was aware of was a blur of movement just at the edge of my vision. I looked up to see Jeanne, now on her feet and squaring up to Pip. He reeled backwards as she pounded on his chest, whilst simultaneously peppering him with a verbal assault. Sadly this was in French so I couldn't understand exactly what she said, but the message was clear – she wasn't happy. By the time he'd backed away as far as the door he'd managed to grab her wrists to fend off more blows, and then he started to shout. This I could understand.

"Fuck off! The lot of you! Get out of my fucking flat!"

We sat in Marcel's kitchen, nursing our wounds. Jeanne's bump was still tender, following our head collision. Mike's leg had also flared up again, the pain having been somewhat aggravated by the speed of our exit.

Now here we were in the house of a stranger, Bobbi's new *ami*, sifting through the wreckage of our recent experience.

My pain was more emotional than physical. I felt totally flat and dispirited. My beautiful guitar was no more. Apart from Mike she had been my constant companion since we had left home, and I felt strangely vulnerable now, without her. I kept thinking of the newness and shine of her when I first bought her, and the sheer sensual pleasure of savouring the aroma of her new sweet-smelling beech wood body. Now she was in pieces, quite beyond repair, quite dead.

Jeanne had come with us, mainly because she didn't want to be with Pip anymore. None of us had any idea what had sent him into such a frenzy. A series of frustrations, a spell in prison, being cold wet and hungry would naturally take the sweetness out of any one's mood, but all that hardly merited a descent into madness. From what I knew of Pip though, I wondered if it was possible that drugs might be involved at some point in the story.

Mike and I had managed to get out with all our stuff, or at least what was left of it. I had scooped up the remains of my guitar, and they now lay in their plastic case in a crumpled heap. There was little hope of recompense – Pip was hardly likely to repent and offer to replace her for me, I had no insurance, and going to the Police wasn't an option. The reality was that my busking days were over. I wondered how other rambling boys managed. Guitars were not the most robust of instruments and being thrown about in box-cars and bumping down dusty roads must surely have meant that casualties were common. Yet no-one ever sang about broken or damaged guitars. Then again, I guess if you lose your music, you lose both the means as well as your will to write such songs anyway.

Jeanne on the other hand had been given no time to pack. She only had the clothes she was able to hurriedly dress in before we left. So we knew that one of our first tasks was to return to the studio to pick up her stuff. Bobbi had persuaded Marcel to put Mike and me up for a couple of nights, and Jeanne for as long as she wished.

Marcel was a confident, extravert sort of chap, probably in his mid-twenties. He had some kind of job in tourism and travel, based at the harbour and it was easy to see how Bobbi had been attracted to his strong, containing sort of presence. Partly to my surprise, but mostly delight, Jeanne wanted to go and sort Pip out, but Marcel had intervened and talked her out of that. That was a great pity of course, as I would have been right behind her on that one. Then again, none of us really wanted to clap eyes on him ever again. In any case a phone-call had summoned Marcel to the docks at short notice, so the plan was that Bobbi and Jeanne would go back to the studio to pick up her stuff, whilst Mike and I waited chez Marcel. I wasn't at all convinced about this, but the general view was that any sighting of Mike or me would only re-ignite Pip's jealous passion, or whatever it was. In any case Jeanne felt confident she could handle him should he appear and really, I had no cause to doubt it. There was a chance he would be out anyway, so they'd be able to sneak in and out quickly.

Just before they left we amused ourselves by swapping insulting descriptions of Pip. It started with Mike calling him 'a stupid pratt', and Jeanne asking for a translation.

"Probably it means *stupide … idiot*", I said.

"*Ah*", said Jeanne, "*conneau!*"

"*Voilà. Quel conneau!*" said Bobbi laughing, and then added one or two more of her own. "*Connard! … Couillon!*" I hadn't a clue what they meant but they sounded really good, especially given the venomous way in which she spat them out.

"*Emmerdeur!*" shouted Jeanne. Where do young girls learn such language?

Then I heard Bobbi whisper something which sounded like '*moyenne?*' whilst holding her finger and thumb about half an inch apart. '*Ah non,*' said Jeanne, '*minuscule,*' and they collapsed in a fit of giggles. I assumed they were discussing the size of Pip's equipment.

It would have been OK and perhaps ended there, had I not then had the witty idea of suggesting that Pip was probably short for 'Pip-squeak'. I waited for the snorts of approval but all I got were blank looks. I appealed to Mike for help.

"What is a pip-squeak anyway?"

He shrugged, "Kind of like a pompous prick I suppose."

I found this oddly helpful, as I was fairly sure *hauteur* covered 'pompous', and they'd just been talking about pricks. I did think *moyenne* sounded like a strange word for penis but I decided to take the risk so, putting them both together I announced, "*Pip est un moyenne de hauteur!*"

The girls both fell silent and looked at each other. Bobbi's expression was one of blank incomprehension, Jeanne's was more … well, one of pity. My bubble burst with a loud pop.

"Er … excuse my French," I added feebly.

After a few more minutes of aching silence Jeanne came over and gave me a hug. "*Oh Nigel,*" she said, "*Ne t'en faites pas.*" Then they left, their girly laughter fading into the distance as they resumed their pillory of Pip's short-comings. I prayed that my pathetic attempts at French didn't mean I had now joined him in the stocks.

"Moyenne de hauteur!" scoffed Mike. "Where on earth did that come from?"

"I was trying to say pompous prick," I protested. "I heard Jeanne say 'moyenne' ... when they were talking about Pip's willy. I thought it was some sort of slang ... you know, as in 'member' or something. And hauteur means ... "

"Well, as far as I recall," he said interrupting, "when we covered willy sizes in our French lessons, *moyenne* meant average. In short, dear friend, I think you just described Pip as 'a man of average height'." He shook his head wearily. "That acid tongue of yours will get you into trouble one day."

I had to agree that, as insults go, it didn't quite hit the spot.

I went into the kitchen and made a cup of coffee, leaving Mike idly picking out tunes on his guitar. After a while, he said, "So what do you think you'll do then?"

I hadn't given it a thought, and I was alarmed by how 'we' had now become 'you'.

"What do you mean?"

"Well, are you gonna go home or what?" The jolly atmosphere had clearly left the room with the girls. He had turned irritable again. I just looked at him.

"Well if you can't busk, there's no bread. No bread, no living".

"I thought we were in all this together".

"I'm going to Italy. I told you. You said you didn't want to come".

"I didn't think you were serious".

"Course I'm bloody serious, especially after last night. Christ, how many times do I have to tell you? I want to get as far away from this bastard country as I can".

"Perhaps it's me you want to get away from?"

"Oh, for God's sake. Why does all this have to be about you? The fact that you're a miserable, whingeing old bugger has nothing to do with it".

I winced, but tried to lighten the mood. "Hey, who are you calling 'old'?" He didn't seem to hear me, so I tried another tack.

"We could hitch back up north, back to Paris. We've only got about another month or so anyway, before we're due to go back. I thought we were road buddies."

"Piss off!" he shouted suddenly, "Why don't you ever listen?" And he slammed his coffee cup down, stood up and walked over to the window.

"It's finished", he said. "We're not road buddies any more. I've told you I'm not going back! So just piss off and leave me alone".

His outburst left me feeling as hurt and shocked as I had done when I'd sat on my guitar. First Pip had crushed my music, now Mike was squeezing the life and spirit out of our friendship, and our whole reason for being here. I felt totally confused, and overwhelmed by a feeling of emptiness and futility. I sat down, bent forward, and buried my head in my hands. After a little while, he came over and put his hand on my shoulder.

"Look I'm sorry mate. But I just don't know what to do. It's just a big fat mess. Here, if you really want to know, read these bastard letters. Poste bloody Restante." He handed me two envelopes, both severely crumpled. "Anyway, I'm going out for a bit." Then he was gone.

I sat and stared at the letters for a minute or so, with various thoughts crashing through my head about what could possibly have happened. Had somebody died? I opened the one that had been sent to Poste Restante first. It was from his Dad, and had been posted about 3 or 4 days after we'd left home.

Dear Michael,

I hope everything is going well. Before you left you told us you were hoping to get as far as Nice, so I'm risking sending this letter to you there.

I won't beat about the bush, but will tell you straight. The reason I'm writing is to let you know that, just after you left, Sandra's mother called to see me to tell us that it wasn't possible for Sandra to go ahead with the abortion, so she has decided to have the baby after all. You may not be pleased to hear this but I thought it was only fair you should know about it before you got home, so it does not come as too much of a shock. Obviously it means you are going to have to pull your weight when you get home. There will be a lot to talk about in more ways than one, but if we pull together I'm sure we can find a way to manage.

In case you're wondering, your mother and I are pleased that Sandra has changed her mind, as you know how much it all upset your Mother when we found out. Still that's water under the bridge now and life has to move on. She is a lot stronger again now by the way, and I know she is looking forward to helping you to do your bit with the baby when it comes. In fact we will all be pleased to see you back home. Little Rosie keeps asking after you too.

Anyway, I hope everything is going on alright, and that you have been able to earn a bit of money. We'd be pleased to hear from you, if you can find the time to write.
Love Dad.
P.S. Mum sends her love too.

What a sad little letter. I read it through twice, trying to take it all in, whilst searching for more detail, more information. A bomb had been dropped, something with major implications for Mike and his future, and yet it was just set out in a few simple words … *she has decided to have the baby after all.* And there was nothing very clear about his parents' attitude to it all. Was there some understanding and support, or were the phrases he'd used to be understood as challenges and accusations … *you are going to have to pull your weight … there will be a lot to talk about …you know how much it all upset your Mother.* The whole tone seemed vaguely intimidating to me, perhaps finally captured by the sarcasm in the sign-off … *if you can find the time to write.*

It all brought back a vivid picture of Mike's Dad – the brisk, authoritarian figure who stood solidly behind the protective glass shield in the Post Office, challenging you to ask for anything difficult. I used to hate going round to the house in case he answered the door. "I'd invite you in," Mike once said to me, "only my Dad would just throw you out again." I took it as a joke, but I was never sure, particularly as it was never properly tested. His Dad was generally in the Post Office when I was invited in to the house – by the timid, shy little woman that was his mother. She never seemed altogether there, but was still kind and friendly towards me. She always seemed to be distracted by Rosie, Mike's needy little sister, who took up most of her time and attention with her exuberance and unpredictable emotional outbursts.

No wonder Mike had been in such a foul mood after reading this. It clearly accounted for the sudden darkening of his mood, and his touchiness and temper. And now I understood his keenness not to go back home - this was what he wanted to get away from – not France, not me, but Sandra Maddison and her threatening little bundle of joy.

I opened the other letter – the one that had been sent to Jeanne's *studio*, and read it next. Again it was from his Dad, and had been posted about 5 days previously.

> *Dear Michael,*
>
> *I've been trying to contact you for a couple of weeks now. I got this address from Mrs Broadbent who was in the Post Office today and she told me she'd had a letter from Nigel, who had told her it was alright to send mail to you here. I am disappointed that you have not thought to write home yourself yet. We've all been wondering how you are getting on, especially little Rosie who keeps asking after you.*
>
> *Anyway, I'm just writing this to let you know there is a letter for you at Poste Restante in Nice – c/o the Post Office, Place Wilson, 06 Nice – in case you haven't picked it up yet. I tried St Tropez at first but apparently the Post Office there is too small and there is no Poste Restante facility, so I took the chance of writing to Nice. I know you said you thought you'd be sure to be there at some point. I wrote it about 10 days ago so it should be there by now.*
>
> *Please go and collect it – you will see why when you get it – I won't repeat it all here, but it's about Sandra and the baby. Hope all is well,*
> *Love Dad.*

So it was, as Mike had said, a double check to ensure he got his Poste Restante letter. That was thoughtful wasn't it? I didn't think much of his letter-writing style. Again, it was a letter that didn't contain much in the way of concern or affection – mainly a critical tone, crisp and business-like, and then this horrible little suspenseful hint - *it's about Sandra and the baby*.

I re-played the events of the last few days in an attempt to iron out some of the muddle that was still in my mind. Now I understood that Mike had got the Poste Restante letter *first*, when he went out with Steve, and that had given him the 'full' details – or all his Dad was telling him anyway. So that did explain his attitude towards the second letter, the one he'd got via Jeanne, when he'd crumpled it up and told me he 'knew what was in it'. Of course he didn't know exactly, but he knew it was from his Dad, so perhaps just guessed it was some sort of back-up. As I mulled it over though, I thought it was quite an unnecessary and heartless touch on his Dad's part not to give Mike the full story in that letter. Since he knew Mike was more sure to get a letter at Jeanne's, why just say 'it's about Sandra and her baby' and not spell it out a bit more? Perhaps he was hoping Mike would get that letter first, and then be filled with anguish and uncertainty till he was able to find out more. It was just a sneaky way of inflicting torture on to someone as far as I could see. I wondered if perhaps his intention was to pay Mike back for re-directing his Hospital bills to them, although there wasn't any mention of those, or even his accident.

Jeanne and Bobbi returned before Mike did. There had been no sign of Pip at the studio so Jeanne had been able to gather up her things unhindered. I couldn't think of anything helpful to say so I just made them a cup of coffee and left them to it. I told them Mike had slipped out for a walk and, mainly because I couldn't cope with the discomfort of being in the flat, I said I would go out and meet him. In fact I just walked down to the sea front and sat on a bench, looking out to sea.

At first I thought of Morecambe and the hours I used to spend leant on the railings there, staring out into the mist and imagining what wonders lay beyond the horizon. I was fascinated by the endless landscape of water before me, how it seemed to go on forever - like a future where there were no limits, where all things were possible. I'd ponder the mysterious whirling sea beneath me too, and imagine what secrets it held, what wonderful things were hidden in its depths, what strange and exotic life forms were waiting to be discovered.

In reality of course, I knew exactly what was on the horizon all the time because, when the mist cleared, there they were staring back at me - the shipyards of Barrow-in-Furness. And, to tell you the truth, Morecambe Bay is tidal and not a deep blue ocean of possibility at all. In fact, if you go for an unguarded stroll when the tide goes out, there is the distinct possibility that the treacherous quick sands will swallow you up. And if they don't get you, the tide will when it comes back in – it's said that it moves faster than a man can run. Reality can be such a pain sometimes.

It was quite overcast now, and I felt as if the sky was pressing down on me. I stared into the distance. The sea was still disturbed from the storm of the previous night, and spray pounded into the air every few minutes as the waves collided with the rocks on the shoreline. The breeze also had a bite to it and found its way under my skin to mingle with my inner chills. The loss of my guitar now seemed not to matter. In the space of one short night Mike had lost his sense of freedom and faced a very uncertain future, and Jeanne had lost her home and her partner. I consoled myself with the thought that at least Bobbi had found some sort of security, although who knew how long that would last. Then I became aware of someone standing next to me. It was Mike, almost as if I had conjured him up.

"I thought it was you", he said. "Sad lonely bastard gazing wistfully out to sea".

"I'm sorry mate," I said. "Thanks for showing me the letters."

"Oh don't be sorry. If that's what the silly bitch wants, it's nowt to do with me is it?"

"What do you mean? It's everything to do with you. You can't just walk away".

"Watch me", he said. "It's her sprog. She wanted it. Let her get on with it".

I was horrified, but not surprised by his cold, callous tone. It was Mike after all.

"You don't mean that".

"Actually, I do. I showed you the letter so you'd know why I'm not going back, not so you could go all sentimental and righteous on me. What's gonna happen if I go back? You saw the way he thinks – 'pull your weight'... 'lot to talk about'... he's gonna want me to 'do the right thing' isn't he?" he said in a mocking contemptuous tone, "and marry the silly cow".

"Not necessarily. He might just be talking about agreeing ways you can support her and the baby."

"What, with money? She's had that – I haven't got any sodding money."

"Well, you know, emotionally or something. It is partly your responsibility you know."

He visibly stiffened, drew in his breath, and spoke to me slowly and deliberately. I was taken aback at the venom in his voice. "And that's EXACTLY why I wasn't going to tell you about this. I don't want YOU, or any other WANKER lecturing me about MY RESPONSIBILITIES!"

"O.K, O.K mate, calm down, sorry, I didn't mean ..."

But by now he had slid down on to the floor and was sitting with his back against the rail. He had buried his head in his hands and, although he wasn't making a sound, I could see his shoulders were shaking. I felt stupid and didn't know what to do. I suppose the grown-up thing might have been to sit down next to him and put my arm round him, I don't know, but for the next few moments I just stood there, paralysed. Eventually I put my hand on his shoulder and squeezed it.

"It's all such a mess," he said at last. "It was just a stupid one-night thing. I don't even like her. Why couldn't she have just got rid of it like we said."

"It's a life, Mike. Look, I don't want to lecture you and God, I don't know anything about it, but getting rid of a baby can't be an easy thing to do. They might not have been able to arrange it or something, Sandra might have been too upset, or maybe the doctors ..."

"Yeah, I know mate. I know it's not her fault. And it's not yours either. But who else can I shout at right now?"

He struggled to his feet and wiped his nose and mouth with the back of his hand.

"Sorry about that – must be the cold and the wind making my eyes water."

"Yeah sure," I said.

As we walked back he asked me what I thought of the letters, so I told him I didn't think much of his Dad's technique of breaking bad news, and that it was hard to tell what sort of support he was offering.

"Yeah that's what I thought. But that's how it's always been," he said softly. He shot a quick glance in my direction, scanning my face as if he was trying to decide how much to say. Then he looked down again and continued. "After Rosie was born I never knew where I figured anymore - you know? I mean at first I thought sure, Mum's had a really hard time, her and Rosie need all the love and support they can get, but it never changed, it just went on and on like that. When Rosie was off it, Mum was tied up with her, and when Rosie was settled, Mum just wanted to be left alone. Dad was just happy selling stamps all day. That's why I didn't mind about sending them the Hospital bills – let them worry about me for a change."

I found myself thinking about his Mum, and wondering how she'd feel when he didn't come home with me. I also thought of Jeanne and the example she'd set of facing up to conflict rather than shrinking away from it. So I took the risk and said, "Do you remember, on the way down, how you were worried about your Mum?"

He turned and gave me a warning look. "Ye-es? What about it?"

"Well your Dad's letter said she's really looking forward to having you back home - so she can help out with the baby and everything. It'll be really good for her I should think. She'll want to help won't she? And she'll want you around so you can help too. You wouldn't have to marry Sandra or anything. You just have to be there Mike."

I tried to say it all this as quickly as I could, either before he could interrupt or shut me up. To my surprise he actually seemed to take it all in, but then he looked away again and said, "I know. You're probably right. And I do feel bad about it ..... but what can I do? I just can't face it mate, I just can't. I'm not going to go back, at least not for quite a while yet."

We walked on slowly for a while, each lost in our own thoughts. I felt very anxious for him. He was about to get himself into difficulties – again - and it was up to me to save him. I'd done it before – saved his life that is. At least I might have done.

It was a hot sultry Sunday afternoon, the day after my 13th birthday, and we were out for a walk in some woodlands on the outskirts of town. We had celebrated the night before by blagging some bottles of *Scrumpy Jack* cider from the local off-license, and I had woken up with a pounding head-ache and nausea. I'd left the house early and was hoping that the fresh air of the countryside would blow away my symptoms enough that I could hide my fragility from my Aunt and Uncle.

Mike had insisted on the hair-of-the-dog remedy, but whilst he guzzled down 3 more bottles I struggled to manage just one. The remedy seemed to work for him anyway. I recall him bouncing along beside me, slashing wildly at the cow parsley with a stick he had found, and then rushing off into the long grass whooping at buffalos, apache warriors and God knows what. Meanwhile I just crawled along desperately trying to hang on to the will to live. As the whooping noises faded I felt an overwhelming urge to rest, so I flopped down in a heap, lay back in the grass and closed my eyes. A soft breeze brushed against my cheeks and I became aware of a wonderful peaceful silence descending.

I would have stepped into the dark abyss that was stretching out before me had not the sudden crack of a gun-shot shattered my peace. My eyes sprang open and I sat bolt upright, searching the echoing silence for clues. Nothing – except the rustle and flapping of the stampeding birds, startled as I had been by the sudden noise. Then, softly on the breeze, came the sound of a voice.

"N-i-g-e! .... N-i-g-e!"

At first I wasn't sure what I was hearing. Then the voice came again, this time more urgently.

"NIGEL!!! OVER HERE!"

"Mike?" I yelled. "Is that you?"

"I'm over here, you daft bastard! Hurry up! For God's sake! I need some HELP!!"

That'd be a yes then. I lurched to my feet and ran towards the sound, leaping through the long grass, dodging shrubs and fallen tree stumps, and into a copse behind which gurgled a little pond. Here Mike stood, up to his chest in the water, with a frightened imploring look on his face. I couldn't believe it.

"What the hell are you doing in there?"

"Picking cotton you dozy sod, what d'yuh think? Get me out. I can't bloody move!"

"How did you get in there?"

"Never mind that! Just get me out will you?"

It took me a while to grasp the situation. The pond looked quite harmless and my first thought was that this was just another of Mike's silly attempts to wind me up. I tried some levity. "Why don't you just walk towards me? You'll find that the water will get shallower as you get near the edge of the pond. That's what ponds are like. We learned about it in Geography ….."

Bad idea. He gave me such a withering look of loathing and contempt that I thought I'd better start to take him seriously. Through clenched teeth he spelled it out.

"I - can't - move! Right? Don't be a smart arse, just give me some help." Then his tone softened and he sounded scared and vulnerable. "Look, I'm really cold and I seem to be stuck. Can't move. It's like I'm standing on a ledge or something. I – I'm scared that if I step the wrong way I'll go under."

Neither of us could swim. Strange that, living so close to the sea as we did. I looked round and saw the stick he had been using to terrorise the buffalos, abandoned on the ground. I picked it up and waded into the water. It was surprisingly cold, and I shivered as the icy fingers of reeds brushed against my legs. The water deepened quickly too and I was up to my waist within about 3 steps, yet still about 6 or 7 feet away from Mike. I stretched out the stick, but it was too short and he couldn't reach it. The mud beneath my feet gave way and I felt myself sinking. I panicked and stepped back, almost losing my hold on the stick in the process as I struggled to regain my balance.

"For God's sake!" he said. "You useless get! Can't you - -" Then whatever else he was about to follow this up with froze on his lips as he suddenly lost his balance himself and plunged forward into the water. He thrashed about, neck-high in the water now, arching his head back as he tried to prevent himself from going under. Luckily the momentum of his fall brought him a little closer to me so I took another step forward and, clutching on to a nearby bunch of reeds, thrust the stick towards him. He kicked out and heaved himself towards it. I felt it jerk as he grasped it, threatening to wrench it from my hand. Soon he was alongside me, spluttering and coughing.

"Put your feet down," I said. "It's not deep here."

He didn't answer, but with a sudden lurch momentarily disappeared under the water and then, just as quickly, re-appeared and crawled crab-like on to the bank, dripping in mud and slime.

We didn't talk much on the way home, and in fact neither of us referred to the incident ever again. I guess we both just felt stupid and ashamed – me about my feeble rescue efforts, and him about getting himself into such a predicament in the first place. I still don't know how he did it. Nor do I know who fired the shot that stirred me from my slumber. At least that woke me in time to … well, do something to help. I don't know if I actually saved his life on that day, although I suppose it's possible.

"So what are you going to do then?" he asked me.

"I don't know. I really don't think I can come to Italy though. I don't really want to go that far. I might just stay and then head on back in a couple of weeks or something." I decided to try again. "Aw, come with me mate. Don't go off on your own. I … "

"Just leave it Nige! I've made up my mind."

But he needed me. He was teetering on a ledge again, in great danger of launching himself into a deep pool of trouble. He needed me to keep offering him an out-stretched hand, a rescuing stick.

"It doesn't seem right," I said. "We should stick together. How are you gonna manage? You're gonna need me … "

He gave me an exasperated look - and I realised he really was determined, and there was nothing I could say. It was over - we were about to go our separate ways. And then it hit me, an understanding that

132

had been staring me in the face all along, and I wondered why I hadn't seen it before now. Mike was just like my Dad, *wandering off to who-knows-where at a moment's notice.* Perhaps that was why I had been so drawn to him as my mate, why I had been so willing to follow his lead and be with him, why I had been willing to take so much crap from him. It was inevitable that he'd abandon me one day. I should have seen it coming.

"I'll go tomorrow," I heard him say. "No point hanging around."

I was suddenly aware of feeling very lost and alone.

Again.

11

He asked me not to tell the others about Sandra and her pregnancy. Since he was denying the fact to himself I suppose it made sense for him to deny the knowledge to others too. We shambled back together through dark streets that were steadily becoming alive with the night-timers, and the cafes and bars which were now lighting up the gloom. I wanted more. I didn't know what to say to him, but I knew I wanted him to tell me what to do, to perhaps persuade me to go with him, or at the very least to sense my vulnerability and offer to stay with me a while longer. I thought that, like Sandra and her baby, I too had now become unnecessary baggage, not wanted on voyage.

Then a sound came drifting towards us out of the night. I think we both heard it together. It was the distant strain of a blues tune being played on a wailing harmonica. I recognised it as one of the tunes that Patrick and André had played that night at *La Grange,* although now there didn't appear to be any guitar accompaniment. We quickened our pace, the sound grew louder, and eventually we found the source. It was coming from a hunched-up figure, sitting on the floor with his back up against the wall, seemingly lost in his music and oblivious to all around him. It was Patrick.

We both sat down beside him and eventually he stopped playing and turned his head slowly towards us. He looked weary and ill. His face was pale and drawn, he was unshaven, and it seemed to be an effort for him to even hold his eyes open.

"Patrick?"

He stared in a bewildered sort of way for a few seconds, then his weary face broke into a smile.

"Hello my boys", he said. "How are you going?"

"Well, better than you mate", said Mike. "What happened to you, and where's André?"

It seemed like an effort for him to speak. Again he looked perplexed and eventually said, *"Pardon?"*

"What happened Patrick? Where is André?"

He just smiled and went back to his blues tune. Mike looked at me and delivered his diagnosis.

"The stupid bastard's stoned", he said.

After a while, and without much resistance on his part we were able to get him on to his feet and, supporting him between us, we shuffled off towards Marcel's flat. Luckily it was only about 100 yards away. We arrived to a shocked reception, not least from Marcel who, nice guy as he was, had clearly had enough of being constantly invaded by Bobbi's refugee friends. We could plainly hear their raised voices in the lounge as he and Bobbi 'discussed' the situation. Meanwhile Jeanne, Mike and I sat in the kitchen with Patrick, trying to revive him. In fact it was amazing what a bit of bread and a hot cup of coffee was able to do for him. His recovery was so quick I decided Mike had been wrong, and that it had been chiefly the combined effects of cold, hunger, and general fatigue, rather than any chemical, that had been responsible for the 'altered state' he was in when we'd found him.

Eventually the raised voices quietened to a more hushed sort of tone, then Marcel and Bobbi came into the kitchen. Marcel looked genuinely upset.

"I'm really sorry", he said, "but all of you will have to leave – tomorrow. Of course you can stay here this night. But I have my work, this place is small. It is very difficult – "

"Hey, it's O.K." said Mike. "No problem. You've done us a big favour already. I was thinking of moving on anyway. I can go tomorrow".

"Yeah, and I will too", I said, without knowing exactly where I was going to. I figured I could cling on to Mike for a bit longer, at least as far as the leaving of Nice was concerned. Then Jeanne spoke.

"Yes, and I will go too. I was thinking I will go back to Paris. I don't know why I am here now. I don't know why I stay".

I was about to plead with her to take me with her but Bobbi spoke first and said something to her in French, which had an earnest, intense tone to it in itself. A longer conversation followed, with Marcel joining in, until I gathered they had come to some sort of conclusion. Jeanne looked at me and translated.

"They think I should stay but it's O.K. It is more good for me to go. So I am going to return to Paris".

"Would it be possible for me to ....?" I began, but I never got to finish. Almost as soon as I started to speak, Bobbi rushed towards Jeanne and, flinging herself on to her, they both dissolved in tears. At that point Marcel, presumably overcome by a pang of guilt, started babbling about how sorry he was and how none of us need rush, and maybe it would be O.K. for us to stay a couple more nights, if that would help.

Patrick meanwhile had laid his head in his hands and had fallen asleep on the table, oblivious to it all.

The next morning felt as ordinary as usual and not at all like the momentous day it was supposed to be. After all our weeks on the road, it was the beginning of the end for Mike and me, and it looked like I was about to say a final goodbye to both Jeanne and Bobbi too. Overnight I had lost the courage to ask Jeanne if I could go with her – on the grounds that hearing her say no would be too much to bear. As for Patrick, he awoke as if transformed. I couldn't imagine that he had had much time to orient himself to his surroundings the previous night but, if he had no clue as to where he was and how he'd got there he didn't show it, but just conducted himself in the flat as if it was his second home. He made coffee for us all, and sat and chatted to us like an old friend catching up on past times. His mood dipped more than a little when we asked him about André. There had been a falling-out apparently, although what about was not clear, but it had resulted in André heading off for Italy. We gathered that Patrick had then spent about 3 or 4 nights on the streets before being arrested for stealing, of all things, ice-cream from one of the hotel's private beaches on *Promenade des Anglais*. He'd tried bumming change off passers-by without much success, and then tried to busk a few coins with his harmonica, but again without success. There was no mention of drugs in his story, so it looked as if the generally wasted state we'd found him in was down to 'natural causes' after all. Certainly a good night's sleep and, I presumed, the boost of being among friends again, had restored his flagging spirits.

I listened to his story though with a growing sense of internal despair. In Patrick's plight of the last week or so, I could plainly see my own. The prospect of an imminent parting had made me realise just how much I had depended on Mike's companionship and, just as Patrick had fallen apart at the loss of André, I feared this might be my fate too. I had precious little money left, no guitar and therefore no means of making a living (if you can call it that), and somehow I had to get from the South of France back to the North of England – on my own. Being with Mike had felt like we were a pilot and a co-pilot travelling in a vehicle that had been fuelled by the friendship and warmth of those we had met along the way. I realised I had felt vulnerable all along really, only ever emboldened when a network of friends or supporters had been around me. I would never have pulled that crazy stunt at Mistral's had Sue and Steve not been there, providing their secure base and back-up.

When we had brought him up to date with our own situation, and Mike mentioned his plan to head for Italy, Patrick seemed somewhat crest-fallen, but then he suddenly brightened and said, "Hey man, let's go to Spain!"

"Spain?"

"Oui, oui, l'Espagne. It is coming close to the time of picking the grapes. There will be many many jobs. We can make money, play the music, meet the senoritas. Monte Carlo is bad place and you should not go to Italy. Italy is ... is too much of the olive oil".

Too much olive oil? That didn't seem like a very sound argument to me. My guess was that olive oil consumption was equally as high in Spain as it was in Italy, and my suspicion was that, since André had headed off toward Italy, he simply wanted to go in the opposite direction. We never did get to find out what had caused their rift, but we all got the impression that it had been a pretty fatal one. Mike was, perhaps predictably, very excited by Patrick's idea. He'd banged on about Ibiza from time to time, so I suppose in his mind it was a step in that direction. It also occurred to me that, with Patrick, he now had a new busking partner – a ready-made replacement for me, his tuneless ex-road-buddy. Mike must have sensed my despondency because he said, "Come on, it's a great idea, man. Don't go home yet, we can all go to Spain instead.!"

I found myself very tempted – particularly after my attack of pessimism at the prospect of being left alone. But it was what Jeanne said next that changed my mind, and probably my life.

"Or you could come to Paris with me ..."

Excuse me? *Or you could come to Paris with me* ... Did I hear that right? And was that Jeanne talking? I'd imagined it surely.

"Pardon?"

"You could come to Paris with me if you like. I'd feel safer if we went together. I remember you said you wanted to go back to St Trop. We could go there, and then to Paris ... if you want".

I felt my heart soar. Like Patrick the night before, a drop of the right sort of medicine and I was a man transformed. The picture from the sleeve of *The Freewheelin' Bob Dylan* flashed into my mind, then gave way to a fantasy of Jeanne and me walking down a dusty road together, her hands are clutched tight to my arm, her head is on my shoulder and her hair is flowing freely. We are ... together. She looks up at me tenderly, and whispers my name ...

"Ni- jjelle ..... Nigel!?"

"Oh yes, sorry. I was ... er ... miles away. Yes. No, I mean. No, I don't need to go back to St Trop. Yes, I think going back to Paris - with you - is a great idea".

Mike looked at me and smiled. I felt as if he'd also seen the picture I'd conjured up in my head, and I felt myself blushing like a stupid schoolboy.

I don't know why I felt so embarrassed. I suppose it was something to do with the fear that I was exposing my true colours. First I had been a folk-singing Dylan-ite, a restless drifter, struggling to survive in a hostile world. Then I'd tried to be the cool street busker and beach bum, dodging convention and Authority. Then I'd had a go at being the modest mild-mannered hero bravely rescuing Bobbi's honour from the clutches of the evil Mistral. But none of it had been a rip-roaring success, so I probably felt that I was now about to be 'found out'. All I really wanted was the security that comes with the love of a good woman – and to get back home.

In the end it all became decided and our future paths got mapped out very quickly. Bobbi and Marcel would stay in Nice and continue with whatever it was they both did; Mike and André would head off for Spain; and Jeanne and me would hitch to Paris. Mike didn't want to hang around anymore than he had to and, ever one for the quick goodbye, he was packed and ready to go in an instant. Patrick on the other hand had nothing to pack. God knows what had happened to his clothes or what belongings he once had, but he didn't seem to care. Bobbi was able to provide him with a blanket and that was apparently all he wanted. She was also able to make up a package of baguettes, cheese and paté to see them on their way. Then, all at once, it was time to say goodbye.

Mike and Patrick were the first to leave. Bobbi threw her arms round Mike and sobbed. It seemed a bit extreme, but I thought it was perhaps something to do with her being French.

"Thank you for looking after me ... you too, Nigel. I am very sorry that I get you into trouble, and ... that I do not speak to you ... *la verité.* You have been very kind to me."

Not speak the truth? I thought that was an odd thing to say, but Mike ignored it. "Hey, there's no need to be sorry," he said.

"But you only come to Nice because of me, and everything goes wrong for you here ..."

"Not at all. We've had a great time. We always planned to come to Nice. Meeting you and Jeanne was the best thing that happened to us. We wouldn't want to change anything – would we Nige?"

"Absolutely not."

Then she threw her arms round me and started sobbing all over again. Jeanne then stepped forward to Mike and kissed him on both cheeks.

"Au 'voir Mike. It has been good to know you, and don't worry about Nigel. I will take good care of him."

"Yeah, thanks for taking him off my hands," he said.

"Are you kidding?" I said. "I'll be able to get on now ... you know ... now that you're not holding me back anymore."

I could feel something falling away inside me, like the calving of an ice-berg. I forced my mind on to practicalities, frantically searching for some solid ground. What did he want me to say to his Mum and Dad? Did he have any message for Rosie? Did he want me to go and see Sandra? I struggled but couldn't seem to translate my tumbling thoughts into the actual spoken word. Will you be alright, Mike? I think I knew he would be, but it was a strange reversal that I seemed to be worrying so much about him. The truth was I didn't know how to say goodbye. Did I give him a manly hug, or shake hands, or what? I just stood there feeling awkward and self-conscious. All I could manage was to ask him if he was going to write home.

"Sure. I'll write a long letter when we get settled. I'll explain to the folks, don't worry. Anyway, it's not like I'm going away forever is it? I'll be back home inside a year or so."

"You are being a bit of a sod you know."

"I know mate, I know. Well, see you around."

And he and Patrick walked off together up the street. He didn't look back.

PART THREE

BRINGING IT ALL BACK HOME

12

Jeanne and me left the next day. For reasons which I guessed were to do with their friendship, and the fact that they were female and know how to do these things better than us chaps, Bobbi and Jeanne wanted to spend some time together before they finally parted, so they went off into the town for the day. Marcel had to go to work so I just moped around the flat.

It was strange to be on my own, but also good to have some quiet time. I wrote home again and told them I was now heading back, although didn't know how long I'd be. I didn't mention about Mike and me having split up, or about my poor dead guitar, but I tried to keep it light and positive – which took some effort actually, considering it wasn't at all how I was feeling. How was I feeling? There was some comfort at the prospect of having Jeanne to myself for a while, but mainly I felt depressed about heading for home, and fearful at the thought of being on my own now that Mike had gone. I felt sad for him too, that he had felt the need to turn his back on his family and wander off like that. I felt alone, but he seemed to struggle with a much more painful kind of loneliness. I remember once walking home from somewhere, fairly late at night, and coming across him sitting by himself on a bench. It was on the sea-front at Morecambe, in the middle of winter, and there he was - just sitting by himself in the dark, eating a bag of crisps. It was the crisps that stuck in my mind. He was cradling them in an odd sort of way as he ate them, and it was as if something cold and hard, and without much nourishment, was all he had for comfort.

I left the flat and went out for a walk, and to post my letter. It felt good to just walk along without having to hump baggage around, without having to worry about where I was going to sleep that night, and to just feel part of the general activity and movement in the streets. It occurred to me that going with the flow was a whole lot easier than going against it.

Jeanne and Bobbi came back in the late afternoon. They both looked pale and unhappy, and it didn't take a genius to work out that they'd both been crying. On the other hand, whilst I could see that they were upset about separating, this was clearly intense stuff for them, and I found that I couldn't really understand why it was such a big thing. I wondered if it said something about a possible superficiality about my relationship with Mike that we had been able to part without this kind of upset.

When Marcel came back the rest of the evening passed quietly. Bobbi and Jeanne cooked a delicious pasta meal for us all, and we ate it round the kitchen table in a subdued, but relaxed atmosphere. They talked together in French mainly, translating for me where necessary, although the gist of it seemed to be about Marcel's working day and the cruise ships that came and went. What was lovely to see was how close he and Bobbi were – he was sort of caring and paternal towards her.

We also spent a bit of time plotting our route back to Paris. Jeanne wanted to go via a place called Brive where an Aunt of hers lived. Apparently this particular Aunt was always pestering her to visit so, when she'd found out about her trip to the South, she had made Jeanne promise to call in, either on her way down or on her way back. It was fine by me. It was a somewhat twisty route across country to get there, but once there, the route from Brive to Paris looked to be more direct.

So the next day we set off. In some way I was dreading the goodbye scene – if it was going to be very emotional I felt it was only fair that I should show some emotion myself, although I wasn't quite sure what would be appropriate.

"Au 'voir Nigel," Bobbi said, as she flung her arms round me. "You are a very good person, and I always remember you. You are very kind to me and I wish you do not go. But you will write to me, yes? And you take care of Jeanne, ah? You are both my dear friends."

Her eyes had welled up with tears by this time, and I could feel myself filling up too. I managed to splutter something like, "Merci bien Bobbi. I will miss you too," but Jeanne and her had already fallen into an embrace, and they both began to sob. They drew back after a while and spoke together in an urgent whisper. I was caught between wanting to pull away in embarrassment and straining to hear, but their French was too fast and fluent for me. It sounded as if Jeanne was giving Bobbi sisterly advice of some kind, and then Marcel joined in, putting a protective arm around Bobbi's waist in a *'don't worry, she's with me now'* kind of way. Eventually we shuffled off up the road, looked back and waved one last time, then turned the corner and headed down towards the Promenade.

How different it is to hitch with a girl – and a French girl at that. We hadn't stood for more than 10 minutes before a car pulled up. The trick was for me to lurk in the background whilst Jeanne stood up front

143

and thumbed down the cars. Mike and I must have put people off with our scruffy over-laden beatnik appearance, whereas stopping for a pretty girl was clearly a more attractive proposition. Our first lift was with two blokes in a fairly smart car who were actually going to St Tropez. I felt a pull to go back there myself, but at the same time knew that it wouldn't be the same without Mike and would only add to the sense of separation from 'old times'. Jeanne felt the same. Basically neither of us had any good reason to go back there – which was a sad thought in itself.

Of course the other big advantage of hitching with a French girl - in France - is that you've got someone with you who can actually speak the language. This is also helpful if you happen to be in the back of a car with the windows wound down, since you have to shout to make yourself heard at all. I had little choice but to opt out and leave Jeanne to it, and they all seemed to get on famously.

After about an hour they dropped us off at Fréjus, just outside St Raphael, where they intended to take the coastal route on to St Trop. The town centre we walked through had a sort of medieval feel about it, with a massive cathedral flanked by other ancient-looking buildings. We didn't linger though, and headed out towards the edge of town, passing what looked like Roman remains as we did so. We had to walk quite a way to get where there was any chance of further lifts, and it was only when we stopped and I looked at the map that I realised I had just walked the last 5Km or so down the National Seven! There was a sense of anti-climax about this realisation, especially as I couldn't really share the significance of the moment with Jeanne. Nevertheless I felt the occasion should be properly marked in some way – so I went behind a tree and had a pee. It seemed oddly appropriate.

Despite our sprint start it then took us quite a while to get the next lift. I sat on my rucksack and watched her as she stood by the road-side, thumb at the ready. I asked her if she was sad to be leaving the South, and especially Bobbi.

"Yes, of course," she said. "Why do you ask?"

"Well you are clearly very close friends, and it seemed very hard for you to say goodbye. I was just wondering …"

"Yes, Bobbi and I have known each other all our lives. We … " She broke off to yell some insult at a car that streaked past honking its horn.

"Go on. What were you going to say?"

"Nothing. It doesn't matter." Now I was even more curious, so I tried a slightly different tack.

"Do you think she'll be alright?"

"Yes, yes, she will be fine now. Bobbi can get herself into trouble very easily, but she will be alright with Marcel."

I was puzzled by that too – what made her so sure? She'd only known him for a couple of weeks, or even less so far as I could see. Another car approached, slowed, then seemed to change its mind and roared off.

"Merde!" she said, but I was relieved. I wanted to pursue this if I could.

"It seems like they hit it off very quickly – Bobbi and Marcel."

She looked round at me affectionately, then came and sat next to me. "O.K." she said. "I tell you. It is no big secret really. She knew Marcel in Paris."

"She knew him in Paris?"

"Yes, that is what I say. Listen, and I tell you. Marcel came into the bar where she worked, and they went out together, a few times. One day he says he is leaving Paris to take a job on La Cote d'Azur. He asked Bobbi to go with him, but she says no. At that time she did not want to leave Paris, but I know she liked Marcel very much. I also tried to persuade her to go as he is a very strong man as you have seen, and I am sure he would look after her. They were a good couple. But still she says no. Anyway, when Bobbi and I come together to the South and she is at last in Nice, she telephone him, and they meet again and, oh là-là, everything is good again."

I waited to make sure she'd stopped speaking, then asked her why she hadn't told me this before. Why pretend they met in Nice?

"I don't know," she said. "It did not seem important."

Maybe not I thought, but why make a secret of it? It was clear that Bobbi and Jeanne generally liked to play their cards close to their chest. I realised I'd seen several examples of this now. In the end I cheered myself up by thinking that, if she was willing to tell me stuff like this, perhaps it indicated a shift towards greater intimacy in our relationship. Then she was on her feet again, there having been a sudden increase in the volume of traffic, strangely reflecting the increase in the volume of my curiosity. Recalling Tim's story about Bobbi running away from her drunken father I tried to probe that one a bit.

145

"So is that why Bobbi finally decided to come to La Côte d'Azur, and leave Paris – so she could meet up with Marcel?"

"No," she said. "That is another story. I tell you later."

I would have persisted but, just at that moment, our next lift arrived.

It was an elderly couple who had stopped for us, on their way home after visiting their son in St Raphael. Luckily however their home was in Aix-en-Provence, about 100 Km further on, so by the end of the ride we felt we were making good progress again.

They were the sweetest couple and made every effort to include me in their conversation with Jeanne. The old lady looked a bit like old photos I had seen of Queen Victoria – short, grey-haired, and with a slight stoop even when sitting. She wore black too, and had a pair of those curious little wire glasses perched on her nose. Her husband was small too, equally kind and softly-spoken. When they asked me about England though, and where I lived, I suppose you could say I was not amused. I actually started it by being negative about Morecambe with its cold winds and frequent rain, but then they seemed to get unreasonably snobby I thought, and started to bang on about the beauties of Provence, the sunshine, and what they called 'les richesses'.

"La Morecambe – elle n'est pas la Côte d'Azur, eh? Hé, hé, hé!"

Perhaps it was homesickness kicking in again but I suddenly felt very protective of my little home town, so I tried to tell them about the 5 miles of promenade, the fabulous views across the bay, the joys of Happy Mount Park, the easy access to the Lakes, not to mention the world famous shrimps and cockles. My French wasn't up to it though, especially when I got to 'cockles'. I appealed to Jeanne. She wasn't sure either. So I just took a risk and told them that Morecambe was *'fameux'* for its *'grandes coqs'*. I immediately panicked at the thought that I might well have said something very obscene. Indeed they both looked bemused, Jeanne looked shocked, and my comment just seemed to hang heavily in the air. I also noticed that we drove along in silence for a bit after that.

Jeanne had told them that we were heading for Paris, and when they dropped us off they were very apologetic about just abandoning us and being unable to offer us a place to stay. For their penance they handed over some francs to Jeanne, driving off before she could protest. We both felt guilty at taking money from elderly people, but then again they looked fairly well-heeled, so maybe it was alright – particularly as we were both hungry and in need of a meal. I asked Jeanne if she knew where we could get some nice *coqs*, but then *she* wasn't amused.

"So, tell me about yourself."

I'd been longing to know more about her ever since we first met really, and now sitting in a quiet café, and emboldened by half a carafe of wine, I felt brave enough to blurt out the question. Also I'd once seen Clint Eastwood use this simple line very successfully in an episode of *Rawhide*. The woman concerned went all coy, seemingly thrilled that a handsome man was taking such an interest in her. Perhaps my delivery lacked the seductive quality of Clint's. She just looked shocked.

"Quoi?"

"Sorry. I was just thinking that, with all that's been happening, I don't know much about you or your family. It's O.K. if you don't want to tell me."

Thankfully she laughed, and then relaxed. "Oh, it is O.K. Nigel. You are so funny. It is the way you say 'Tell me about yourself'" and she mocked me, speaking in a gruff, deep voice with a tone that was more interrogative than seductive. Clearly my technique needed honing up a bit.

"Of course I tell you. And you tell me something of your family too. Well, I live in Paris all my life – not far from La Gare Montparnasse, you know? When I grow up there is just me, my mother and my father."

She pulled out a crumpled photograph from her purse and handed it to me. It was an old black and white picture of a happy little girl in pigtails sitting on a bicycle, with a man holding and steadying her. He was smiling broadly and looking towards the camera. There was also a woman standing behind them, looking on approvingly.

"It's lovely," I said. "You all look very happy."

"Yes we were. It was ... *mon anniversaire* ... my birthday?" I nodded. "I was 10 years old. My parents, they bought for me this bicycle."

She looked at the photo herself in a wistful sort of away. Then she quickly put it back in her purse. I thought I noticed a tear.

"Do you know, only two months after this photograph, my father is dead. He was *un pompier* ... you know? He put water on the fires?"

"Oh, a fireman."

"Oui, oui, a fireman. One day he was trying to rescue people from a factory, and ... it was very tragic. One day I come home from school, and he is not there anymore. My mother tells me that he has ... gone away

…. she says he is gone to Heaven …" She tried to smile. "It was a very bad time for everybody. Oh, I am sorry…"

She broke off to get out a handkerchief which she used to dab at her eyes.

"It's O.K." I said, not really knowing whether it was or not.

She paused and we sat quietly for a moment or two. I kind of wished that I hadn't started this, but at the same felt pleased that she was trusting me enough to tell me these things.

"But it was how he lived. He cared about so many things, and he had a strong passion for everything that he does … do you know what I mean?"

"Yes I do. I think you are the same."

"Oh I hope so. But it makes me sad. I miss him. I can't talk to him about the things I do … my plans … I want him to be proud of me … do you know?"

"I'm sure he would be very proud of you now."

"Oh Nigel. That is very sweet. I don't know it is true, but it is very sweet."

"Of course it's true. You are a very nice person." God, did I really say that? I can't imagine Clint telling anyone they were 'a nice person', especially not after they'd just poured their heart out. But she took it well.

"Thank you Nigel."

"And what about your mother? Is she all right?" As soon as I'd said that I cringed again. It was like I was asking if she was still alive, which I was actually, although my other intention was to help her think of something more comforting. Reassuringly, she gave a little laugh.

"Yes she is fine. She still lives in Paris. It is her sister that I want to see in Brive – my Aunt. She came to live with us for a time after my father died, so we are all … close."

She excused herself and went off to the Ladies. I hoped it wasn't to have a good sob but in fact she wasn't away long, and if she had been crying she seemed quite together again when she got back.

"Thank you for listening to me," she said. "It is nice to talk about my family. I tell you more another time. Now you must tell me something of you. Do you have brothers and sisters?"

I suddenly felt uncomfortable, not expecting the spotlight to be turned on me. I hated to talk about my family. I looked around anxiously, and then at my watch, hoping that the café was about to close or something, and that we'd have to leave.

148

"Qu'est-ce qu'il-y-a?" she asked. "What is the matter?"

"Oh nothing. I'm sorry. There's not a lot to say. I'm not really used to – "

"Tell me," she said gently.

"Well, my father was in the Merchant Navy when he married my Mam ..."

"Excuse me?"

"He was ... at sea a lot ... a sailor."

"Ah oui, *un marin*?"

"Yeah. Anyway he was always away from home, often for months at a time. He could never settle – all he wanted to do was sail off to sea. I don't understand why he ever got married to my Mam really – he didn't seem to want to be with her – or me for that matter. She hated it when he was away, and was always trying to persuade him to get a job at home. But he never would. Anyway, when I was about seven he ... well, he left us ... completely. I don't know the details but he just wrote to her one day to say that he wasn't coming back. Can you believe that? What a bastard."

I wasn't sure if Jeanne was understanding everything I was saying. I was speaking to my hands and I was aware of her listening very quietly. At that point I didn't want to risk looking at her, so I ploughed on.

"She - my mother - just sort of stopped coping. She certainly couldn't cope with me anyway, so I went to live with my Aunt and Uncle. I thought at first it was just for a short time, but my mother never really recovered and she died when I was twelve."

I looked up and risked a glance at her. Her eyes had widened and her face was frozen in an expression of amazement.

"Do you understand me?" I asked.

"Yes, yes, of course," she said. "Of course I understand. I had no idea of this. Oh Nigel, I am so sorry." Then she reached out her hand and placed it on mine in such a tender way I felt something give way inside me and my eyes misted up. I coughed in an effort to clear my head.

"So you see sir, I'm an orphan," I said, trying desperately to lighten the mood. Of course it didn't work. She just looked puzzled. "Sorry," I said. "It's a Dickensian thing."

"Dickensian? Qu'est-ce que c'est, Dickensian?" Actually she said it in such a French way - '*Deek-en-jeunne*' - I spluttered out a laugh.

"Why do you laugh?" she said. "You are telling me something painful for you."

Now I could feel my cheeks burning.

"Sorry," I said.

"And all the time you say sorry!"

I was on the verge of apologising again but managed to stop myself in time. We sat in silence for a moment or two. Embarrassed as I was for irritating her, and at my total mishandling of my feelings, I was thankful that at least she had kept hold of my hand. I found myself drifting off into a *David Copperfield*-type fantasy, imagining that I could perhaps wrest more sympathy by playing up the part of the poor lost orphan dominated and abused by his mercenary step-parents. Poor Aunt Doris and Uncle Fred hadn't been like that at all. Eventually she asked about my Dad.

"Do you see your father?"

"No, no," I said. "I have no idea where he is. He never kept in touch, just ... sort of ... vanished. Actually I don't remember much about him at all – he just wasn't there when I was growing up. I'd really like to meet him again though."

"Of course," she said kindly.

"Cos then I could bash the stupid bastard's head in," I said with vehemence.

I don't think she understood the words, but my tone of voice was fairly clear. She looked momentarily shocked, but then smiled.

"Is that *Deek-en-jeunne* too?" she asked.

"Sort of," I said.

It was time to go. The woman at the counter came over to clear away our glasses and said something about being *fermé* whilst pointing at the clock. Although I felt relieved not to have to say anymore, I was also sad to be released from the gentle hold of her hand. Actually I was aware she had been surprisingly easy to talk to. If we'd stayed for much longer I'm sure I would have been willing to tell her anything. I had certainly never talked about my family to anyone like that before. As we got up to go she reached over, squeezed my cheeks in her hands and kissed me on the forehead.

"We will talk more later," she said, "but now we must find somewhere to sleep."

I left wishing I'd told her I was an orphan sooner.

We were in the northern part of the town, near a huge and very ancient cathedral which we walked past on our search for a quiet resting place. I thought again what a pity it was that there wasn't the time to explore these ancient towns and buildings more thoroughly. Aix in particular seemed stunningly beautiful from what I had seen of it and it was clearly steeped in history. Mike would have scorned such rubber-necking inclinations, whereas Jeanne on the other hand was an informative and enthusiastic guide, proud of the history and cultural traditions of her country.

"Not far from here," she said, "is where Cézanne has his house."

"Suzanne?"

"Oui, oui, the famous artist?"

"Oh yes, *that* ... Suzanne, yes."

"Yes, he painted some very famous paintings here. *Les Grandes Baigneuses,* you know? ... *Le Jardinier Vallier?"*

Of course I didn't know – the only painters I knew were the ones that did the outside of our house every three years – but I was still very impressed, as much by Jeanne and her knowledge, as about being near a famous man and his work.

Not long after we came across a little orchard, which was quite secluded from the road, and appeared to offer good shelter. We dossed down near a wall, and as we lay down she gave me a little goodnight kiss. I'd been sort of wondering whether we would curl up together 'Babes in the Wood'- style or something, but in the event we just lay side by side in the quiet of the night. It felt good just to be next to her, and to imagine that we were both lying together in the middle of a Cézanne painting.

It took me a good while to drift off. I lay on my back gazing at the night sky, and thinking further about the memories that Jeanne had brought to the surface in the café. I remember it all vividly – it's fixed in my mind as my last clear memory of my mother, and as the moment my whole world changed.

I had just come home from school. I remember the door being half-open as I walked down the yard, and I remember seeing my mother hunched over the frying pan, spoon in hand, poking absent-mindedly at the contents which were hissing and spitting like a nest of snakes. I can see her turn as I walk in, her face brightening into a smile, and I can feel her warmth as she stoops down and kisses me.

'Alright son?' she asks. 'Had a good day?'

'Yes,' I say.

But I am more concerned about her. For a few weeks now I think I have seen a change in her. She's started to look pale, is always tired, and

151

doesn't talk to me as much as usual. Sometimes when we are watching the TV I notice that she's just staring, and not watching the telly at all. As she smiles at me now I quickly scan her face for clues, or at least some sign of the sparkle I used to see there, but there is none. Then the snakes spit at us angrily so she gets up to give them another poke.

My thoughts make me feel uneasy so I find myself idly scanning the room. Everything else seems normal. Everything in its place. The pots and pans are ranged together on their usual greasy shelf. Mugs droop languidly on the wall. The work-top space supports its usual clutter having been steadily invaded by various containers, trays, tea-pots, and over-spill from the cupboards.

My eyes then fix on my mother's back and I just stand still, watching her. She senses me staring I think, because her head suddenly spins round and, just as quickly, I jerk my head down to look at the floor. She laughs.

'Oh I know what's the matter with you!' she says. 'You're not looking forward to your tea are you? I saw you scowling at the pan. Well don't worry son, I've got a surprise for you tonight ......' Her voice trails away. She goes silent and then drifts again into one of her trances. I see her wipe her brow with the back of her hand.

'Look!' she says. Then she stoops down to open the oven door and, using her pinny as an oven-glove, she slides out a steaming casserole dish which, by its topping of rippled mash potatoes, is instantly recognizable as a Shepherds Pie.

'It's a special treat for you tonight', she says. 'I know its your favourite ...'

I feel my heart leap for a second, but I don't understand.

'It's a special treat tonight', she repeats slowly, 'just for you, my special little boy...'

She closes the oven door and stands up, her back turned towards me. I hear her sniff, see her hurriedly wipe her eyes with her pinny, and then hear her carefully clear her throat. Slowly she turns round and looks down at me, smiling. Then she hunches down so that her eyes and mine are on the same level — except that she isn't looking at me; she is looking down at the floor. She gets hold of both my hands and rubs their backs with her thumbs. Slowly she raises her head and our eyes meet. I can see clearly now that she has been crying.

'I've got something to tell you', she says, 'and I need you to be brave ...'

152

Next morning we got up early and, after a quick *toilette* and *chocolat chaud* in a little back-street café, we were on the road again. Sensibly Jeanne suggested we should try to avoid getting lifts into big towns.

"If you go too far into the town, it is a problem sometimes to get to the … *extérieur*? .. of the town. Of course you cannot get rides from the *Centre-Ville*, so it is mistake to go there."

Yes indeed, that was the mistake Mike and I had happily kept making. So, although the first car that stopped for us was going right to the centre of Avignon, about 50 Km or so from Aix, we got out at a little village called Plan d'Orgon, from where we struck out west towards Nimes. We then by-passed Nimes by changing our course and heading north, before turning west again for Alès. Here we stopped or lunch.

"Are you pleased to be going home?" she asked me.

We had bought some bread, paté and fruit, and had set up a little picnic by the roadside.

"Yeah, in a way. It's all very different from what we planned though. I'm sorry Mike went off by himself, well with Patrick, in the way he did."

This journey felt much more stream-lined, and I felt safe in a different way with Jeanne, but the manner in which Mike and I had scraped along had a sort of edge to it that I missed now it had gone.

"You know Mike for a long time?"

"Yes. Most of my life really. We went to school together. I think we sort of adopted each other. I've always been a bit … sort of shy…?"

She nodded her understanding. Oh, she was so easy to talk to! I ploughed on.

" … and Mike liked to take the lead in things, so I was quite happy to let him. He was always good at things too, especially at playing the guitar, and he was popular with girls – so I followed on from behind. But he was lonely in his family too – like me, but for different reasons. There is just him and a very young sister, so I think he was pleased to have me to boss around. We were a good mix really."

"Yes it seemed like that to me," she said.

I felt sad as I said all this, because the thought hit me that it was unlikely to be like this again – something had changed.

"And you?" she continued.

"Me?"

"Yes. You tell me yesterday that you went to stay with your Aunt and Uncle – after your father left. You were lonely in your family too?"

I thought about that for a bit. I knew that Uncle Fred and Aunt Doris had provided me with huge helpings of love and stability just when I needed them most, but I can't say I ever felt free enough to share my thoughts and worries with them. Both were controlling in their own way, and I mostly just went along with what they said, doing my rebelling in secret. I didn't want to think about it all just then though. It was different in the café, sitting in the half-light, holding her hand. This draughty roadside with the hum of traffic around us didn't quite conjure up the same atmosphere, so I just said, "They were difficult to talk to. They always thought they knew best."

"*Oui, c'est ça*", she said meaningfully. "Like Mike, I think?"

"Yes, I suppose so." I played that thought through my mind for a moment before she surprised me by asking, in that strangely perceptive way she had, "You miss him?"

"In some ways," I said, "but actually it's good he's not here right now. He'd have been, kind of, in the way."

She laughed and gave me a playful thump of mock outrage.

"Ni-gel! Actually," she went on, "I think Mike will miss you too. I think he needed you to guide *him* more than you know."

Now I was starting to feel embarrassed so, partly to distract her I said, "Is it like this with Bobbi and you?"

"I suppose it is really. I came to the South to look after Bobbi, you know?"

I was surprised. "Did you? I thought you came because of Pip."

"Pee-eep!?" she said, in such an astonished and high-pitched way that it made me laugh. "Non, non, *Peep* can look after himself."

"Tim told me that his mother got you the job so you could be with him in Nice."

"Oh Pip's mother is just like him – *dominante*."

"Bossy?"

"Oui, oui, bossy. It suits me to say yes when she tells me about the job, because Bobbi is coming here and I want to be with her."

I wanted to ask her more about why Bobbi had changed her mind about leaving Paris, but I put that to one side. At that moment I was more interested to close the case on Pip. Since his name had come up I wanted to be sure she still thought he was *un connard,* or whatever it was she'd called him.

"So you didn't mind – leaving Pip behind?" I asked hopefully.

154

She smiled at me. "Of course not. It was O.K. at first – he was funny and perhaps a little exciting. But Pip loves only one person – and that is himself. We were friends, that is all, until he turned into a … crazy monster. I hate him for how he was when he came back and found you in the room. And I hate him for what he does to your guitar."

I thanked her as I took a very satisfying bite off the end of my bread. I can honestly say bread and paté had never tasted so good.

In the afternoon we proceeded on up the road, heading in a kind of north-westerly direction according to the map. We didn't make such good progress at first since, although we were avoiding the big towns, we were also on a quiet country road where traffic was thin. We ended up travelling about 100 Km though, via 2 lifts and some extensive walking, before the daylight started to fade. Both lifts were fairly uncomfortable so I was glad when it was time to stop. The first was a tractor ride, echoing an early experience with Mike, and the second was in one of those upside-down prams. Inside it felt like a very basic and thinly-constructed sort of vehicle, and I was disturbed by the long umbrella handle sticking out of the dash which appeared to double as a gear stick. Anyway it did the job and we all bounced along as if we were on springs of elastic. I just hoped we didn't bump into any flies or anything.

When we were dropped off we found ourselves standing at some crossroads in the fading light. It was quiet and eerie. Then, just as we were wondering what our next move should be, a man appeared as if from nowhere. It was another priest. This time I knew immediately as he was dressed in the same way as the one Mike and I had encountered outside Orléans. After he and Jeanne had a brief conversation she explained to me that he was offering us a meal at the vicarage (or wherever it was he lived), and the opportunity to doss down in a hay-barn nearby. I was a little suspicious at first, but he turned out to be everything he said he was and we spent a very pleasant evening indeed in his company. It was like a miracle, a man truly Heaven-sent at just the right moment.

He lived in a little stone-built cottage which had a charm all of its own, and we shared stories about our adventures to date and where we were now going. He and Jeanne seemed to enjoy each other's company too, and I thought I caught her looking at him in an odd wistful sort of way from time to time. She kept calling him 'mon Père' too and, in the light of what she'd told me about her father, I found that particularly poignant. I got the impression that his was a very quiet country parish, and

I wondered perhaps if he didn't get much company. Or perhaps his way of doing his Christian duty was to spend his time lurking behind a bush or something on the off-chance that some weary traveller would stumble by that he could assist.

I have to say though that I was moved by his acts of kindness towards us. Not only did he give us a meal and a place to stay, his whole demeanour was gentle and kindly. He even offered us a lift the following day. He explained that he and a neighbour were due to go to a place called Espalion – which was on our route about 60 Km further west – where they each had some business to do. It was strange how, when I was with Mike we mainly seemed to provoke suspicion if not hostility, whereas with Jeanne we just seemed to attract people who felt compelled to perform some spontaneous act of kindness towards us. It was partly my idealisation of Jeanne I'm sure that I felt this but, even so, for the first time I felt that I should perhaps review my suspicious and cynical stance toward the world.

Something else was about to change too – my relationship with Jeanne during the night in the hay-barn. We didn't have sex or anything, but we certainly moved up a level or two on the intimacy scale. Le Père Albert, as he was called, settled us into the barn and joked about us being like *Marie et Joseph* with there being *'pas de place dans l'hôtellerie!'* It was an interesting association particularly as, given the milk of human kindness that was flowing freely in our direction, I wouldn't have been too surprised if three wise men and the odd shepherd had turned up in the night. On the other hand, if Jeanne had given birth, I would have been very worried – particularly as, like I said, we didn't have sex.

As it was, as we lay together in the dark, I heard a whimpering coming from her direction.

"Are you all right?" I whispered. She made a strangled little noise in reply.

"What's the matter?"

"I'm sorry," she said. "Le Père Albert reminds me so much of my father, that is all." Then she started to sob and I could see the outline of her sleeping bag begin to shake a little. It seemed obvious what I should do, but I felt very hesitant at first. Then I shuffled over to her and put my arm around her. She responded immediately and held on to me tightly. I suddenly felt aroused, then ashamed, but was reassured to think that at least I was still in my sleeping bag so she probably wouldn't notice. I tried to concentrate hard on Jeanne and her tears. After a while she released her grip, and apologised again.

"I'm sorry Nigel. I don't know how this happens. Usually I do not cry so much about my father. I think it is because Le Père Albert is so kind and he is so gentle like my father, that I start to think what it will be like if he was here. I have thought about him many times recently because, do you know, it is this week - 8 years ago only – that he died."

"Oh I'm so sorry, Jeanne. I didn't know."

She set off sobbing again and we held on tightly to each other. Then when her tears had subsided, she lifted up her head and looked at me.

"You are very kind Nigel."

Then she kissed me and I kissed her back, and it was just the most lovely feeling.

"We are a sad pair," she said at last. "But it is through these experiences that we become strong."

She was ahead of me on that one. I didn't feel strong at all. "I wish I could be more independent", I muttered, "stand up for myself more."

"Oh but you do! I think that sometimes you are … how do you say … *determiné* .."

"Determined? Really?"

"Oh yes. I know you are frightened, very easy to frighten. You need *beaucoup de l'assurance. Comprends?*" Only too well. "Well you are brave for Bobbi, yes?" she continued, "when you tried to steal from Mistral?"

"Brave or stupid?"

"Well perhaps both," she laughed, "but you were … how do you say it … *le champion* for Bobbi. You faced danger for her."

I wasn't sure that was entirely true, but it was a sweet thought. In my mind I wasn't much good at facing danger. A real *champion* would have confronted Mistral directly, faced him down, and demanded the return of the photos. I had skulked into his office under cover of darkness. It was always like that – when I rebelled and protested it was in a passive sort of way. Back in Morecambe I was the kind of chap who would take revenge on Aunt Doris by dunking the cat's spoon in her tea when she wasn't looking. The cat's spoon was one of those old and worn-out pieces of cutlery that spend their retirement doing mucky jobs, like spooning the Kit-e-Kat out of its tin. Actually I only did that once – and have regretted it ever since.

"And you have come to France," Jeanne said sleepily. "You are away from home, away from your *securité*. This is good. You are learning to be brave."

"I wish I was brave," I said, "and stronger. I've never really felt that I could ... never mind ... let's go to sleep."

"No, tell me," she said, and she snuggled her head deeper into my chest.

I loved talking to her like this. She made everything feel so ... safe. I stared up at the barn roof and the grainy blackness of the night. A little skylight was letting in misty shafts of moonlight. I thought I could hear the distant hoot of an owl and everything just felt so peaceful. So I told her.

"Well after my Dad left, my mother dissolved into a sadness that I couldn't get her out of. No matter what I did, nothing seemed to help. I know I was only a kid but I just felt so useless and helpless, and ... scared. I even went to the Police Station once, to see if they could help me find him ..."

She murmured something and I felt her squirm slightly.

"I know, I know. Daft thing to do. Some old sergeant chap listened to my story, then he took me home and talked to my mother for ages. When he left he said – I'll never forget – he said, *'I'm sorry son – it looks like you're the man of the house now. You look after your Mam now, and be strong. He'll come back one day I'm sure'*. But he didn't. And Mam got worse – sitting about, crying, not sleeping, doctors coming and going. Then this one day I came home from school and ... and she told me she'd arranged for me to stay with my Aunt and Uncle for a while.

But then, the next day, I came home and saw a coat, just like the one my Dad used to wear, hanging on the banister. And I could hear voices in the sitting room. It sounded like Mam was talking to someone. I could hardly believe it! I was so excited, thinking all my wishes had come true and everything was going to be all right. I burst into the room ... except it wasn't my Dad. It was my Uncle Fred and my Aunt Doris, come to fetch me.

After that, I never lived with my Mam again. I think that was probably when I finally decided that, since I clearly couldn't control anything, it was best not to even try. So I let others take the lead – and that's what I do now, all the time. I came to France really because Mike said I should, that's all."

I wasn't sure what sort of a response this true confession would prompt so I stopped speaking and waited for her to say something. All I could hear was her breathing, and I realised that she had fallen asleep. I smiled to myself and closed my eyes. Whatever had happened in the past, right now there was no-one else I needed and nowhere else in the world I wanted to be.

When we awoke next morning we were still curled up together, my arms around her, and her head snuggled into my chest.

13

She raised her head slightly, looked up at me and smiled.

"Bonjour."

"And bonjour to you too," I said.

She sat up and bent forward, resting her arms on her knees as if giving herself time to adjust to the day.

"Oh Nigel," she said at last. "I am sorry I get so sad. It is silly."

"I don't think it's silly," I said.

"I'm sad for so many things," she said. "I am sad for my father, I'm sad for Bobbi, and I am sad for me …." then she turned slightly and looked at me "…and I am sad for you."

"For me? Why would you be sad for me?"

"I like you Nigel. I like you a lot. But I think I might cause you pain."

"I don't mind," I said. "You can even fall in love with me if you want." I flushed up at my boldness. Did I really say that? She just smiled and looked away again. She didn't look as if she was going to speak again, so I continued, "I really like you Jeanne. I like you a lot."

"I know," she sighed. "I like you too. But we are in two different countries. You have to go back to England and I have to stay in France. We cannot let something happen between us that will just cause us pain."

"It could work," I said, possibly somewhat eagerly. I was also thrilled to hear her talking like this – to think that she actually thought something *could* happen between us.

"No, I don't think so. I think because my father died when I was young, I have learned to be a strong person. I am … what do you say … *indepéndente*. There are many things I want to do. Last night you see my … my … *vulnerabilité*, and I am glad you were with me. But it is over now." Then, as if to offer me a consolation prize she added, "We can be good friends though, eh?"

"Of course" I said, "I hope we will always be good friends."

It hadn't occurred to me before, but I suddenly saw that she was a lot like Mike. This is exactly what he does I thought – he pretends he doesn't need anyone and puts on a big show of strength and independence, when all the time he's … well, basically hurting underneath.

160

Unlike Mike however, I was impressed that she could at least find some way to acknowledge her pain. He'd have poked me in the eye by now.

As if it was all sorted, she got up and started to busy herself with packing up. Fair enough, but we *had* got closer and I hadn't given up by any means. Besides, like the Bogart *'We'll always have Paris'* line in *Casablanca,* I eventually wanted to be able to say something similar to her, but more than *'We'll always that night in the hay barn somewhere on the way to Brive'.* It didn't have the same romantic kick to it somehow.

Le Père Albert arrived soon after, a passenger in another of those flimsy cars. This one belonged to his neighbour, our driver, a slightly older man with a warm, weather-beaten face and a hearty laugh. They had also brought with them some croissants and a flask of coffee, and again I felt very touched by their kindness. The journey to Espalion was a pleasant one – it was still quite early and the strength of the morning sun was such that it gave a sharp focus to the fields and houses we passed by. Le Père Albert did most of the talking, chatting mostly I think about the countryside we were passing through. We said a fond farewell to them both at Espalion, and then had a brief rest before heading out of town in search of our next lift.

"Why is it important to you to visit your Aunt in Brive?" I asked.

Up to now I'd been very happy to go wherever Jeanne led without much question, but given our earlier conversation I thought it was about time I made more effort to take charge of things.

"Oh my Aunt Sylvie, she is a lovely lady. You will like her, and she will like you! She has had a very hard time in her life. When she was young she had a baby who died, and then her husband leaves her because of this. When my father died she came to stay with us, and she is very kind to Bobbi and me. Then she meets a man, my dear Uncle Gustav, who brings her to Brive to live. She has been there about 5 years now. It is a long way from Paris, and many times she asks for me and Bobbi to go and live with her, but of course we cannot. So this time I promise that I will visit her on my return from La Cote d'Azur."

"How long did you intend to stay in the south then – you and Bobbi?"

I realised I hadn't followed up the hint she'd dropped in our conversation at the Alès picnic that she'd actually gone to Nice for Bobbi's sake rather than for Peep's, so I added, " Did you go there for a special reason?"

She looked down and fiddled with the bread she was eating, and I worried that I'd been too pushy, although it also seemed an innocent enough enquiry.

"It is a long story," she said in a thoughtful sort of way. Then, as she often did when she wanted to distract me, she became more bustly and animated and got up to go saying, "Come on, I tell you all about it soon. We are not far from Brive now. Show me the map."

It certainly seemed a do-able journey, and with a bit of luck we would get there before nightfall. We were about 150 Km away, with a town called Aurillac at roughly the halfway stage. It wasn't long before we had thumbed down our first lift – a lorry that was going about 25 Km in the right direction. After he'd dropped us off we then had about a 30 minute wait before we got into a van with a young chap on his way to Aurillac itself. I assumed he was an electrician, or maybe a TV repair man, from the gear he had in the back where I sat amongst the wires, screws and general debris whilst Jeanne sat and entertained him in the front. The road was undulating and twisty, and I felt quite ill by the time I got out. Still, it was now only 4 o'clock and we were well in striking distance of our goal.

We finally arrived in Brive another three lifts and about 4 to 5 hours later. Again the roads were steep and, in places, not very wide – the last leg of our journey being about 40 Km of narrow country road in fact. The lifts we got were pleasant enough though, with the exception of one where we were trapped for about 45 minutes with a rather rotund chain-smoking dog owner who not only filled up his car with the pungent heady stench of Gauloises, but installed me on the back seat where I spent the whole journey being stared at by a sad, miserable-looking cocker spaniel. Given the smoky atmosphere it had to exist in, I imagined it had long since lost the will to be unfriendly to strangers.

Jeanne had called ahead from Aurillac to give Sylvie and Gustav some prior warning of our arrival, although of course we didn't know exactly when we would land. They were looking out of their window for us when we walked down the street, and in no time we were being warmly greeted by a cheery and welcoming middle-aged couple. Gustav shook me firmly by the hand whilst Jeanne and her Aunt collapsed in floods of tears as they fell into each other's arms. Gustav and I looked on helplessly. I saw him shaking his head as if, like me, he was bemused by the uncontained way woman dealt with their feelings.

162

Once we got inside the house Jeanne and her Aunt huddled together and talked in hushed tones. It was obviously about something serious and difficult, and more than once I saw Jeanne's hand fly to her mouth as she took a sharp intake of breath. Gustav did his best to distract me although his English wasn't too good, and when we got past my opinion of France being a 'très belle' country, we found it difficult to find common ground. Eventually Sylvie and Jeanne disappeared off into the kitchen whilst I sat awkwardly with Gustav.

"What is the matter?" I asked him.

He looked blankly at me.

"Qu'est-ce qui s'est passé? Est-ce que ... un problème?"

"Ah oui," he said, but then he just shrugged and smiled, shaking his head as if to say it was classified information he had not been given permission to disclose. I looked anxiously towards the kitchen. Eventually Sylvie emerged, her eyes looking red and swollen.

"Je suis désolée," she said. "It is ... euh, un problème de famille. To-night, sleep ... tomorrow ... Jeanne, she explain you."

"Is she alright?" I asked. "Has something happened? Where is she?"

"She sleep. Elle est très fatiguée. Toi aussi, n'est-ce pas? Tomorrow... Jeanne, she explain you."

I lay in bed staring at the ceiling, feeling very unsettled. What on earth could it be? It seemed certain it was something to do with her mother and, given the dramatic way it was all being handled, I felt she either had to be seriously ill or, heaven forbid, was already dead. But I also found myself feeling annoyed that I was being excluded from it all – I was Jeanne's close friend, surely if she was upset I ought to be sharing it with her. And then there was this half-story I'd been given about her and Bobbi's trip to the south. Why did she have to make such a mystery out of everything?

It was no good, I couldn't sleep, so I got up and switched on the light to see if there was some book or something I could thumb through to take my mind off it all. The room was a small box-room at the top of the house and, besides the bed, the only other furniture was a small dressing table and a bookcase, which was stuffed with books. When I examined them I found they were all either novels or reference books, in French of course, and not a lot with pictures. So I gave up on that. In fact there wasn't much of interest in the room at all.

Then I noticed two framed pictures on the dressing table, so I picked them up to have a look. One was clearly of Sylvie and Gustav, sitting on an armchair and smiling out at me, and the other was of two little girls building a sand castle on a beach. I was fairly certain one of the little girls was Jeanne, and the other looked oddly like Bobbi. Not so surprising I thought. They had clearly known each other a long time. But, seeing them together like that fired up once more my sense of irritation that I was now being excluded from something important. I considered going to seek Jeanne out for myself and to offer her some comfort, but at the same time I knew that was a bad idea, so I lay down again. Eventually, with an image of Jeanne and me playing on a beach taking shape in my head, I went to sleep.

I was awoken by a gentle tapping on the door.

"Nigel?" The door creaked open and Jeanne's face appeared from behind it.

"Are you … awaked? *Ne dormez-pas?*" I sat up immediately.

"Yes, yes" I said anxiously. "Are you alright?"

She slowly edged her way in carrying an enormous cup which, from the way she was carefully cradling it, was clearly full of something hot. "Yes I am fine now. Here I bring you this – *le chocolat chaud* – to warm you, and to say sorry."

"Oh that's alright Jeanne. I was just very worried about you. What on earth has happened? What is all this mystery?"

"Exactly," she said. "That's what I've come to tell you." As she sat down on the edge of the bed she picked up the picture of the two little girls. "You see this?"

I nodded.

"You know it is a picture of Bobbi and me?"

"Yes, I guessed."

"So you know we are … les *cousines?*"

No, I didn't know, and my face must have registered my surprise as she continued, "Yes, yes. My father and Bobbi's father are brothers."

"Why didn't you say?"

"It did not seem important … two friends, two *cousines* … it is the same thing."

Well, not entirely I thought, but why all the secrecy? Still, there were more important things for her to be telling me. Like what had caused her to be so upset and to disappear so quickly the previous night. What had happened? But before I could ask anything, she said,

"When we arrive last night, my Aunt Sylvie tells me that Bobbi's father, that is my Uncle Georges, has ... gone to see my mother ... to find where Bobbi is gone. But Maman and Uncle Georges, they do not like each other I think, they are angry with each other for many years. And so, when he goes to see her, they fight."

I must have looked puzzled because she went on, "Yes, I know, it is strange. I do not know everything about it, but I can tell you what I know.

"When his wife died, Georges came to my house often with Bobbi. It is a comfort for them, and we have nice times together. Then my father died, and everything is changed. Aunt Sylvie – she is the sister of my mother – she comes to stay with us to comfort my mother and me, but then when Georges comes with Bobbi, he is angry all the time. He is shouting, he is in a bad temper, and he is all the time drinking. Maman and Aunt Sylvie are frightened for Bobbi and they want to take her away from him. Of course that is when he does not come to see us anymore."

She was starting to look doleful as she recalled all this, and she paused as if other memories were flicking across her mind. I suspected she might also be distracting herself from the matter in hand.

"So what happened Jeanne ... last night?"

"Oh yes, sorry," she said, and she shifted her position as if bringing herself back into the present.

"Last night my Aunt Sylvie tells me about the fight between Maman and Georges. Maman does not tell him where is Bobbi. She does not even open the door to him. So he shouts and he bang, bang, bang on the door. Then he throws a bottle through the window, and my mother has to call for the Police to come."

"Was she hurt?"

"No she was not hurt but of course she was very frightened. But there is more. My Aunt Sylvie tells me that, afterwards, my mother is sad for what she has done, so she goes to see Georges to say sorry. She has to say sorry to *him*! Isn't that strange? And she tells him that we have gone to la Côte d'Azur, where we hope to find work. He is upset of course. And then I don't know what happens, but they have a long talk together or something, and now ... now he has come to stay with her! She has let him come into the house! Foolish woman! Now he drinks of course, and she is frightened of him again.

"So, you see, I have to go to Paris quickly now. I am going to go on the train today. I must be with her. And you – you can stay here for a few days if you want. You do not have to come with me."

"Don't be silly Jeanne. Of course I will come with you. Perhaps I can help ..."

"No, it is not necessary. It is our problem ... *en famille*. It may be trouble for you."

"Not at all," I said, feeling a little hurt. "I want to be with you, and I want to help if I can."

She brushed her hand across her forehead and sighed, as if resigning herself to her fate. "O.K. If it is what you want," she said. "I will go and find the time of the train, and then we go." She got up to go but then stopped. She turned to look at me and, with an affectionate smile, bent down and gave me a kiss on the forehead. I reached out and pulled her towards me to give her a hug. I thought I sensed a slight resistance at first but then thankfully she melted and clung on tightly. I thought I could feel the hint of her warm tears on my shoulder.

I lay back in the bed and mulled it all over. I admired her spirit, and her wish to rush to her mother's aid and to rid the house of an unwanted invader. Again it had a certain *Maid of Orleans* feel about it, which was nice. But is that what her mother wanted? What on earth had persuaded her to go and seek out a drunken bully, and then invite him in? Did she feel she owed him something? I began to wonder if our intrusion may not be welcome. Then it occurred to me that it all had an echo of Jeanne and Pip about it – what had possessed *her* to link herself to a loser with a bad temper?

I was sad to leave Aunt Sylvie and Uncle Gustav who, although I hadn't been able to spend much time with them, had struck me as warm and generous people. It was clear they wanted us to stay much longer too, Sylvie especially. As we prepared to go, she and Jeanne continued to have long conversations together in fact, so Gustav took me out to show off all the things he was growing in his garden. It was a situation that leant itself to gesturing and miming, and as long as I smiled and looked impressed at the things he showed me, we got by. The worst moment came when he pointed at something and let out a sort of exclamation of surprise. I thought he was particularly pleased at the progress of a clump of flowers so I clapped and smiled enthusiastically. He gave me a withering look and disappeared into his shed and, still eyeing me suspiciously, scooped up a dog-turd from the soil. I tried to apologise and to explain that I really did know the difference between a daisy and a dog-turd, but I suspect he wasn't convinced.

It wasn't long before we were on the train – a 5 hour trip was ahead of us, straight through to Paris. It was lovely to think I would have Jeanne to myself for all that time.

"Are you very worried about your mother?" I asked.

"Of course. Why does she do this? Everybody knows Georges is a selfish, angry man, and she invites him to stay in the house … I don't understand."

Who knows the secrets of a woman's heart I wondered, as I again thought about her and Pip. Perhaps if I was shirty a bit more often she'd fall for me too. Was this where I was going wrong?

"You are very sweet to come with me Nigel."

Well that was alright then – sweet was in the lead over shirty, at least for the moment. I felt myself blushing a little, so to change the subject I asked her to tell me more about herself and Bobbi.

"I didn't know you were cousins," I said, "you must be very close."

"Yes we are, although Bobbi goes her own way now. Actually, when we were younger Bobbi was always impulsive, *impétueuse* … she like to … how do you say, have risks? I always try to look out for her, so that she is not in danger."

That fitted of course. I recalled Bobbi saying how she would hide her father's shoes and then watch him rant and rage in frustration. And the whole business with Aimée and Antoine seemed to indicate that her talent for getting into risky situations hadn't waned too much. It also had an echo of me and Mike.

"It is a pity you weren't there to stop her getting involved with those photographers in St Tropez," I said.

"Ah," she exclaimed. "Perhaps I should tell you about that too."

I wondered what she meant, and then I listened with some amazement as she talked. She told me that Bobbi's 'chance' meeting with Aimée and Antoine in the streets of St Tropez had, by no means, been their first meeting. Antoine was in fact an old school-friend of her father's. He had made something of a name for himself as a glamour photographer, with studios in both Paris and Nice, mostly in the wake of the mini-revolution in attitudes to nudity initiated by Roger Vadim and Brigitte

Bardot. When in Paris he had been a frequent, if not entirely welcome visitor to the house and had watched Jeanne and Bobbi grow into attractive young girls. His jokes however, about one day recruiting them as models, had apparently not gone down well in the family – except with Georges, Bobbi's father.

Recently they had again tried to entice both Bobbi and Jeanne to the Cote d'Azur, promising them steady modelling work and help to get settled there. This time, according to Jeanne, Bobbi had been very keen to go. I suppose it wasn't that difficult to see why. She had been flattered to be asked, was very unhappy in Paris at the time, and was being offered the chance of an easier, more comfortable life in the sun. Even so, it was odd to think that she had been keen to accept this offer after turning down the one from Marcel. Perhaps this one offered the chance of more excitement or something.

Anyway, Jeanne had tried very hard to talk her out of it, but Bobbi had remained keen. The row with her father and her subsequent flight to Jeanne's house had finally forced the issue. They had already met Pip, Tim and Simon, so Jeanne had thought that if she went along with Pip, as his mother had arranged, she would be able to keep an eye on Bobbi. Then if the whole thing with Aimée and Antoine went awry, she would at least be there to support her and help her get out of it.

"Wow, you really do care about her don't you?" I said.

"Of course. Isn't it the same with you and Mike?"

I was quite taken aback at first as a surge of anxiety for Mike shot through me. Perhaps I should have tried harder to persuade him to stay with me. I tried to brush it off.

"I don't think so," I said. "We were just travelling together."

She laughed. "Of course not. I told you before, Mike relied on you a lot. He needed you to guide him more than you think. And I know you were very worried for him when he went off with Patrick."

Well, that was true certainly, but was that for his benefit or mine? Anyway she seemed to be far too much on 'girly' ground for my liking so I urged her to go on with her story.

Things had changed on the way down to the South. They'd had lots of opportunities to talk of course, and Jeanne had worked hard to convince Bobbi that, given her vulnerability, glamour modelling was not really the way to go. As for Bobbi, being away from Paris seemed to have a therapeutic effect on her generally so, to Jeanne's relief, she had finally gone cold on the idea herself. It was also nice to hear at this point that

168

Mike and I had been slightly influential in her decision – when we had turned up again in St Tropez after their brief meeting with us at Orléans, Bobbi had decided that tagging along with us might be a better option for her. That's really why she had stayed in St Tropez, and Jeanne had been able to go on to Nice without her. Although we didn't know it at the time, and God knows what Mike would have said if he had known, Bobbi was effectively being left in our care.

All had then proceeded smoothly until this chance meeting with Aimée and Antoine. The story was that they had just been driving through St Tropez after a day spent location spotting when they 'happened' to see Bobbi. They were happily renewing their contact with her when Mike and I had shambled up – a rather unwelcome complication as far as they were concerned. So they'd taken Bobbi off to talk to her in peace, and Aimée had returned to deal with us. The whole story of them owning a café where they wanted us to play was of course a complete fabrication - merely a means of distracting us. None of that came as much of a surprise, but my jaw dropped at the next bit when she went on to explain that Aimée and Antoine had actually paid for the Hotel for us in advance – it was simply being used as a convenient dumping-off place for us whilst they spirited Bobbi off to Nice.

"They paid for the Hotel?"

"Oh yes. Bobbi insisted. They have plenty of money and of course they are good friends with Bobbi and her father. But in any case, they did not want to make a situation bad for you so that you would involve the Police. The plan was that Bobbi would telephone you and explain that she was going to Nice, and that everything was all right. They thought you would be happy to have a free night in the Hotel and would not cause a fuss."

Of course everything had not been all right. Bobbi had changed her mind and would not agree to be a model for them. She did not want to just abandon Mike and me either. Eventually, after much debate, she had agreed to operate as a courier and salesperson for them – they persuaded her that she owed them something – and this is of course where Mistral had come in. Aimée and Antoine worked through him as their printer, and one of the 'outlets' for their work was the cruise lines that regularly called in at Villefranche, just up the coast from Nice. Jeanne didn't know how it all worked, but somehow or other Bobbi's job was to act as a go-between for Mistral and the crew of the cruise ships, popular customers of his apparently. As far as Jeanne could tell it was all a legitimate operation.

As Jeanne told her tale, several things started to slot into place in my mind and make a bit more sense – why no-one had been bothered about us fleeing the hotel, why Bobbi had been so keen to go to Nice, my 'sighting' of Aimée at Mistral's, and Bobbi's strange appearance there in the middle of the night. I wondered then if perhaps there never were any pictures of Bobbi to be liberated, and that presumably my escapade at Mistral's had been in vain.

"So has Bobbi ever been a model for Aimée and Antoine?"

"No never, only a courier."

"But she seemed very upset when she came back to us at the Hotel. She kept saying that she felt very ashamed."

"I think she wants to convince you that she really had agreed to posing for the photographs. But in any case, she is really sad because she had been tempted to leave you, and ashamed that you and Mike had been so kind to her, and she was going to betray you."

"But she didn't. She came back."

"I know. And I love her for that."

"Yes I do too", I said spontaneously and I felt grateful that I now knew more about all the things I'd been involved with over the past few weeks. But there was still one burning question.

"Why all the secrecy Jeanne? Why did you not tell Mike and me all this before?"

"I promised Bobbi I would not tell you. She felt as if she had made use of you only, and she was upset that she had made danger for you. Then when you tried to break into Mistral's ..." I could see the smile playing on her lips.

"But I wouldn't have done that if she'd been straight with us from the start."

"Straight? What do you mean?"

"If she had told us the truth. Then I would not have gone to steal photos from Mistral."

"Ah but that made it worse. It made it harder for her to tell you the truth. And then Pip broke your guitar, and that was all because of me. So both of us felt very bad that we had spoiled your time in France."

"No, no you haven't done that," I said. "You have made my time in France wonderful actually. I ..."

"Shush, shush," she said. "I have told you that ..."

I think I knew what she was going to say so I just broke in and thanked her for telling me all that she had.

"O.K." she said, "but I am sorry I do not tell you sooner."

Yes, I wondered about that too, but as I thought about it, I came to understand it as a way Jeanne and Bobbi had of functioning. They certainly liked their dramas, as well as their secrets, which they used to cultivate an air of mystery around themselves. Perhaps it was to do with the atmosphere they had grown up in. Anyway, if I was honest, it was another of the things that appealed to me about Jeanne – never quite knowing where I stood.

14

We arrived at about 5 in the afternoon at the busy Gare d'Austerlitz, Paris. After the relative calm of the French countryside the bustle and noise of the city hit me like a rainstorm as I got off the train. We then had to fight our way to the Metro so we could transfer over to 'chez Jeanne' at Montparnasse. It was a quick and efficient journey though, and we were walking down her street within the hour.

My heart was pounding as we got near the house, not knowing what sort of welcome we were going to get. I didn't fancy meeting Uncle Georges at all – would he be sober, would he be ready and waiting for us with another bottle to throw, would Jeanne's mother be alright or would she be cowering in the attic whilst Uncle Georges rampaged through the house like a rabid tiger?

Although Jeanne had a key I suggested she should ring the bell, so that Georges and her mother would at least have some time to adjust to our arrival.

"This is my home!" Jeanne said indignantly. "I do not need to be invited in!" and she seemed to make a point then of creating as much noise as she could as she pushed the door open and shouted, "Maman! Maman! C'est moi!" Her shout echoed through the house then faded into the silence. There was no reply.

"Perhaps they are …." I started to say but Jeanne shushed me and, cocking her head on one side she looked up the dark stairs. Then she looked at me as we registered the muffled sounds of someone moving about. A picture flashed across my mind of a murderer desperately trying to conceal the body of his victim. Jeanne had her foot on the first stair as I tried again to plead for caution.

"Jeanne, I …."

But before I could finish a door in the hall-way opened revealing a shadowy form standing in the half-light. I was desperately trying to remember how to move my legs when Jeanne let out a scream, ran towards the figure, and embraced it.

"Maman!" she cried, and amongst other words of affection and welcome the two of them burst into tears. It was like the meeting of Jeanne and Aunt Sylvie all over again, only this time with the added bit of

Hitchcock-ian suspense. I leant against the banister for a moment and tried to calm my beating heart.

Jeanne's mother was very clearly the woman from the photograph – tall and attractive, but now beginning to show signs of age with her dark hair pulled into a bun at the back, and a face that was drawn and care-worn. Even so, it was the sort of natural pretty face which stays attractive even when age and time take it over. I reached out my hand to greet her but she just took hold of my shoulders and kissed me firmly on both cheeks, and then thanked me for bringing Jeanne home.

When we were seated in the lounge they fell into an intense conversation which mainly seemed to consist of Jeanne asking lots of questions and her mother answering them. The odd thing was the contrast between Jeanne's earnest, almost pleading tone, and the calm and controlled tone of her mother's replies. She didn't seem to be communicating fright or upset at all. This wasn't what I had expected. I also gathered from the nods in the direction of the stairs, and the mention of Georges' name, that the mystery noises were actually being made by him. Jeanne was gradually becoming more upset as the conversation continued and when she started to say things like, "tu es folle!" and "ah non, non, non, alors!" I sensed that some disagreement was creeping in.

Then there was the sound of footsteps on the stairs and Georges himself appeared. At least I assumed it was him. Standing in the doorway was a thin, wiry-looking man with rat-like features. I just had time to make out an anxious, worried look on his face as I saw Jeanne push past him and run out of the house in tears.

"Qu'est-ce qu'il y a?" said Georges as Jeanne's mother covered her face with her hands and flopped down on to the settee. He immediately rushed over to her to comfort her, and she buried her face in his chest. Since I had come to help, I felt sure my duty was to chase after Jeanne but, also feeling a pressure to make a polite exit, I first put my hand awkwardly on her mother's shoulder and told her not to worry, then grabbed Georges' hand to shake it, whilst saying, "Je m'appelle Nigel - ami de Jeanne. Excusez-moi." Thank goodness us English remember our manners in times of crisis.

I found Jeanne leaning up against a wall in an alley way about 2 or 3 houses further along. She was sobbing enthusiastically. When she saw me she just fell against me and clung on tightly. It took a while for her tears to subside, then we just set off walking towards the lights of a café, my arm locked firmly round her shoulders. Once we had got settled in the café, and she had composed herself, we were able to talk.

"Why do you get so upset?" I asked her.

"Oh Nigel, she says she loves him." I still couldn't really understand why this was such a painful thought, but since I didn't know what to say, I just waited for more.

"How *can* she love him? He is a ... a... *brute?*"

"A brute? You mean he hits her?"

"Mais oui!" she said quickly, but then her voice softened. "Perhaps he does not. She says he does not do this. But it is possible! He drinks too much, and he is cruel."

"In what way – cruel?"

"He shouts. He has very bad temper." She looked at me and said sharply, "You do not believe me?"

"I don't know Jeanne," I said. "I don't know. I am confused, that's all. When you were talking to your mother, she seemed very calm. When Georges came in, she didn't look frightened like I expected. In fact, after you'd gone, they kind of ... fell into each other's arms. I wonder what it is that makes your mother say that she loves him."

"That is the problem. It makes no sense."

"Tell me what she said to you." She went quiet for a moment or two, as if gathering her thoughts.

"She tells me that he has changed. He is not an angry man any longer. Since Bobbi left he has been to see her often and she says she *likes to talk to him!* He has bought for her presents, they go to a restaurant, she says he has made her laugh again. She calls him a good friend. A good friend! I hate him! It is so stupid," and she started to wind herself up again as she went on, "My Aunt Sylvie says he is a bad man, he drinks, and he is cruel. How can Maman say that she loves him?"

"She says she *loves* him?"

I had no answer. In fact all I had was a head full of questions. In particular, how did her mother's relationship with Georges fit with what Jeanne had heard from Aunt Sylvie? I tried to make some sense of what she was saying.

"Perhaps she has felt very lonely since you and Bobbi left, and he is good company for her? He must be lonely too; perhaps they help each other in the same way." It was a fairly simple analysis, but seemed reasonable.

Jeanne looked at me and said, "That is what my mother says, that she is not so lonely when he is there. He first came looking for Bobbi because he was unhappy that she had left and he did not like to be at home on his own."

"When he first came looking … was that when he flung the bottle at the window?"

"Oh, my mother says this does not happen. When I ask her about this, she does not know what I mean. I say Aunt Sylvie tells me about this, and she says Aunt Sylvie is lying."

"Why would she do that?"

She looked thoughtful, and then said, "I don't know. But I know Sylvie does not like Georges. When she came to stay - you know, after my father died - they were all the time arguing, especially Georges and Sylvie. I do not know why. I know that Sylvie wanted Bobbi to come and live with us, and he would never allow it. She called me and Bobbi 'her girls' and he hated that."

This was interesting. I don't know why, but it then occurred to me to ask whether Sylvie ever had any children herself.

"No, I told you, there was some problem, I don't know, but her baby died. Then her husband goes away, so she came to live with us. She spent a lot of time with Bobbi and me, and I remember Georges did not like that ……"

"Perhaps she cannot bear the thought of your mother and him getting together because it takes you and Bobbi away from her. Do you think it is possible that she has been trying to turn you against him by telling you bad things about him?"

"But why would she do that? This is all when we are children. It cannot matter so much to her now we are all grown up. What does it matter to her if Georges and Maman are together …."

She trailed off, looked thoughtful, and then continued, "Actually, Maman told me just now, that Sylvie is jealous of her."

We sat in silence for a few minutes, and I tried to puzzle it all out. I don't know who had the answers, but it wasn't me.

"You need to talk more to your mother, I said at last.

Jeanne was lost in her own thoughts and I'm not sure she heard me. "It is true," she mused. "I only know about Georges what Sylvie tells me. I have not seen him much these past few years, not since Sylvie came to live with us. I know he drinks a lot and he has a bad temper. That is what Bobbi says too."

175

I dimly recalled the things Simon had told Mike and me back in St Tropez, about how Bobbi's stories of her father's 'rages' might be a little embellished.

"But Bobbi isn't frightened of him, is she?" I said. "And he has never hit her?"

"No, he does not hit her. Actually, when we were going to the south, she says that she misses him. I could not understand why she said this."

"So how likely is it do you think, that he would throw a bottle at a window?"

"I don't know."

"Well, shouldn't you give him a chance at least, to put his side of things ….?"

"What do you mean?"

"Well, you've just run out of the house because you think he is a cruel and violent man who is going to make your mother's life miserable. But you don't know him. Neither do I. All I've seen is the loving embrace he gave your mother. You only really know the man Sylvie has told you about. I think you should talk to him – and make up your own mind."

She looked at me with her tearful, brown eyes and I suddenly became aware of a strange sensation. My heart beat faster and I felt light-headed and vaguely dizzy. My mouth went dry. She gave me a long, lingering look, and smiled. "I told you that you looked after Mike well. Now you look after me. Thank you Nigel." And she leaned over and kissed me. Then she blew softly into my ear and my skin started to prickle. And then we kissed again, properly kissed, and I felt myself evaporating somehow and being carried away on the wind.

We walked slowly back to the house, my arm round her shoulders. This time we rang the bell. Georges answered the door and immediately stepped aside to let us in, expressing obvious delight at our return. Jeanne's mother also quickly appeared. She looked anxiously over to Jeanne who went over and embraced her. They exchanged some clear words of apology and we all sat down. The atmosphere was tense and heavy, a bit like four Heads of State all sitting down to decide the fate of Europe. I felt decidedly spare, however, and wasn't sure what my role should be.

As it happened all I had to do was hold Jeanne's hand and listen while everybody else talked. As usual most of my understanding of what was going on was determined by the non-verbals – the body language in particular, and the tone of voice they used to express themselves. In this respect Jeanne showed the most varied mixture, the ingredients mainly consisting of anxiety and passionate angry tears - and a lot of the initial action took place between Jeanne and her mother. Bobbi's name cropped up quite a lot too, although Maman pronounced it 'Bay-bay' for some strange reason.

As they talked I watched Georges taking it all in. I thought my first impression of his physical appearance as rat-like was accurate enough, given his sharp facial features and his twitchy, jerky way of moving, so I kept on the look-out for ways this might be reflected in his personality. Was he something of a scavenger, a predator, or ready to desert at the first sign of trouble? But so far as I could see he was none of these things. He was a bit inclined to jump in and interrupt, but he always drew back graciously if checked by Jeanne's mother.

I did notice that he bristled whenever Sylvie's name was mentioned. Then, when he was given the opportunity to put his side he spoke in a moderated tone, head bent at times as if he was ashamed, and at least on one occasion struggling against tears. There was a tender sort of vulnerability about him which I found strangely endearing, and I noticed Jeanne listened to him avidly whenever he spoke.

The evening eventually drew to a close with mutual hugs and apologies, whilst I looked on smiling stupidly. "I am very sorry for all this Nigel," Jeanne said to me tenderly. "I am very glad you come with me. Tomorrow we will talk. O.K?" When I left them to pad off up to bed Jeanne was curled up on her mother's lap being comforted like a frightened child. Georges was laid back in his armchair looking on, and smiling.

"So what do you think?" I asked Jeanne next day when we at last got a moment to ourselves.

"I think you are right Nigel."

"I am right?"

"Yes. You said perhaps they are both lonely and that they rescue each other."

"I said that?"

"Mais oui. You are clever Nigel."

"Clever?"

"Why do you repeat all time what I say?" and she leaned over and kissed me. "I think you are clever, and I think I am very glad I meet you."

I felt my heart skip its usual beat. Could this be a sign that she now wanted to be with me as much as I wanted to be with her? I was her clever problem-solver – except I hadn't a clue what problem I'd actually solved. I had picked up odds and ends, but a lot of the pieces were still missing.

"Oh I think it is complicated," she said. "But the important thing I learn is that, when Sylvie first came to stay with us .... I don't know how to say this in English ... *elle en a pincée pour lui* ... she like him very much, she wanted to be with Georges ..."

"She fancied him? You mean ... like me and you?"

"Yes perhaps," she laughed. "But he does not 'fancied' her, and he is not kind when he says no. But she torments him I think, she is persistent, and he keeps saying no. Maman says Sylvie was very hurt. She loved him, and she loved Bobbi. She can be complete again – you know? – if only she can marry him! But he says no, no, no. She was very upset for a long time about this, saying that Georges is a very cruel man. There was also a difficulty between them because of Georges' friend Antoine."

"Antoine the photographer?"

"Oui. Sylvie does not like him and his photos of the young girls. Especially, she does not like him to be with Bobbi. Because instead of 'Bobbi' he would say to her 'come here my little Bé Bé' – you know? like in Brigitte Bardot? Sylvie would say 'non, non, Bob-beee, Bob-beee, PAS BÉ-BÉ, PAS BÉ-BÉ,' and Antoine and Georges would laugh and laugh. It's strange, all this happened but I never really noticed when I was a child."

"You were probably too occupied playing with Bobbi."

"Like the time before my father died, you mean? I was too busy to spend time with him ..."

"No Jeanne. I'm sorry. I didn't mean ..."

"It's O.K." she said. "I know. But anyway, I think I understand now why it is so hard for Sylvie to see Georges and Maman together now."

It started to make sense – except the bit about Georges' ability to get women to fancy him. I couldn't really see how that worked.

"So Sylvie was lying about him drinking and throwing the bottle?"

"Oh he has always drunk too much. But I think it is not as bad as she says. And no, he does not throw the bottle. But I do not blame Sylvie.

She has had a sad life." Although she smiled, her look was a sorrowful one. "We are a sad family. We all have problems because of what happens to us. Bobbi's mother is dead first of all, then my father, and then of course Sylvie's baby. Everyone is sad and frightened for themselves. And I think, instead of finding comfort in one another, when we all come together there are battles and conflicts. Georges is scared he will lose Bobbi, my mother is frightened for me, Sylvie is frightened she will lose everybody – and so it goes. Sylvie especially does not like Georges because he push her away from him, and she is angry because he has Bobbi for himself, and now he has my mother."

I thought the saddest thing was that, amidst all their losses, they hadn't been able to find a way to talk to each other and comfort each other, without their anxieties getting in the way. And the secrets they all seemed to keep! I found an echo of this in the way Jeanne and Bobbi had related to Mike and me – the tendency to keep us in the dark about things, the web of mystery they liked to spin around events, and the tendency for no-one to be straight with anyone else. I thought I had been attracted to this way of being. Now I wasn't so sure. Families can sometimes sink under the weight of their own silences I fear. Hearing about her family made me think of Mike's family for example – especially the enduring unspoken grief about Rosie's brain damage, which had resulted in increasing isolation for Mike and his mother in particular.

It took a little time but, over the next few days, things gradually found a sort of equilibrium, and what remnants of tension there were between them gave way to a generally more relaxed and harmonious atmosphere. I liked the way Georges tried to make contact with me too. He didn't speak much English but he tried hard to talk to me, and to ask about our time in the South, and of course about Bobbi. Having temporarily forgotten that he was her father I came to notice more similarities between them as I got to know him better. There was the inquisitiveness, the quick darting movements suggesting a certain impulsivity, but mostly the air of sadness that seemed to accompany him. I did also witness occasional bursts of temper and frustration from him, when he stubbed his toe or lost his keys or something, which were sudden and startling when they occurred - a bit like thunder-claps. But, thankfully they didn't bring a prolonged storm with them – when they were gone they were gone.

"When do you go back to England?"

I felt my heart jump. Her question sounded like a gun going off, with the bullet speeding in my direction. The anxiety must have showed in my face.

"Don't look so worried," she said. "It is only a question."

My vague aim on leaving Nice had been to head straight back home, now I wanted to stay with Jeanne as long as I could, but I wasn't sure how much she wanted me around. I knew it wasn't that long before I was due to start at University, but I had been studiously avoiding thinking about it. If I was to give myself time to prepare properly I guess I needed to be back home within the next three weeks. To my relief she said, "Three weeks! That is good. I can show you something of Paris."

Like a fool I just repeated what she said, "Show me something of Paris? Are you sure?" She rolled her eyes.

And so I became a rubber-neck. She took me to Notre Dame, the Arc de Triomphe, le Sacré Coeur, and Montmatre. Here I even had a charcoal sketch done for 5F. Jeanne pushed me into it and I only agreed because I thought she was going to sit with me, but she ducked out at the last moment, only to hover behind the artist grimacing and pulling faces in an effort to spoil my concentration. Another time we spent a whole day strolling round the Latin Quarter, losing ourselves entirely amongst the many little bookshops and cafes. There was a brilliant vibrant atmosphere and an immediate sense of welcome and belonging, unlike anywhere else in France I had so far experienced. There were even buskers on street corners playing all kinds of instruments - from accordions to xylophones. Strangely however there was no sign of a single Dylan copyist – a gap in the market that Mike and I could surely have exploited.

I was thinking about Mike and wondering how he was getting on when we were suddenly approached by a tall, curly-headed youth. He was scruffily dressed in a brown corduroy jacket which was emblazoned with various badges. He reminded me of the kind of nerdy chap who sometimes used to turn up at the Merry Neet Club, trying to persuade people to go on CND rallies or whatever. His main distinguishing feature was an enormous dark beard which was threatening to colonise his entire face. He thrust a leaflet into my hand and then rattled on in French. Jeanne talked back to him while I examined the leaflet. It shouted out its message in bold letters - "HALTE AU CRIME"- and then went on to announce details of a 'Meeting de Protestation' against French nuclear testing, so far as I could make out. Eventually, when The Beard rushed off to accost someone else, Jeanne said,

"There is a lot of this just now. At Easter there was a very big march through the streets of Paris – it was against the nuclear tests, and for the peace in Vietnam. It was very exciting."

"You joined in?"

"But of course. And if you were here, you would have come too."

"Of course I would," I said, without conviction. She must have noticed as she looked at me and shook her head knowingly.

"And do you think you will go to this meeting?"

"Of course. That is what I was talking to Jacques about."

"Jacques?"

"Yes, the man who gave you the leaflet just now."

"Oh. Was he Jacques 1, or Jacques 2?"

"Pardon?"

"You know, *Tale of Two Cities?*" She looked blank – why wouldn't she? "It's another of those *Deek-en-jeunne* things, remember?"

Her eyebrows furrowed and she studied me carefully for a moment.

"*Tale of Two Cities* is a book by Charles Dickens – he's very big in England. You really ought to read him sometime."

Clearly we weren't on common ground and I was aware of feeling anxious.

"Doesn't matter. Do you know this 'Jacques'?"

"No, of course not. I just met him. But he tells me it is a very important meeting and I must give my support."

I marvelled both at the speed with which she made contact with people, and at the way things mattered to her. I also thought it was lucky that the strength of my own commitment to Important Causes wasn't going to be tested as the meeting was to take place after I was due to leave. It struck me then how much of a folk-singer I really was. Wasn't I supposed to relish Meetings of Protestation, and seize these opportunities to change the world? I had a heart-sink feeling that the things I had cared about up to now had actually been quite superficial. There I was striking out boldly in France, making some kind of statement about being an individual, and being free of parental control and the shackles of convention or whatever. In fact all I'd really done was to follow Mike's lead, and sing somebody else's songs.

181

15

Having long played supporting roles in other people's dramas – Mike and Sandra, Bobbi and her photos, Jeanne and her family – now I felt more centre stage in one of my own, and I didn't like it. The thing was, I had come to feel potty about Jeanne and the thought of having to leave her was becoming more and more painful. She had been right – our lives were in separate countries, and it was hard to see a way in which we could really be together.

"I could delay going to University for a year. We could travel around together some more."

"And what would we do after that?"

"Well, we'd have to wait and see."

"No, all we do is put everything off for a year – then we are in the same position as we are now."

I knew she was right but I still didn't want to face it.

"Perhaps I could stay in Paris – or you could come to England! Yes, yes, come to England with me Jeanne!"

"Yes, of course I could do that, but do you forget that we have no money, and it is in any case not the right time for me. I have to live my own life in France. And you also in England!"

I persisted. "But it would be so great. You speak English so well, you wouldn't have any problem settling in I'm sure. You could get a job easily ..."

"Oh yes, what do you want me to do? A waitress perhaps? Or perhaps I can clean houses, or do you want me to do the busking with you?"

She seemed to be getting a bit edgy now, and I was starting to feel uncomfortable myself.

"Well no, I mean ..."

"Do you know what I want to do? Do you find out? Do you even ask me ..?"

"Sorry Jeanne, it's just that I feel very secure when I'm with you. I don't want to lose you."

"Nigel! You are so selfish! All you think is what you want! What about *me*!?"

She was shouting as if something had exploded inside her and I found myself feeling shocked and embarrassed. I realised she was right – I hadn't given much thought to plans she might actually have for herself. I suppose I didn't want to consider that she actually might have something in her mind that didn't involve me.

"I'm sorry Jeanne, I …"

"And all the time you say sorry, sorry, sorry!"

We both fell silent and I was unsure what to do next. Eventually she seemed to calm down again and then she apologised herself. "I am sorry too. I should not shout at you. But I warn you about this, that I might hurt you if you feel too strongly for me. You have been very kind to me and so helpful with my family. I love you for that … but I think we want different things Nigel. I want to see more of the world …"

I leapt in without even thinking. "Perhaps I could come with you! Yes! What a great idea! We could travel together …" *Oh Jeanne, we could stay together, just you and me, we could do such exciting things, we would be unattached and free, travelling from town to town* … and for a brief moment I was entranced again. *Yes Jeanne yes, wherever you want to go, just say the word and I'll follow…*

She looked at me long and hard, and as she did so I felt my frantic thoughts drop to the ground like chicks tumbling out of their cosy nest.

"Nigel," she said tenderly. "You must listen to me. First, my plan is to train how to become a Nurse, then I want to go to countries where there is trouble and, if it is possible for me, to help the people … all this is important to me now … you are different … you need more … *de la sécurité* …"

"Security? No … I mean … when I said I feel secure with you, I didn't mean …"

"Nigel … why did you come to France?"

I didn't have a ready answer. I stumbled through some of the first thoughts that came into my head. "I don't know really … for the adventure … to get away from home for a bit … to see if we could manage on our own …" Of course the real reason was that I came because of Mike. But I wasn't going to tell her that - except she knew anyway. I'd already confessed.

"Yes, perhaps," she said, "But that night, when we slept in the barn – chez le Père Albert – you tell me that you come because of Mike. He said come, and you followed him."

I cringed and could feel myself shrinking. "I thought you were asleep," I murmured. She smiled. "But, that same night" I hurried on, "you told me that I was brave, that I had been *un champion* for Bobbi. Please Jeanne, we could be strong together."

"Perhaps," she said softly. "But I think this is the trouble. You are not ... *un explorateur,* Nigel. You do not like to be on your own. You need to be with other people too much. Do you know what I think?"

My heart sank. I thought she was making it very clear already what she thought. She looked at me and smiled.

"I do not want to be cruel, Nigel, but I think ... you follow Mike, and now you follow me."

I didn't want to hear this, so tried to pretend she was wrong. Being with Mike was very different from being with her. And although it was true that I did have more confidence when others were around me, I thought I'd also been quite bold in doing things on my own and taking risks and such. Deep down, I was a life-saver, wasn't I?

She carried on, "I am not the answer to your happiness, Nigel. No-one is. You must go back to your home and lead the life that is right for you."

Well, sort of, I thought. The trouble is I don't know what 'the life that is right for me' actually is.

"And you Jeanne?" I asked her. "What will you do?"

"In my life I have worried a lot about my family, especially Bobbi, and Maman, and my Aunt Sylvie. But they are all settled now I think, and that is very good. I am free now to make my own choices. I cannot do that if I come to England with you."

She had me there.

Our last few days and hours together passed very quickly. Having found our matching patterns and come together like jigsaw pieces, we had to accept that what we had found was more like an illusion, a false fit – we were pieces in two different puzzles. Now we started to be uncomfortable with each other, not knowing exactly how to be. On the night before I was due to set off for home I lay in bed, mulling things over in the quiet of the dark old house. Clearly the sensible, logical thing to do was for Jeanne and me to separate, and create our lives in two different places. Perhaps there could be a place for us to be together later on. But if we really loved each other wouldn't we feel this as a certainty now? Wouldn't it be something that was beyond question, because we'd be bound to each other no matter what?

The more I thought about it the more I realised that what really troubled me was the fact that everybody seemed to have a direction, or some course mapped out – except me. The first to go were Steve and Sue, who had both gone back to America with clear ideas of what they were going to do - Steve was going to Law school and Sue was going to be a teacher. And even little wayward Bobbi had found some stability with Marcel and, under his guidance, had got herself a settled occupation. How different from the little girl who ran around passing the hat, and who dallied with dodgy photographers and printers! Jeanne was going to undertake some professional training, become a nurse, and then apply her skills to a noble cause. I knew of course that I was going to University – to read Chemistry - but there was no grand plan, no career path. I was cheered momentarily when I thought about Mike - at least he had no plan, except the negative one of making everybody in his family suffer. Then, as I thought about that further, I found it disturbing to think that, even though he was behaving independently, he wasn't actually going forward at all – all he was doing was rebuking his parents for letting him down.

Then I started to think about whether it was actually best to make things up as you go along, and how much it helped to have a route planned out. I once saw a cartoon of an Arab sitting on a camel in the desert reading an 'A to Z'. The caption said something like, 'A sure way of getting lost is to rely on a familiar map in unfamiliar territory.' On the way down to St Tropez it was only when we got a map that we really lost our way – going on trains and stuff, because that looked like the easiest thing to do – travelling a familiar route because we knew it would get us there. A proper Ramblin' Boy would never have bought a map – he'd have gone with the flow, allowed himself to be blown along by the wind and, unshackled by structures, he'd have been open and left himself free to make new discoveries. Perhaps that's what I'll do when I get home I thought – I'll have no particular goal in mind. I'll just free-wheel it, and lay myself open to experience, and go wherever life leads me. I shivered at the very idea.

As I lay in the dark I thought I heard a noise outside my room. I sat up and listened. There was a little rustling noise and the door creaked open gently.

"Ni-gelle?" she whispered.

"Jeanne! Is that you?"

She gave a quiet little laugh. "Of course. Who do you expect to come?" and she tip-toed over to my bed and climbed in.

"I feel sad tonight that we do not have much more time together. So I come to be with you tonight." Then she cuddled up close to me.

We lay in silence for a while.

"I'm sorry about these last few days," I said.

"Sorry? Why sorry? All the time you say sorry ..."

"Do I? Sorry ... oops, well you know what I mean. I've just felt a bit awkward. It's really hard to say goodbye to you Jeanne. You make me happier than I ever thought I could be. In all my life, I never thought ..."

"Shush, shush," she said. "I know. But we don't say goodbye ... we say 'au revoir' ... it means, until I see you again."

"You think we will see each other again?"

"Of course. You do not?"

"I don't know Jeanne. I hope so, but lots of things can happen. I just know I love you, and I want to be with you ..."

I shivered a little at my boldness, but isn't it strange how these things are always easier to say in the dark. Unfortunately though, she didn't say the same thing back as I hoped she might.

"I tell you before you are not *un explorateur* ... I think this is not true. I think you are ... we say ... *en francais* ... *hardi*. Do you know what it means?"

"Hardy?"

"It means when you can face things, with courage..."

"Oh, like 'daring' you mean?"

"Oui, oui daring."

That sounded good to me, particularly given the sensual way she said it. What with that, and the way she was lying next to me I thought to myself that I was well on the way to being *hardi* as it was – if you know what I mean.

"Then you can think of me," she said. "We have some nice memories."

"But I don't really want memories," I said. "Well, I do, but really I want you, the real you. I ..."

"Shush," she said again, "let's just stay with the memories shall we? We'll always have these moments."

"Yes," I said with a sigh, "We'll always have Paris."

We kissed, and snuggled down into the warmth of the bed and each other. I caressed her, running my hands along the smooth silky lines of her body. It was as if, all around me, the world was slowing down and holding its breath. Then, out of the silence, I heard a distant sound – like

186

the gentle rumble of a train approaching. At first it is just a rhythmic drumming sound, but gradually it becomes louder and louder as the train appears to get closer and closer. Somehow I fancy I can see the hot steam coursing through the boiler, and I can feel the fiery breath of the engine rolling across my skin. Then there is a sudden change of pace. It feels as if the train has altered its course and is bearing down upon us with unconscious speed. No force on earth can stop it now. All at once it has burst into the room with an urgency that sweeps me away, and I am deafened by the sound of the heavy wheels pounding remorselessly against the tracks. The whole room is shaking, vibrating.

Freight Train, Freight Train, going so fast,
Freight Train, Freight Train, going so fast.

Suddenly a squeal breaks above the noise of the panting engine. I hear the shrill sound of a whistle as the train hurtles by, and I am swept away in its motion. A fierce blast of hot air scoops me up high into the sky, there is a blurring of all my senses into one soaring moment, and I lose all contact with my surroundings. I feel like I am falling and falling. A bell is clank-clank-clanking, and all at once the room is filled with a blinding white light. I am lost.

And then it is passed. Slowly I became aware of the wind dropping, the light fading, and the air becoming still. The shrill sound of the whistle has faded and died too, swallowed up in the darkness.

I pull Jeanne close to me and, as I close my eyes I feel the warmest feeling I have ever felt engulf me. Inside I am smiling my widest smile.

The Midnight Special has finally shone its light on me.

16

I awoke, dimly aware of daylight creeping into the room and faint noises somewhere in the distance. The rest of the world was getting ready to carry on with its daily business-as-usual. But in the room there was just Jeanne and me, and things had changed. She was cuddled up to me, her head on my chest, sleeping soundly. It was wonderful. I lay in the stillness, listening to her sleeping, and hoped the moment would last forever. Then she squirmed a little, slowly opened her eyes and smiled at me.

I whispered an affectionate 'Bonjour, chérie'. I was Charles Boyer, moody and mysterious, driving my lover wild with my sultry French accent and irresistible eyes.

Except I wasn't.

All of a sudden the beatific smile vanished from her face, her eyes popped open as if a gun had gone off in her brain, and she jerked up her head.

"Oh là là!" she said, and leapt out of bed so quickly I didn't have time to unravel my arms from her shoulders. The next thing I knew I had fallen out of bed, my nose buried in the carpet and my bum sticking in the air. My fantasy shattered in a million pieces – as far as I know Charles Boyer never appeared in a *Carry On* film.

Meanwhile Jeanne had reached the door. She was half-way through it when she turned to me and said,

"Pardon, Nigel ….. *désolée* …. Don't worry, I come back soon."

"But Jeanne" I shouted helplessly after her, "What's the matter? Are you all ri…?"

But she was gone.

I crawled back into bed, my mind in a total spin. What was that all about? Hopefully her sudden exit hadn't been prompted by the shock of waking up next to me. Perhaps she was mad with me? Had we gone further than she intended? Did she think I had taken advantage of her? Perhaps I had actually – perhaps I had sensed her vulnerability and cashed in. Oh my God – perhaps I was just like Mike after all. I heard the toilet flush. Perhaps she had just needed the toilet urgently. God, it hadn't been that much of a shock surely? And still she didn't return. A big black cloud of gloom filled the room and I felt bleak and wretched. The elated feeling of well-being I had been basking in was no more; instead my mind had become invaded with worries and anxieties like an army of marching ants. But the worst thing of all was the crushing sense of guilt.

After what felt like an age she finally came back, fully clothed, and with a hot drink cupped in her hands – just as it had been when she came to me at Gustav and Sylvie's. She sat on the edge of the bed and looked at me. I searched her face for disapproval, disdain, anger, hurt – something – but found nothing.

"Why do you look so worried?" she said at last.

"Because I think you are angry with me."

"Angry? Why am I angry?"

"Because of what happened…"

"I don't understand."

"I feel ashamed."

"What? *Qu'est-ce que tu veux dire?*"

The fact that she lapsed into French only confirmed my worst fears. Something serious was going on. But I still couldn't see why she was being so obtuse. I tried to remember the word Bobbi had used when she'd come back from her supposed photo shoot with Antoine and Aimée. *'Hunter'*, or something, only with a French accent.

"Je suis *'onterre'*…" I said, "I don't know what you must think of me …"

She clapped her hand over her mouth as she spluttered into laughter. I could hardly bear it. I lay back down, turned away from her and screwed my eyes tight shut.

"Please don't laugh," I whispered.

"Idiot!" she suddenly exclaimed. Then she put a firm hand on my shoulder and pulled me over to face her. She cupped my face in her hands and looked me straight in the eye.

"Now! Monsieur Nigel!" she said, "*Now* I am angry! Why do you say these things? *Honteux*! How dare you! Why do you think I come to you, ah? I want us to share some tender moments together … before we say au'voir. I want to be with you. A beautiful thing happened last night. A beautiful thing! *Nous avons fait l'amour.* Do you understand?"

"Mmmph", I said, my lips constricted by the vice-like pressure she was now exerting on my face. "Mmmph, ay uh-er-sand."

Mercifully she smiled and released her grip.

"Nous avons fait l'amour," I repeated, just to show I had got the message.

"So what is this with the *honteux*? What is this … *idioties?*"

189

I wished she wouldn't keep calling me an idiot, but I tried to explain.

"I was scared Jeanne. When you left so suddenly, I thought you were upset and angry with me. I'm sorry, Jeanne ..."

"And again you say sorry. You are sorry for everything you do, I think. You are sorry for making love to me?"

"No, Jeanne, no ... never ..."

"Of course not. And I am not sorry. It is not because I am '*onterre*' that I leave you. I simply remember that this week I have to go to the University. There is – I don't know how you say it – a meeting before the start of the class. I forget which day so I run to my diary."

I started to feel ashamed at my stupidity all over again. On the other hand I reassured myself with the thought that a naked girl running away from one's bed would probably unnerve any man. Mainly you want them to be running *towards* your bed, or so I imagine. Still, what she said was a bit of a blow. She would rather enrol at the University than be with me. It meant that, for her, her life plans were more important than being with me, she was moving on, moving away from me. I had just wanted to stay and lie with her forever.

"But I don't really understand, Jeanne ..."

She cocked her head to one side with an expression of mock-enquiry on her face. I hesitated, but decided it was the only chance I was likely to get, so forged ahead.

"You don't want me to stay here with you ... yes, yes, I understand that ... but we are more than friends now, especially now, especially after ..."

"After we have made love?"

"Yes."

"Of course. But because we make love, we are not ... I don't know how to say in English ... we are still two people. We are not one person ... *pour toujours*. We have shared a special moment of love ..."

Yes that sounded nice, '*a special moment of love*'. But why did it have to be only the one special moment? I can have trust in the world Jeanne, with you beside me.

"You fall in love too easily Nigel. Actually, I like this about you. You have ... *loyauté* ... you know? You find someone to trust, perhaps to love, and then you do not let go. Then you follow. The other person leads the way for you. You follow because you think you do not know yourself what to do."

"Well, not all the time …"

"Yes, yes. O.K. maybe not all the time. I know you can be *hardi, non?*"

I thought for a brief second she was flattering me on my sexual prowess, but then remembered that the pun was entirely in my head, and she was using the word in its classical French sense.

"*Hardi* .. daring, yes." I said.

"So why do you wait all the time, eh? Why do you wait?" There was a pause. "Do you know what I think?" she said. I said nothing, and waited to hear what she was about to say.

"You follow because you do not have the faith in yourself. You want … *l'assurance, l'assurance répetée.* You are frightened to have your life. You are frightened to let your life begin!"

She was right of course. The truth of what she said hit me between the eyes and something clicked inside my head. My life to date could probably be described by two words … "wait" and "follow". That's all I ever really did. In fact, if 'following' was ever to be made an official sport, I figured I'd probably make the Olympic Team, always just a few steps behind someone else, always efficiently dogging the crowd in front. And, sure enough, when I looked I could see them all there, up ahead, leading the way. There was Bob, Bert and John, Woody, Ramblin' Jack, all the American Dust-Bowl heroes, and of course there was Mike, and then Jeanne, and oh my God, I could even see Miss Benson, my Chemistry teacher. Yes, when I thought about it, even my choice of University course had been determined by my following instinct. Jeanne looked at me tenderly.

"Do not wait for your life to begin Nigel. This is a mistake. In French we say *fonces-y!*" and she made a fist and shook it above her head. I recalled the last time I saw a gesture like that – it was when John Glenn was about to be launched into Earth orbit. *Bring it on! Make it happen! Let's get this baby on the road!* The Astronauts' salute.

"Fonces-y?"

"Oui, *fonces-y!*"

I looked at her, probably in an unhelpfully awe-struck way, but I couldn't help but marvel at the certainty with which she said things, and at her ability to understand things about me I didn't really understand myself. She got hold of my hand and squeezed it.

"O.K. I will try. I will go back to England, I will go to my University, and I will be … *hardi.* Thank you Jeanne. But most of all, I will

191

have you in my mind, I will have our tender moments, our memories, and I will not need *l'assurance répetée*, not anymore."

She smiled.

"Just one thing though ..." I said. She looked momentarily anxious. I paused for dramatic effect.

"Was I any good?"

She gave me a puzzled look.

I nodded towards the bed. "Was I a good lover?"

She rolled her eyes and sighed in a what-am-I-going-to-do-with-you sort of way.

On the way back to England I came to a momentous decision. I wasn't going to University to read Chemistry. I was going to go back, cancel my place, and see if I could get in at Medical School instead. I'd never been that convinced that Chemistry was the way to go. Because of this trip I realised that I actually quite liked being involved with other people and their lives. Up till then I had tended to live my life in a fairly tight boundary and, Jeanne was right, just waiting for something to happen. Hearing her talk so enthusiastically about her Nurse training and what she intended to do with it had inspired me too.

Oh but wait a minute. Wasn't I just being a follower again? Was I just trying to impress her by going for Medicine, trying to be like her, following her lead? I knew I still had a yearning to be with her, that I wanted to be around her constantly. She just made me feel so secure and safe, especially when I was being ... well, a Nigel. But no, this was different. This wasn't blind following. This was a major life choice I was making. I knew it was different because it felt so much more scary than any other choice I'd ever made in my life.

I especially found myself wondering what Uncle Fred would say. He wouldn't be able to understand why I'd changed my mind of course, and he'd have plenty of things to say about my giving up a perfectly good University place, but I hoped the inducement of eventually having a Doctor in the family would win him over. Anyway what did I care? I was my own man now. I had a mind of my own. Finally I knew where I was going. I gave the Astronauts' salute in my head.

PART FOUR

MAMA YOU BEEN ON MY MIND

17

Manchester, England
10ᵗʰ May 1967

> *Dear Mike,*
> *Hey partner and road buddy – glad to hear you got back O.K.*
> *I was worried that you wouldn't – come back that is. Do you think Sandra might have been doing you a favour actually, going off like that? According to my Ma, your Ma is looking really well and happy too. Pleased to have the prodigal home again I guess.*
> *That's the formalities over with then. I hope you don't mind if a lot of this letter is a bit sort of serious, but I'm in a funny mood. But not, I hasten to add, in the sense of having lots of sharp and witty things to say. Just the opposite in fact.*
> *I'm enjoying myself here, even though it's a one-horse town and there's bugger-all to do, but you'll be pleased to know that I've made some nice chums here. The teachers are O.K but the prefects are rotten – and there's too much homework. But I'm learning all the time – cell structures, muscles, bones, we've got them all covered. Ha! Oh and did you know that, apparently, the leg-bone is connected to the … knee bone, and the knee bone connected to the … thigh bone?*
> *But what's it all about? Alfie.*
> *Something funny is happening. I keep switching moods. One day I don't care and it's great, the next I feel down and miserable. I suppose it has something to do with Jeanne – I miss her a lot in a way, but there's something else too. I just miss something. Perhaps it's to do with leaving everything behind in France after we came back, and coming back here to this routine-y way of living. I guess you'll understand something of that in the light of what happened with Sandra.*
> *Anyroads-up, I'm not asking for advice, I'm just talking to you to gerrit off my chest a bit. I hope you don't feel embarrassed at this letter, and definitely don't write back in the same genre. Thing is – Jeanne was – oops, is – such a good girl, she really is, but I don't see how we can make it work. She only writes once every two weeks now – well, alright once a month – actually yes, she did miss last month if you must know – but I can sense something changing all the time. And I'm scared now, like I'm walking in the dark and I don't know what's out there that I'm gonna bump into. If Jeanne was here, I'd hold her hand and talk to her and smell her Jeanney-ness and it'd all be O.K. And if you were here, you could swear at me like you used to, tell me to stop being a tosser all my life, and buy me eleven-teen pints in that kind and sensitive way you have of dealing with people's woes.*

But before we parted she really set me thinking – she told me I wasn't an adventurer. She seemed to think I was just looking for soft options all the time, and for others to lead me on. Thing is, I probably was at the time but I don't feel like that now. What with all those adventures we had, and seeing how kind people basically are, and doing the right thing, and how confusions mainly arise out of fear and not knowing enough about what's going on, and what it means to really really care about someone and something, I feel more sure of where I'm going now – except I don't either, if you see what I mean. Uncle Fred said he'd give me 6 months (I thought that was the kind of thing us doctors said), but it seems to me I'm in it now for life.

I owe a lot to Jeanne really – and to you of course. You coming back made me see that there was hope. But Jeanne gave me a trust in myself and in what I am and want to be. God I think I'm going to cry.

Actually, I feel a bit less depressed now – if this continues I'll probably feel dead happy tomorrow, and I'll tear this up for being such a tit, or with admirable fore-sight keep it till I feel the same again and then just pop it in the post. Just read it, it's a load of unlinked ramblings like we used to do in the olden days. And 'on va voir', as we used to almost never say.

Thanks very much,
Yours, being a pillock of the first water,
Nigel.
P.S. I know I'm doing the right thing cos I've got a mind of my own. Jeanne told me so. What do you think?

Morecambe, Lancashire
20ᵗʰ May, 1967

Dear Pillock of the first water,
Stop being a tosser all your life and go and have a pint. Sorry to hear you're like that – as for me, I'm like this. But even though you said not to write in the same genre, I will tell you this. It's great having a kid. If you want to have no money, or you want your shirts to always smell of puke, and you never want to sleep again, you should get one. It'd fill your obviously empty days up nicely. Actually it's not that bad. I've only seen it in bursts (as 'twere) – me Mam pretty much does it all, what with being a girl and all, she knows about these things. Incidentally, since you forgot to ask, she is bright as a veritable button, and she's called Angie – what else? As for me Mam, you are right, she is happier than I've seen her in ages.

So perhaps Sandra did us all a favour going off like that. Given the attitude of her parents to the sprog, who clearly just wanted shut of it altogether, the issue was forced rather. Even I couldn't be that big a bastard - although I tried, God knows I tried. Anyway, it's all working out. (Why does everybody keep leaving me anyway? Is there something you need to tell me?). Incidentally I also realised (and you've NO IDEA how much it grieves me to say this) that you were right in what you said just before I went off with Patrick - what was really bothering me was me Ma. I hated what all the baby business was doing to her, and by coming back I thought that maybe I could perhaps do something right by her.

So - basically - what I have to do is get to the end of this year, put a bit of the old dosh aside and, when I go away again, keep some sort of contact with home — birthday cards and the odd Christmas present ought to do it. Of course there's other stuff to sort out, but you can't rush these things. In short, I'm glad I came back. Just think, I wouldn't get angst-ridden letters from you otherwise, and I'd only be in Sicily, or Ibiza, or Tangiers, or somewhere boring like that. And next year I'll be joining you as a stooodent — well, not at your place natch, I'm off to a proper school, where there's so much to do there won't be time for 'missing' things that can't be named, or having feelings, or girly things like that.

So look, tosser, go and be Dr Broadbent if you must. Just stop going on about it — I mean it's hardly a matter of life and death is it? Jeanne was nice but ultimately just a sub-plot in the great book of life, a wonderful page or two maybe, but just a sub-plot — now you've started a whole new chapter. (tilt head back at 45° angle, and assume faraway look).

O.K? Now go and have some more adventures.

Yours, pretending to be a reformed character,

Mike

P.S. Your Uncle Fred says to tell you to get your hair cut.

PART FIVE

MR TAMBOURINE MAN

18

She offered me coffee and we sat together on a sofa under the soft glow of an old-fashioned standard lamp.

"I like your Restaurant."

"You do?"

"Yes, very much."

"We have been here about 10 years now, and we are quite well known in the area. In fact we are mentioned in all of the Guide books of Provence and La Cote d'Azur."

I smiled to think how I'd long since given up on consulting such things.

"You must have worked very hard."

"Now it is easier, now we have our reputation, but it was hard at first."

She went on to tell me how it had all come about, talking quickly and excitedly. I suppose it helped her to get re-acclimatised to me. After all, we both had to bridge quite a big gap between the past and the present. Meanwhile, I was longing to ask about Jeanne but thought that it would be impolite to give in to my impatience so soon into our renewed contact. Plus I knew that particular part of our conversation was likely to be painful.

"Do you have any children?" I asked at last.

"No, we have no children. My husband and I, we were both very busy with our jobs, and then it just became too late. But I don't mind," she said, shrugging off what still seemed to me like a pang of regret. "And you?" she went on, "Do you have children?"

"Yes I have three."

"Three? That's wonderful."

I told her a little about them, and the course my life had taken since we'd last met, and my emigration to the States in 1975. She seemed surprised.

"But Nigel, you are now an American!"

"I don't think so. You can take the boy out of Morecambe, but you can't take Morecambe out of the boy."

"I don't understand."

Neither did I really.

"Never mind," I said, "The main thing is, I still feel very … English."

"No, it is not true. To do what you have done, you are not a typical Englishman! Many Englishmen come to *La Côte D'Azur* – they are … how do you say it … *timides* … *et réservés*." She laughed again. "Actually, when we were all together, I remember that you were always trying to be brave, but really, you were always worrying about everything. Where are the Police? I will be deported! We have no money! We have no food to eat!"

I laughed along whilst thinking that she was slightly over-stating the case. Although the trek to the South of France all those years ago showed me I was never going to be a famous singer/guitarist/rambling boy, I had gained things that actually turned out to be of much more enduring value. Basically I had met Jeanne. I can't really explain what happened – all I know is that she freed me up somehow. She connected me with a realisation that I did have some courage inside me, that despite my stupid nick-name, I wasn't actually a jelly-fish, and that basically I was all right.

I became aware of a pained, wistful look on Bobbi's face as she picked up her coffee cup and cradled it in her hands. I guessed it was because we had started to recall memories of our time together.

"I guess you miss Jeanne a lot," I said.

She ignored my question and changed the subject.

"What about Mike? How is he doing?"

"I don't know actually", I said. "We lost contact. He came back to England for a while, even went to University for a year or so, but then he dropped out."

"What does that mean?"

"Oh, he left his course, left the University. He played in a band for a while … they were quite popular actually - in our local area anyway."

"What is it, a 'band'?"

"Oh .. er .. music .. a group?"

"Ah, *un orchestre de jazz* … yes, he was a very good *musicien*."

"Yes he was – very good. But he was always restless, and I saw less and less of him. He never settled down with anyone, and he was always going away, then coming back, then going away again. The last I heard was that he had gone to live in London, but sadly I don't know what happened to him."

"Oh Mike could always look after himself."

"Yes," I said, feeling somewhat ashamed that I hadn't made more effort to stay in touch with him. I realised that I'd started to feel anxious again. It was probably sparked off by the uncertainty that hung in the air following her sudden diversion away from Jeanne, but a certain bleakness had also descended on me as I thought more about Mike. To me he had sadly wasted his talents, and although I didn't know for sure, probably his life as well. My sense was that he had tried to maintain the illusion that he was somehow inviolate, and had persisted with his efforts to prove he had no need of others, no vulnerabilities or yearnings that others might exploit. The self-imposed exile this produced had been temporarily suspended on his return home but, for whatever reason, he'd gathered up his defences around himself again fairly quickly.

"I liked Mike a lot – did you know this?" she said.

"Yes I knew. He was worried about that." She laughed again.

"Oh wasn't it funny when we ran away from the Hotel in St Trop."

"Yes they were good times."

"Yes … good times."

Without looking at me she then said, "Yes Nigel, I still miss Jeanne, very much."

The moment had come we had both been avoiding.

"Yes," I murmured. "Me too." We lapsed into silence each lost in our own thoughts.

"She talked of you often you know? Of course I was in Nice and she was in Paris so we did not see each other a lot, but we wrote lots of letters. And she was full of such ideas! Oh what she was going to do! She was going to make money for the orphans, she was going to work with the children on the streets, go to Africa …"

Yes that was my Jeanne, I thought. My Maid of Orleans.

"She wrote letters to you too?"

"Yes, yes," I said. "I still have them." After I had got back Jeanne had written to me about once a month or so. Not love letters as such. They were more like letters between two close friends exchanging news of their plans and adventures. The ones I wrote back to her probably erred on the mushy side, and I never quite lost the habit of burdening her with my woes, but hers were always full of life and energy and, ironically, so forward-looking. I shared some of these thoughts with Bobbi, still avoiding the question I really wanted to ask.

Eventually I had to say," So what actually happened Bobbi? I so wanted to come and see you after … you know … but I couldn't. I had very little money, and I was so busy with my studies and …"

"It's all right," she said. "I am sorry too. I should have written to you myself, but I could not bear to do it. It was a horrible horrible time, and there was the family, and my work with Marcel and…"

"Listen to us," I broke in, "We are apologising to each other like two frightened children. Jeanne would not have liked us to be so broody. She would have wanted us to get on with it. Life was to be lived she said. *Fonces-y* she used to say."

Bobbi smiled, as she repeated the words over to herself. "*Fonces-y.* Yes she would say that to me too. *Fonces-y dans le brouillard!*"

She took a deep breath.

"Well …you know she was always involved in … *les protestations* … and the politics. So of course when all the students were fighting, and there was the battles in the *Quartier Latin* she was … what do you say … *en plein cœur de la révolte.*"

At the heart of it. Yes, that sounded like her.

"And there were the demonstrations, the barricades, the throwing of the stones, the burning of the cars … oh so terrible."

I had of course heard all about the famous Paris uprising of 1968 at the time, and seen pictures on the news. Revolution was in vogue in 1968. Even my University had once staged a 'sit-in' although it had seemed more like a silly game compared to the seriousness of what had happened in Paris. They had been on the brink of Civil War. I remember thinking at the time that Jeanne would probably be involved somehow and now cursed that, despite making the connection, it hadn't spurred me into an active effort to make contact with her.

"So, one night, after Charles de Gaulle had spoken on the television, many people attack *La Bourse*. Do you know what it is?"

"The Stock Exchange, yes."

"And soon it is on fire." She paused and seemed to struggle to gather herself together. "Then … nobody knows exactly what happened … Jeanne is in the building, I don't know why, and then something falls on top of her, I think … " She broke off. "Oh it is so horrible to think of it," and she covered her face with her hands. Suddenly she was vulnerable again, like the fragile Bobbi Mike and I had found curled up that time on the hotel bed in St Tropez, frightened and upset.

"I know Bobbi, I know ..." I said, "I'm so sorry." And I had the strange sensation of something falling away inside me.

My poor Jeanne. What a waste. Killed by the fires of her own lust for life. Yet in some ways there was a kind of poetry in it. She had died in a fire – like her father had done before her, and like the other strong-willed and uncompromising Maid of Orleans had done. Goodness knows how she had found her way into the building. I thought it was highly likely she was trying to save someone, perhaps some poor soul who had just found themselves caught up in the flow of events. Someone who needed a rescuer. Just like me in fact, all those years ago.

We continued our conversation long into the afternoon, reminiscing about the good times and sharing our stories, particularly our memories of Jeanne. I told her how I hadn't wanted to leave her at all, and how I had tried to persuade her to come to England with me, and then offered to stay in France with her. She told me some more about their childhood together and, although they had been cousins, how Jeanne had been like her tough and protective big sister. In a strange way, I think talking about her helped us both to come to terms with her loss, even though it had happened so many years ago.

"Oh Nigel," she said at last. "She made the wrong choice! If only she had chosen to stay with you!"

At first I thought that was a lovely compliment but in the quiet of my Hotel room later that night, I realised how wrong she was.

In Paris, Jeanne was the one with all the certainty, sure of her heart and what she wanted to do. I was the lost romantic, ready to do anything just to be with her. But she urged me to follow, not her, but my self, my own mind. By doing that, she somehow grounded me and I became the one who had direction and focus –a focus which, as things have worked out, has served me well throughout my life. It's funny really. At the time I kind of felt that she was depriving me of what I wanted more than anything – her. Instead she actually gave me something much more enduring.

When it came to it, Jeanne probably didn't have a choice about her own future. The more I thought about it the more it seemed to me that the course of her life had really been determined by what had happened in her past – in particular the loss of her father all those years ago. I remembered her telling me how affected she had been by this, how she felt she had let him down in some way, and how much she wanted to be like him. In that she had surely succeeded. When I was with her I was regularly struck both by her passion for life, for the things she believed in, and her compassion, her fierce protectiveness of others and especially those she loved. In the end it had been these qualities which, like her father before her, had sealed her fate.

It also occurred to me that this was how I had often thought of Mike – someone whose fate was determined by his past. Although there had been some signs of hope when he changed his mind and came back to England, in the end he had never really found a way to overcome that hostility towards closeness and intimacy which he'd carried forward from his childhood. As a result, the cynicism and passion for isolation which went along with this had ultimately been his undoing.

And what of me? When Mike and I were in France all those years ago, our most frequently requested song was Bob Dylan's *Mr Tambourine Man*. Dylan-ologists will tell you this is chiefly a song about drugs. It may well be, but I just like the image of a magical 'Tambourine Man' whose musical energy somehow carries you along, with a promise of something wonderful. *Cast me under your dancing spell and I'll follow you anywhere* kind of thing. It seems to me that being an adolescent is like that; that strange sort of time when you're searching for something that goes beyond who you are, for someone who really knows where they're going, for someone who can tell you what to think whilst your busy making up your own mind. But I didn't know what I was searching for. How to move on from being a kid I suppose, some sense of who I was, what I could do, what I wanted to be. But basically I was still happy for others to mark out the trail for me – until I met Jeanne. She refused to be a Tambourine Man for me – she urged me probably for the first time to play my own song.

Of course in many ways I'm still a Nigel at heart. I have to acknowledge that the reason I enrolled for VSO was because, at Medical School, I fell under the spell of the peppery little ball of fire that was Rhiannon. From fairly early on, she was set on doing VSO as soon as she qualified and, my impulse to 'follow' not having entirely left me, I applied to go with her. She was never as keen as I was on it being a joint venture though, so it was probably a good thing in the end that we got different allocations. Otherwise I wouldn't have met Ken who, I suppose, I ended up following over to America once I'd heard him rave about the opportunities there.

So it goes.

203

I lay in bed in the quiet stillness of my hotel room. There was the vague sound of traffic gently humming up and down the *Promenade des Anglais,* just as it always did and then, whether I imagined it or not I'll never know, I thought I could hear the distant wail of a harmonica drifting through the night.

That's when the tears came – at first a pricking behind the eyes and then fuller, flowing tears. Tears for my lost youth and tears for my precious friend. I had not properly grieved for her before. When I first heard of her sudden death I had been too stunned, and then too busy to cry. Images of her now assailed me – her lovely smiling face, her long brown hair, her laughter, her strength of purpose, her tenderness, thumping Pip into submission, and squeezing my cheeks together and telling me not to be such an *idiot.*

And doing the Astronauts' salute.